Endpapers

Endpapers

JONATHAN STRONG | TWO NOVELS

DISCOURSES, WITH DONKEY &

PLAYFUL AND THOUGHTFUL

GRID BOOKS | BOSTON

ALSO BY JONATHAN STRONG

Four Last Songs

Quit the Race

The Judge's House

Hawkweed and Indian Paintbrush

More Light

Drawn from Life

Consolation

A Circle Around Her

The Old World

An Untold Tale

Offspring

Secret Words

Elsewhere

Companion Pieces:

   Doing and Undoing

   Game of Spirit

Ourselves

The Haunts of His Youth

   (*expanded from* Tike and Five Stories)

www.grid-books.org

COVER ILLUSTRATION: Vintage 19th c. marbled paper, double comb wave pattern. University of Washington Libraries, Special Collections, UW42258.

ISBN: 978-1-946830-23-4

Discourses, with Donkey

*"It's hopeless and we know it, but not so hopeless
we don't want to find out how hopeless it is."*

WILLIAM SAROYAN

to the memory of O. P. Brown

Day One

I'd been running about in my old New Balances, up and down the dirt roads outside the little Vermont village where I was spending the month of August. I took one promising fork up into the hills, but the road began to peter out past an off-kilter metal shed where a rusted-out silver-gray pickup was stowed. On the tailgate were black letters spelling ISUZU. The grass below was worn down, and maybe I could make out tire tracks.

I ran on as far as I could before the road gave up completely and high weeds and saplings made it impassable, so I stopped to listen. I'm devoted to sounds. I kept my digital recorder snapped around my belt because those woods and fields and brooks and breezes always rewarded me with nice audio to put myself into a meditative state when I needed it.

Back home in Somerville, my partner Robert claims I'm totally weird about sounds. He prefers silence, but I tell him there's no such thing in this busy world. We've been together five years and seven months, since January 6th, 2014, and though we certainly do have our differences, actual unfaithfulness isn't one of them. Not that we don't occasionally go out and fool around some, but it's a deeper sense of staying true to each other that really counts.

For this trip north, Robert gave me a twenty-ninth birthday present of an Airbnb somewhere out of the city, because he could tell my work was bringing me down. He works obsessively more than I do, but I still had four vacation weeks coming to me and Robert was looking forward to some undisturbed evenings at home without me acting all angsty. I wasn't too worried about him getting into trouble down there, and up in those hills there wasn't much chance of me getting into trouble either.

So there I stood at the dead end of that overgrown road, recording the wind swishing through the trees and the birds chirping, unless they were frogs. I'm not up on flora and fauna, but I love listening to all the mysterious croaks and warbles. Suddenly up ahead, something large crashed through the forest. I captured that too, probably a deer, though for all I knew it could've been a fat squirrel making a ruckus. I decided to turn around and seek a better road.

When I passed the Isuzu again, I noticed a narrow path winding up alongside the shed. Random flat stones here and there made it a kind of stairway. I didn't see a "keep out" or "no trespassing" or "no hunting" sign, so I figured I'd check on what was up there. There were hunting camps hidden away in those woods, shut for most of the year between seasons. I'd snooped around a few on my runs.

First, I came to a leafy-green vegetable patch surrounded by a rabbit fence and then some open ground where a small log cabin stood with a wooden rocking chair on the front porch, and sitting in it was an old man in grubby sweatshirt and jeans. His whiskery chin was nestled onto his chest. I assumed he was asleep, but I didn't turn back. Somehow I decided to keep walking up. Then I realized he was actually staring through eyeglasses at an open book in his lap.

"Hey hello, sir," I said in a cheerful voice. "I hope you don't mind. I didn't know there was a house up here."

His head popped up, a knobby hand to his forehead shading his eyes. With the afternoon sun behind me, I must've seemed only a black shape. "Yes, indeed, there is a house," he said in a not unfriendly tone and, after my own hesitant pause, added, "and we live here, me and Hank."

Was it possible that two old men had retreated to those woods to live out their lives together, safe and off the grid? I'd taken him for a mean-spirited Take Back Vermonter and expected to see a shotgun leaning against the cabin wall, but now it seemed okay to step closer. The sun was glinting off his silver-rimmed glasses, so he set them up on his wrinkled forehead and I got near enough to make out his pale blue eyes.

"Need these to read," he said. "Cataract surgery. Had to choose, near or far. Chose far. Should've chosen near since all I do these hot days is read."

"Do you mind a visitor?" I asked. "My name is Griffin. I'm up from Massachusetts for the month. I was out taking a jog." I'd forgotten to switch off my recorder, and that's how I began preserving my times with that old man. This is exactly what we said:

"Don't get visitors much, just the old gal down the road, the painter. Always wants to do my portrait, but I refuse. She's done Hank's, though."

"And your name is—" I began as I stepped onto the porch.

"Sam," he said. "Sam Fry, pleased to meet you."

"Griffin O'Dea, thank you, sir."

What he said next put me off for a moment. "Most people know better than to venture up here. I'm a crotchety old geezer liable to get on your case, young fella."

"I can handle it," I said. "I work for the city. I'm used to crotchetiness. I simply go home and meditate to recover."

"So you're one of those," Sam snorted, and then out of nowhere he said, "You see, they flee from me who sometime did me seek."

"That sounds like it's from your book?"

"No, fella, this book is Coleridge." At the time what I heard was "Coal Ridge" because Sam Fry looked so much like an old Appalachian coal miner. "He's another Samuel," he added shutting the old green volume with a snap. "Griffin, you say? What kind of name is that?"

"It's my mom's maiden name," I explained. "Griffin Eugene O'Dea. Eugene's my father."

Sam was surveying me up and down, and what he saw, now

that I was out of the sun, was a not-too-tall slightly stocky guy in gray running shorts, a drenched Tufts Jumbos jersey, and my floppy reddish hair dripping with sweat. That's as much of a description of myself as I need to give. Everything about me is what Robert affectionately calls chunky. He can talk, he's a stunner.

"The names kids get these days," Sam said. "Not many plain old Sams."

"Or Hanks?" I threw in.

"Short for Henry. Kings' names. Biblical kings. English kings. David's a king's name. So's Arthur. You Irish?"

"Half, I guess. My father's side."

"I'd offer you a seat but just got the one rocker 'cause I'm the only one to use it."

"What about Hank?" I ventured.

"Oh, he takes his shuteye this time of day." Sam gestured to the porch steps as if I should take a seat there. I wiped my brow with the sleeve of my jersey and settled down. Maybe the afternoon cool was about to set in.

"Can't figure why a city fella would go running about in this weather," Sam went on.

"It's cooler up here than Somerville."

"See, I like it real cold," Sam said and began to rock himself back and forth with the softly creaking sounds my recorder picked up so clearly. That evening, when I played the tape back, it conjured up the sight of the skinny old man, his grubby jeans, his scuffed-up leather boots, his knotty fingers still gripping the closed book with a thumb marking his place. He looked to be tallish, lanky, with thinning silvery hair, more of it than on most oldsters, and his chin and cheeks and upper lip showed only a few days' growth. Because he spoke so sharply, I was aware of his tight narrow lips and the surprisingly white teeth, possibly false, that occasionally caught the angled sunlight. His tongue, coated whitish, stuck out now and then to moisten his lips. I had noticed a half-full drinking glass set on the floor by the rocker. It could've held water or gin. I wasn't close enough to smell Sam's breath.

"Where you staying?" he asked.

"I took a room above the post office."

"How much the Cobbles get you for?"

"Nine hundred for the whole month."

"Nine hundred! For one measly room?"

"It works out to thirty a day. That's not a bad summer rental."

"Musty, moldy, I bet."

"No, it's sunny. I can use the kitchen behind the post office, and the bath in the hall. Nice couple, the landlords."

"Scam artists, those Cobbles," said Sam. I'd begun to notice that his way of expressing himself had two modes. He'd mix backwoodsy with educated, as in what he said next: "I have certain legal issues with this town. Don't mix much with them folks in the village. Fetch what little mail comes and hoof it outta there quick."

"But you drive your truck, don't you?"

"Yes, indeed I do. That's my hootnanny automobile. Still goes. Drove it up here in Eighty-Six. That's thirty-three years ago."

"You retired early, huh?"

"I'll say I retired! Stashed enough away. You pay nine hundred for one miserable room. Back then this whole property wasn't much more—house, acreage, fencing, barn out back, shed down at the road."

"Where did you come from, Sam?"

He shot me a piercing stare as if I'd doubt what he was going to tell me. "The immense city of Chicago!" he proclaimed with obvious pride. "A man could make a small fortune and go live fat and happy up on the North Shore. Wife and a daughter. Wife remarried, then daughter got married, she had my grandkids, two boys close to your age, by now, I reckon. Never seen either of 'em, only in pictures. Maybe some great-grandchildren by now. I'm almost eighty. What do you make of that?"

"It sounds kind of sad, I mean about your family," I said, unsure if that's what he'd want to hear.

Then with a fierce scowl he bellowed, "You bet it's sad!"

I looked down the steps at the path I'd come up. Off to one side, I could see the vegetable patch, maybe with zucchinis or cucumbers or squash or something beneath the leaves. Old Samuel Fry kept up his rocking.

Then out came one word: "Estrangement."

I nodded as if I could possibly share the weight of that thought. "I appreciate you telling me," I said. "Especially since you don't talk much to other people up here."

"No, I do not, Mr. O'Dea."

"Well, I'm honored."

"Phooey!" He chuckled at some private joke. "You see, it's Hank I talk to about these things. He's an excellent listener."

"I'd like to meet him."

"I don't interrupt his nap time. He's as old as me in some sense. Wiser, I give him that."

I waited before asking what was really on my mind, then I decided to go ahead. "Have you two been together a long time?"

"He came late into my life. Don't count the years. Feels like perpetuity."

That was one of his non-backwoodsy words. Of course, a man retired with a Chicago fortune, if I'd understood him, was surely no woodchuck, as they're called up there, but I was only beginning to assemble a sense of who this Sam Fry was. People don't often explain themselves as soon as you meet them. You have to put one hint next to another, like doing a puzzle. Right then, Sam was staring into the trees whose leaves had begun to rustle in the wind, which was picking up and cooling my forehead. I could hear a faint whir when I played it all back. I had considered telling the old man that what he'd been saying was being recorded, but I was afraid he'd yell at me to get the hell off his land. The guilty fact is, I never did reveal what I'd been doing all along.

That first day, I didn't get past Sam's front porch. I didn't meet Hank, and I wasn't offered a drink to replenish what I'd sweated out. I got so thirsty looking at that half-full glass beside the rocker, and it was thirst that made me say I'd be heading back for a cold shower. It didn't prompt Sam to get up from his chair. His thoughts had drifted far from his uninvited visitor. All he did was nod and take up his book again, set his glasses down over his squinting eyes, and open to the page where he'd left off.

"Could I stop by again sometime?" I asked as I stood up from the steps.

"Griffin? That's your name, right?"

"Or just Griff."

"Samuel, or just Sam."

"Sam," I repeated and, with a backward wave, took off at a jog, skipping down the random stones and back to the solitude of the dirt road and the crunching of my rubber soles.

Day Two

It didn't follow directly. The next day was rainy and even chilly, so I stayed inside and read the spy novel I'd picked up at the town dump's recycling barn. That morning, to help out Mr. and Mrs. Cobble, I'd piled the kitchen trash bags into my Smart Car, a normal vehicle in Somerville but exotic up there. "Three bucks," the dump guy said when I threw the bags in the hopper. "I see you got Mass plates. That Death Trap handle these rough roads of ours?" His disbelief made its way onto my recorder because, that first week, I was still planning to capture all the indigenous soundscapes, the locals being part of nature, too. But I gave up such a vast project after I'd become a regular visitor to Sam Fry's cabin. He was a soundscape all his own.

Sam wouldn't think much of the escapist stuff I was reading. The dump's barn had a long sagging shelf of books for the taking. They kept me entertained on dreary days and after dark. There wasn't much else to do with only one grungy general store down the valley, but escape was what I'd come for, not from Robert, truly not, but from the city planning office where nothing ever panned out the way I hoped it would. At community meetings, everyone was always at cross purposes, regular working folks facing off against slick-talking developers, liberal academics allying with the natives while still expecting their trendy coffee shops, rents shooting up, house prices out of sight—lucky we bought our one-bedroom condo when we did! I hate to say it but even some life-long townies were cashing in to get out of a city where all those brown people who don't speak English were crowding into the three-deckers.

It's hard fighting the good fight when you're not sure what it should be. So I was majorly stressed, and Robert knew it. Sometime he gets me better than I get him. He acts like his career is spitball compared to what I do, but wealth management would stress me out even worse than urban planning.

Up there in Vermont, nothing seemed planned or managed at all. There weren't enough people in that village to get on each other's nerves, though I doubtlessly missed some nasty undercurrents. I gathered there were entrenched factions over road maintenance and school fees and animal control and whatever. Aside from those legal issues he never explained, Sam Fry stayed out of it, and all I got from the Cobbles were some raised eyebrows when I mentioned I'd run up past Samuel Fry's place and got to talking with him.

But the next day after the rain, the sun came back and started drying things out, so I suited up and took off running to record the swollen brooks and the trees dripping in the wind. It was turning hot and steamy again, but I made a long loop around the hills, debating whether I should head back to see the old man. I hadn't yet figured out how all the roads connected, so coming down a hill past a derelict dairy farm, with one lonesome horse at the fence and a half dozen cows in the shade of a huge maple, I was surprised to find myself at the fork to Sam's dead end, but from the opposite direction. I turned in without further thought.

I huffed and puffed up to his cabin, and out stepped Sam Fry, clean shaven and taller than he'd seemed in his chair. He took a quick glance at me and said, "Seems you could use a cold beverage." He set a can of ginger ale on the porch railing and ducked inside to get himself another.

What had been in the back of my mind since I stumbled on his cabin was: who is this man Hank and what is he to Sam? I hadn't let on I was gay and wouldn't usually come out to an old geezer like Sam except for this Hank he talked about. Then I realized that the sweaty T-shirt I'd put on had "20 Pete 20" across the chest. Would he even know who Mayor Pete was? Sam didn't seem to care much for the world outside. I'm somewhat of a political junkie myself. Though my policies were with Bernie, one of the reasons I'd chosen Vermont for my retreat, I couldn't help feeling proud of the first ever out gay man running plausibly for president. What if Sam was a Trumper? Or maybe he was a survivalist. But if he and Hank proved to be long-term partners, like Robert Abreu and me, they might be role models for us and we might help bring them out into a more accepting world.

These possibilities went whipping through my head while I waited for Sam to return. "It's too stinking hot out here," he said peeking from the door. "Why don't you get your sweaty ass in here instead?"

Sweaty ass? For a second, I feared what I'd be stepping into.

In the book I'd been reading, the Austro-Hungarians had the British spy trapped in a Tyrolean farmhouse. But I trudged onto the creaky floorboards and grabbed the cool can on the railing. This will all be in a digital file, I told myself, not actually all that apprehensive. Sam was holding the door open.

Inside, my eyes had to adjust. I made out a cast-iron wood stove, cold of course, and behind it a closed door to where I assumed Hank was having his mid-day nap. To my left was an overstuffed couch and armchair, both threadbare, and a dim standing lamp beside a tall book case. To my right, Sam was pulling out a wooden chair for me to take a seat at a round wooden table. He settled himself in the other chair with his own can of ginger ale. Beyond him was a gas stove, a stubby old-fashioned fridge, a porcelain sink on high legs, lots of unpainted cupboards, and windows with curtains drawn against the sun. In the corner, there was also a closed wooden hatch, like the top half of a Dutch door.

So far my host had been silent, not to disturb the sleeper, so I didn't open my mouth either except to take an extended slug from the can. At last, Sam said, "Reckon I better let you meet my better half."

He went to the hatch and swung it open. A pungent draft blew in, not entirely unpleasant, but I couldn't place it. Then came a loud asthmatic yawn, and suddenly a gray donkey stuck its mournful face into the kitchen. It laid back its long ears and brayed another gasping ee-yaw, louder than the first. Now I had to re-calibrate everything. I could tell how Sam was relishing my surprise. All I thought to say was "Oh, Hank's a donkey."

"Yep, there he is, Honkety Hank. He's somewhat around your human age, which in his time of life means he's getting on. Still might make forty, surely outlast me. Haven't a notion what'll become of him then." Sam was fussing in the fridge and took out a peculiarly-shaped carrot to pass over to the animal. "Parsnip," he explained. "Loves 'em, grow 'em myself." He took his seat again while Hank munched, being a good listener.

Now Sam was squinting at my T-shirt. "So you're a Pete man. Twenty-twenty's coming. I'll be eighty next month. Born the day Germany invaded Poland. I find no peace and all my war is done." It sounded like another quote.

That night in my room above the post office, where they have Wi-Fi, I googled those words and up came Sir Thomas Wyatt the Elder (1503-1542). He died only ten years older than me and here's Sam Fry quoting him to this day! In college, I steered clear of literature courses except for Creative Non-Fiction to fill the Arts requirement. I took mostly Urban Studies and Sociology and Econ, which is where I met Robert, though we didn't get together for another five years.

After downing my drink, I asked Sam if I could give his donkey another parsnip. "That would be kindly," said Sam. He warned me to watch my fingers, but Hank took the parsnip gently. His eyes seemed to meet mine, though it's hard to know what a donkey is looking at. I saw he was standing out in a narrow stable that ran alongside the cabin. "He's also got a window over my bed," said Sam, "so he doesn't get lonesome at night." And I'd been imagining two old men in that bed keeping each other company into their last years.

Hank did appear to be listening to us. His ears kept perking up. My recorder captured the ear-splitting yawps, but it couldn't convey that sense of thoughtfulness in the creature. I admit, Robert and I anthropomorphize our cats, and Sam Fry had clearly made Honkety Hank into a life companion, better than human, he'd maintain. Hank's most useful contribution that afternoon and ever after was how he'd deflect us from squabbling, calm us down. His donkey nature, his ever-patient, long-suffering, philosophically resigned spirit put us in perspective. Hank was mulling over his own unarticulated thoughts about parsnips and hay and keeping cool in that stuffy stall, and he must've enjoyed his sense of those two-legged fellow beings in there, his loyal provider and some reddish-haired newcomer reeking of sweat. He had no opinion about a gay man running for president.

But Sam had returned to the subject. "So you like this fella Pete." He gave me a sharp stare. The coming out I'd expected was about to occur. I didn't know what line to take, so I simply tapped the logo on my chest and gave a smile. "He's the smartest one," Sam said, "but this stupid country don't feature smarts."

"I'm afraid you're right," I said "I work for the city, and you wouldn't believe how truly stupid it can get."

"Lots to be said for a king," said Sam. "Least as long as he's me." He leaned his head back and sort of brayed, enough to cue Hank to open his toothy mouth and join in. "That's my pal!" Sam said. "Bet you figured Hank was another old codger like me and we was a couple of backwoods queers!" Sam was having a good laugh now. I could feel myself blushing. "I like my little deceptions, young Griffin O'Dea. I had you there, didn't I?"

"I mean, it did seem a possibility."

"Named him after a song I used to play on the Victrola when I was a kid: 'Honkety Hank and his Hootnanny Automobile.' Know what a Victrola is? Anyways, bet you can find the song on that famous internet I reckon you're addicted to."

I shot a glance around the cabin and didn't spot even a phone, and no TV, no radio, certainly no computer unless they were all in back. I'd seen no electric or phone lines coming up the hill. How did that dim lamp stay lit? How did the fridge keep ginger ale cold? And what would Sam do in an emergency? What if he was dead and Hank was starving? There's no cell reception because of the hills. How did Sam even know who Pete Buttigieg was? No newspapers were lying around. The books on those shelves looked ancient, fat old hardbacks with faded spines.

"I guess you save yourself the hassle, Sam," I said. "I mean, you're not online, are you? But how do you get the news?"

"I'll tell you something, my friend: the news is a misnomer. They should call it the sames. One gander at the valley paper at that sad excuse for a general store and I know all I need. Now, this Pete with the strange name—"

"It's Maltese," I said.

"Portuguese, Maltese, Lebanese, Burmese, all those 'eses. I tell you it's the Chinese to watch out for. They got us by the balls. This Pete's a queer fella, isn't he?"

"He's gay, and he's married," I said as if that would make a difference.

"Marriage!" Sam snorted. "I could tell you about marriage. So you're queer, too, aren't you?"

"I prefer gay, but yes." Phew, now that was over.

"Thought it was 'queer' they're saying now. Can't keep up and don't have to. I grew up politely saying 'colored' for 'black.' What the hell does it matter! Right, Hank?"

The donkey's solemn expression, as I imagined it anyway, proved he never had to make distinctions. His kind have been the most useful but also the most abused of all beasts of burden. They have donkey rescue farms now, so maybe Hank came from one. That evening, I did google "donkeys" (not "asses") and got tons of YouTube videos to watch into the late hours. I also found that Honkety Hank song from Sam's childhood. But I'm not addicted. Sam didn't have any notion of how addicted the generation after me is these days.

He tossed his empty can into a trash barrel and said, "What the hell! I'll call you whatever you like. I'll even call you Griff. Sounds a bit quaint for my taste. Got a boyfriend or partner or husband or take your pick?"

"I do. Robert Abreu. He's in finance. Makes lots more than me."

"I made lots more than her, too, that's for sure. Ay-broo?"

"Portuguese, the way Americans would say it."

"Portuguese, that's nothing. It's the Chinese you got to watch out for. Now, admit I had you thinking Hank was another old man."

"I mean, it's how it sounded."

Sam was so pleased with himself. He leaned forward, elbows on the table. His shabby sweatshirt was loose at the neck where a tuft of gray hairs poked out. He peered at me over his silver-rimmed spectacles, I decided to call them, and said, "Do you think I honestly give a shit about what other people make of me? I gave that up years ago. So should you. Farewell, love, and all thy laws forever. Fuck it!"

That turned out to be by Sir Thomas Wyatt, too. Not the "fuck it" of course. Eventually, I found all the lines Sam Fry kept spouting and also learned how to spell his namesake, Samuel Taylor Coleridge. I'd get him back one day by saying I assumed he was on a Sir Thomas Wyatt kick.

But I began wondering if I was just another sounding board for him, like Hank only less elemental. Or was Sam itching for a worthy adversary to spice up his monkish hermitage? He appeared to want me to come back because he stood up creakily and said, "Kind of you to stop by. Anytime, but now I can use a nap. This heat is getting me down. Quenched your thirst enough, Mr. O"Dea?"

"I could actually use just a glass of plain water, if you don't mind."

"Have all the water you want. Told you I came out east with a small fortune. Did everything right: drilled well, propane tank five-hundred gallons, few years back even put up a set of solar panels in the meadow. You thought I was living in the nineteenth century—gas lantern, hand pump, stinking outhouse? I'm no hippie, fella."

"I wondered about electricity," I said after gulping down the water he handed me.

Sam yawned and nudged Hank back so he could close the hatch. "I'll open the rear one for our nap," he said. "Hank knows the routine. So off you go then, son." I had taken hold of the iron latch on the front door. "You ever run into that Elaine Greene, the painter lady?" I hadn't. "Well, when you do, tell her to do your portrait 'stead of mine. Next house down the way, brick cape with big mulberry out front. She's my bothersome neighbor. Lesbian on top of it." He had another private chuckle. "Now, out!" he barked and flicked his gnarly fingers at me as if shooing chickens.

Days Off

With all that liquid sloshing around inside me, I didn't feel like running. So I sauntered past the painter woman's house, shades all drawn, and when I got out of the woods to the paved road, the lower sun struck me hard. I'd intended to drop a few pounds that month, not that Robert minded. He liked stockiness as long as it was solidly packed.

In the shower, there was plenty to mull over, not just the fact of the donkey. I was annoyed that Sam thought news was more of the same. He must not have been keeping up with it all. Glancing at headlines wouldn't tell him much. Maybe I'm an idealist, young enough not to have seen the long-term picture, but back in August, it seemed a tipping point in history, and now as winter comes on it's looking even scarier. Just because Sam Fry won't have to live as long with the consequences!

I set my smelly running clothes on the windowsill to dry out and put on clean baggies, a plain white T, and flip-flops to go down to the hammock in the yard behind the building with my historical spy novel for distraction. World War One is very "in" now that it's been a century since.

I'd almost decided not to return to Sam's. There must be good reasons why mentioning him raised eyebrows in that little village. But before I opened my book, I pulled my recorder out of my shorts, put in my earbuds, and was soon aurally back in that dimly lit dark cabin, listening for clues in Sam's crotchety voice and wry chuckles.

"It's the Chinese to watch out for... I could tell you about marriage... I thought it was 'queer' they were saying now." If I cared to hear it that way, he could sound racist, misogynist, and homophobic. I'm not that sensitive myself, but the scene at City Hall definitely is. I have to watch what I say, even ironically. My supervisor tries to be inclusive: "How's your husband doing, Griff?" When I remind her we're not actually married, she gets embarrassed.

The more I re-played Sam and the way Hank would suddenly let out a loud honk, I knew I'd be going back sooner than later, but for now I plunged into more gruesome details of the torture techniques used on the British spy in that remote farmhouse on an Austrian mountainside. Why do I read this stuff? I asked myself. And me, swinging peacefully in a rope hammock in a pleasant Vermont back yard on a sunny August day, shaded by the tall maples!

I don't intend to go into my daily life up there. I did have conversations with my landlords and with the cheery postmistress when I got my daily cards from Robert. I suspected she read them. I sent short notes back on the ready-stamped post cards he'd sent me off with, a very Robert thing to do, a bit controlling but lovingly meant. We'd agreed for a month not to use the internet to keep in touch, part of his decompression plan for me. Besides, I didn't know if I'd even have service up there, and he didn't want me driving off to some bigger town to get it. It was our chance to live life as it used to be, proof we had faith in each other. I didn't confess that the post office downstairs did have Wi-Fi. So far in my cards, I hadn't said anything about Samuel Fry, either. Robert's own cards were full of made-up bulletins from the outside world, like that Vladimir Putin and Angela Merkel had been caught in a secret love nest.

I hadn't yet thought of transcribing my tapes. Who'd care what my landlords said or the postmistress or the dump guy? But it soon occurred to me I could do some sort of oral history project on Sam Fry, even turn it into a podcast without his permission because he'd never have access to it. It would depend on how interesting our talks got to be, how colorful or outrageous the old man really was, and I'd begun to wonder if I was in for some major form of enlightenment. But this was my mind running away with itself, not thinking of Sam's privacy. I'd have to stop fantasizing, but I wasn't ready to stop making my secret recordings.

Still, I didn't feel like visiting Sam right away. That evening, after salad from the hippie produce farm and two slices of dry pizza from the general store, I sat up in bed watching donkey videos: over-worked underfed donkeys in Sicily, soulful retired donkeys in manger scenes outside churches at Christmas, donkey rescue farms, a family with a miniature donkey that thought it was a dog, donkey baseball games—too much to take in. I read about literary donkeys: *Travels with a Donkey*, Balaam's ass, Sancho Panza's donkey, Brick le Brit in the Grimms' fairy tales, the wise old donkey of the King of Yvetot, and of course Eeyore, the pessimist donkey in his gloomy swamp. Then I listened to Harry Belafonte singing "Jackass, he jump and bray, let him bray, let him bray" and saw paintings of "The Flight into Egypt" with Mary and Jesus on donkeyback and Joseph leading them, and that's how donkeys got those crosses in the hairs on their backs, and donkeys representing the Democratic Party so I can't help loving them, and Pin the Tail on the Donkey from kids' birthday parties when we'd rather have been on our Game Boys. I listened again to the Honkety Hank song, an earworm by then, and had a hard time falling asleep.

The next day and the next were stormy. De-stressing was in danger of getting boring, but Robert always says boredom clears out your head so you can fill it up again with what you really want to do.

Day Three

The first thing I thought of on Monday, when the air was swept clear and dry and warm, but not yet hot, was to go for an early jog and visit Sam. I found him in his vegetable patch. Hank was grazing in the meadow behind the split-log fence. He didn't look up, but Sam did, shaded his eyes, and said, "My galley charged with forgetfulness." He said "charged" in two syllables.

I apologized for not stopping by over the weekend. "The rain," I explained.

"Don't much feature visitors," said Sam, holding open the rabbit fence gate for me. "Go for weeks unless Elaine stumbles over to bother me."

"Stumbles?"

"She's no spring chicken 'cept compared to me. Feeble for her age, though. Don't mean in the head. Uses a cane. But her eyes, they pick out things, painter's eyes. She saw you first. Day before you showed up here, she comes by with 'Who's the kid that keeps chugging along, short with a dark red mop on his head?' Had no notion what she was talking about."

"She described me as short?"

"Well, she's a real tall woman, six foot, just somewhat stooped.

I used to be six-three. Shrank of late. Spine, knees, gravity, Mr. O'Dea."

He was plucking weeds from around the bigger leaves. I'd never seen close-up how vegetables actually grew. Sam pointed out what was spinach or brussels sprouts or the tops of carrots and parsnips. "Takes a lot of tending, I guess," I said.

"Everything takes tending, young fella," he said.

I checked to make sure my device was on. I didn't want to miss the folksy side of him.

"About done for the day," he said. He had a hard time heaving himself up, so I reached him a hand. "Thank you kindly," he grumbled back, shut the flimsy gate behind us, and turned toward the cabin. I heard him say, maybe grudgingly, "You're allowed to come along."

Inside, he brought me a glass of cold water and set me down, not at the kitchen table but on one end of the fuzzy sagging couch, then he lowered himself into the armchair beside the lamp. He asked me, as if we were already in the middle of a conversation, "Do you have any idea how many galaxies are up there?" He was gesturing to the rough-hewn beams above us. Where did that come from?

"I mean, I know the Milky Way isn't the major one."

"Tens of thousands of galaxies, at least. Know how many stars in each?"

"No, I don't."

"Milky Way's about four-hundred billion. Nothing to the trillion in a truly big galaxy. We're not even the biggest of our near neighbors. You got the Andromeda, can see it with your naked eye. And we're but a crummy little solar system on the edge of a piddling galaxy on a stinking little planet set to disappear into our exploding sun in some millions more years, and we think we're the cat's pajamas!"

"Cat's pajamas?"

"You know the expression?"

"Not really."

"Delighted to introduce you to the colorful locutions of your elders and betters." He gave a private chuckle, staring out the side window where the curtain was drawn open so he could check on Hank, who was standing up there in his own lonesome donkey meditation by the solar panels.

"I would've expected you to have a cat here, Sam, for the mice."

"I snap 'em all dead, any mouse makes its way in, snap! A mouse once chewed up half a page of my poem. That done it. No mercy. Don't need no cat."

"Chewed up a poem by Sir Thomas Wyatt?" I asked to startle him.

His eyes popped wide open. "No! My poem!" he almost yelled. "What do you think I spend my time doing in this one-horse town? You familiar with the expression, one-horse town?"

"I get the idea."

Now Sam was laughing so loud he held onto his belly, which bulged out more than I'd noticed when tucked behind the kitchen table. I don't hear myself giving back more than awkward giggles on the tape.

After he'd taken a deep breath and composed himself again, Sam said, "Thomas Wyatt, eh? Good for you. College class?"

"No, sir, I googled one of those lines you quoted."

"Ah, forgot about your addiction," he said with a snort. "No, kid," he said considering whether he should reveal more, "I been writing a very long poem in three cantos. Any notion what a canto is?"

"A song?" I guessed.

Sam simply blew at his lips and went on: "It's taken years, young fella. Elaine caught me at it once, so I had to confess. You're the second human to learn of my magnum opus. Sworn to secrecy? It's an epic poem called 'Unfaithfulness.'"

"I'd like to read it."

"No, you wouldn't. An ignorant youth like you? Has to google everything. Besides, you might mistake it for decent poetry."

I couldn't tell what response he was fishing for. "I mean, I don't know a thing about poems," I said, "but I imagine it's better than you think. At work, I always think my proposals suck until they go over well in presentation sessions."

"I do not intend to present my blank-verse epic to anyone. You know what blank verse is?"

"Sort of free-flowing?"

"The exact opposite, my ill-educated friend. Though it should read as if it were free. Iambic pentameter? Ever heard of it?"

"Yes, I have," I said but not sure how to define it.

"Ever read Shakespeare?"

"In high school I did."

"*Romeo and Juliet*, right? *Macbeth*."

"*Julius Caesar!*" It had just come to me.

"What else don't you know?"

I sat up straight and took a careful sip of my water to collect my thoughts. "Sam," I said slowly, "I admit I can't know all you do, but I know plenty of things you probably don't and keep learning more. You shouldn't be so critical. I mean, what's it to you anyway? Why are you even talking with me when you go weeks without seeing a soul but Hank? Am I bothering you like this Elaine person? Why did you even invite me in?" I was shocked at what had poured out my mouth. Usually, I'm non-confrontational. I saw the water quivering in my glass.

Sam said nothing for a full fifteen seconds. I timed it on the recording. Finally, he said, "Don't understand it myself."

"But why, Sam?"

"Oh, maybe because in half a century, when you're my age, you'll recall what this old coot, such as you will be by then, had to say once upon a time. That is, if you're alive and the earth's still habitable."

"Our conversation?"

"We're having ourselves a discourse, young fella. I don't waste time on conversations. Don't even mean a discussion. Discussion's a weak sister to a discourse. You know the term 'weak sister'?"

"I get what it means."

"Galileo wrote discourses. You heard of Galileo?"

"Of course," I said with some confidence at last.

"His theories on mechanics and motion. He'd already shown how the earth moves about the sun, heresy that it was, and he paid for it." Sam pointed to the beams or rafters or whatever they're called and above them to the white-painted boards of the peaked ceiling. "Back when I was a boy," he began, "not so long ago in astronomical terms, they called galaxies nebulae, giant gas clouds, but bit by bit they were recognizing how puny our corner of the universe is. No wonder the god people were getting nervous!"

Sam went on. I've transcribed his words from the recording, but I'm cutting the um's and er's and repetitiveness because no one wants to read how much people stutter and hem and haw.

"Naturally, Mr. O'Dea, if you're standing still with the stars revolving around you, you feel like the cat's pajamas. You can make up all sorts of gods of land and sea and sky and, eventually, as if it's an improvement, one single dad-god in control of everything. Revealing choice, eh? Most of humanity still thinks that dad-god is up there among the billions of trillions of stars despite all we've learned! Ever heard such nonsense?"

"I'm not religious myself," I said. "My father grew up Roman Catholic and my mom sometimes goes to the Unitarians. Robert's family's all serious Catholics, but not him."

"Robert?" He rubbed his wrinkled brow until it dawned on him: "I forgot, the husband."

"We're not married. At least not yet."

Sam shrugged inside the baggy gray sweatshirt he wore even in hot weather. "Marriage!" he blurted out with scorn. "'Unfaithfulness'—that's the title of my magnum opus. Spent the last thirty years scratching away at it, page upon page upon page."

"Because your wife left you?" I was trying to sound super sympathetic.

Sam leaned back in silence. We heard a far-off ee-yaw from the meadow.

I dared to ask one thing more: "Unfaithful, as in adultery?"

But Sam said, "Unfaithfulness simply means lack of faith."

"I'm amazed, Sam, that you're confiding this in me. Elaine knows, too?"

"Elaine's a lesbian. Touchy about men. And Hank's heard it all many a time. Seems there's something about you, Griffin O'Dea, that bugs me. That's why."

"I bug you?"

He was staring fiercely across the narrow room where the sunlight formed a bright path on the pine floor between us. I had to say something. Out came: "I mean, if I'm bugging you, I don't have to stay." On the tape, Sam can be heard chuckling to himself. While I waited, it hit me right then that I was, literally, bugging him and he didn't know it. The bug was covered by my untucked dried-out Pete T-shirt.

"Free to leave," said Sam. "I'm no kidnapper."

"Or maybe my bugging you inspires your discourse, or whatever?"

"I'd call you an irritant, as if the world wasn't irritating enough."

"I'm an irritant."

"All young folk are. You think we appreciate your coming along?"

"My grandparents are glad I've come along."

"That's what they tell you."

I leaned back to seem as unruffled as I could be. "You certainly are a crotchety old geezer like you said, Mr. Fry."

Sam smiled his wry smile and, spreading his knobby fingers on the chair arms, pulled himself up. "Time for Hank to get out of the sun."

I followed his creaky legs to the door, out and down the porch steps, and around to the meadow and through the wide gate. Hank loped over for a pat on his shaggy forehead, and we accompanied him into the stable attached to the far side of the cabin where his stall was. He went straight to his water trough. Standing at the stable door I said, "I'd better be off anyway."

Sam nodded and went to fork some hay and pour some grain into the bin under the bedroom hatch.

"Can I ask one thing first?"

"Yep," said Sam, his mind now on other things.

"I notice you sometimes speak like a country bumpkin and sometimes like a professor I had in college."

"Maybe I once was a college professor. Now I'm a country bumpkin."

"Where did you teach? What did you teach? Astronomy, poetry?"

"I said 'maybe' I was a professor. I didn't say it as a fact. See, I can irritate you right back. We're engaged in a subtle war of the generations. So off you go, running and wrecking your knees for all I care."

When I played it back, his last quip sounded almost affectionate.

Day Four

In my room above the post office, I googled "Samuel Fry Chicago" but found nothing. Maybe it was better not to know. He'd tell me what he wanted me to know and when.

I took a long afternoon nap. Why was I so tired? And therefore that night, I wasn't sleepy at all. Relieving some sexual build-up didn't help the usual way. Afterwards, at ten o'clock I went out to look at the night sky. I stood in the center of the small village green, a triangle of grass where three roads met. A week ago a tethered calf had been grazing there. The postmistress told me he was gone to slaughter now. With cattle, that's the fate of most of the males.

I leaned my head back and scanned the blackness above for anything that might be the Andromeda nebula, I mean galaxy. I recognized the more famous constellations, but mostly it was those billions of Milky Way stars and some cloudy patches hiding the moon. I tilted sideways as if to gaze deeper into the heart of our galaxy from the outer edge where we were. Up and down don't mean a thing in the universe, only farther and farther out.

Not a single car passed while I stood there, no lights flicked on in the handful of dark houses that made up the village of this mostly empty town. People went to bed early in Vermont and got up with the light. I tried to feel the earth turning away from the sun, and then, as I stood there a long time, I tried to feel us turning back toward it. Sunrise is a misnomer, as Sam Fry would say. The sun doesn't rise. We're slowly moving back to where it's been all along. Not an original perception, but in daily life I never think of it that way. Sun salutations shouldn't be "Welcome, Sun" but rather "Here we come, Sun, after being away from you all night."

Back in bed, I squeezed a longer than usual note on my daily Robert card about how, on that little village green, I got a better sense of the vastness of the universe than I ever got at home. Did he know it's not just millions or billions but many trillions of stars out there? That doesn't help de-stress me, I told him. In fact, it's begun messing with my sense of who I am. But I didn't mean to worry him. I was doing fine, no problem, just some meditative philosophical bullshit I wanted to share.

Robert knows I'm more of a dreamer than he is. At work, I come up with over-determined unrealistic projects for how City Hall might cope with the housing crisis, with traffic patterns, with all our demographic changes. I'm big into clustering and green space and pedestrian zones and bike paths, the expectable things but made way too elaborate. Still, at the planning office I'm appreciated for opening up the dialogue. Robert thinks my proposals go against human nature. Pursuit of happiness, he says, means getting more than you need with no one telling you what to do with it.

We're used to arguing from our opposing camps. During a rocky spell in our relationship, our counselor assured us that couples do better when they don't totally think the same—as long as they respect their differences, as long as they talk about them and accept where the other's coming from. Especially, he said, when it's two men stuck in a single gender together. The friction keeps it vibrant. I could imagine discussing this with Sam, or discoursing on it, if he liked. He'd had to deal with two genders. To me, that seems much more difficult.

In the morning, I posted my card, but it was too early for Robert's to have come in. He'd stopped sending "fake news alerts" that weren't all that funny anyway. He and I do share a taste for stupid things like Daniel Tosh or the Jackass movies. We pop some popcorn and cuddle up with the cats and our TV with the Roku box. It can't hurt to indulge in offensive videos in the privacy of your own home, but we don't admit it except to our closest friends. People at my work would be appalled.

Up in Vermont, I did miss those mindless entertainments, not to mention us having sex. I hadn't gone without it for so long ever since college. Relieving the pressure by myself was all I could do. I didn't want to resort to Grindr in case it might show up on the post office internet. Robert had plenty of options, and we'd promised each other to report any "adventures" on the side, but so far none. I began to wonder about Sam Fry. Had he been celibate for thirty-plus years? I'm sure it slows down by fifty, and by eighty it must be nonexistent, but still. Maybe he and the painter woman had a thing going once, though he said she was a lesbian. I know women are supposed to be more fluid than men. Maybe I'd knock on her door when I ran by later that day.

But her shades were drawn, and no one answered when I gave a light tap on her door. I didn't feel quite ready to head on to Sam's, so I kept running past the fork and up beyond the dairy farm with its lonely horse at the fence and cows grazing down by the brook. I could've turned left to loop back home, but instead I kept on the same road into higher hills, good exercise working off the pounds. I did feel lighter that day, but not as sweaty. The air was cool enough to have put on my long-sleeve Tufts Jumbos jersey again.

The dirt road crested at an overgrown cemetery on the uphill side, which gave the dead, so to speak, a wide view of a green valley across the road. I found a seat on a fallen tombstone and listened to the country sounds, birds, insects, wind, a distant tractor mowing some field. Everything in sight was a small sample of the whole planet: crops, streams, animals, machinery, a barn roof, a farmhouse way down there, people out of sight. My Econ classes, Micro and Macro, showed how everything large is contained already in everything small. The -cosm is short for cosmos. So maybe Samuel Fry could live up there and not feel he was out of the real world, that everything there was enough, a smaller version of everything beyond.

I stayed half an hour, a half hour of distant moos and tractor rumbles and chattering squirrels and cawing crows and bees buzzing on my tape. (We still call it "tape" though no tape is involved anymore.) The tombstone had fallen face down, so I didn't know who the dead person below me was, but I didn't feel disrespectful. I was partaking in the proper spirit of his or her state of obliviousness.

But I didn't lose myself for good. Before my joints stiffened, I got up and stretched thoroughly then took off retracing my route to Sam's fork. He was standing out on his porch as if he'd known I was coming. I ran up, but he put his hands in front of him, palms out, to stop me right there. In a surprisingly unwavering voice, he started to recite something strange, as if he'd seen a vision:

Westron wind, when will thou blow?
The small rain down can rain.
Christ, that my love was in my arms
And I in my bed again.

I stood in silence not knowing what he expected. Then he repeated the poem more slowly and quietly, to ponder the meaning of each word. The "Christ" had puzzled me, so had "my love was in my arms." What if Sam was having an emotional spiritual crisis and I'd have to cope with it?

But he lowered his hands and said in a more bumpkin voice, "Tend to shoot my mouth off on the cooler days. That was my favorite of all poems. Ancient. Who wrote it? No one. Just is. Well, I do have one more favorite I'll save for later. Not in a nice mood today. I warn you. Maybe best you don't come in now."

"It sounded very sad, Sam, but you recited it like a real actor."

"Maybe I was a real actor once. Are actors ever real? Actors have to make you think they're real, that's all."

"I don't mean to interrupt your day, so I'll run on, but I'll check in tomorrow?"

"See, son, I been immersing myself in the sonnets of Sir Thomas Wyatt the Elder, as you so correctly identified him. Not a body of work to cheer one up. 'Like to these immeasurable mountains—' Look it up on your machine."

With a quick shake of his silvery hair, he turned back into the cabin. An ee-yaw resounded from the stable. Hank could tell his friend was coming over to open the hatch for another chat. The donkey was who he could turn to when he was feeling low.

I remained somewhat shook up, though. There was a depressed side to Sam I wasn't sure I should get involved with. The point of coming to Vermont was for a month without human complications. I'd been returning from the office all discombobulated, as Robert put it, all entangled by the constant drama of who was on whose side or who was undercutting who else. I'd been taking it all too personally. Robert said if he got emotional about his clients' finances, he'd never do right by them. Robert has a "silent" place in his brain that allows him to get things done steadily and efficiently, while I get angsty and upset.

I ran past Elaine's brick house again and caught sight of an SUV parked around back, one of those super-ugly Nissan Aztecs they haven't made for years. She must've been home, but I kept on running. I didn't feel ready to introduce myself right then and get drawn into whatever issues she had with Sam Fry.

When I got back to my room, I took my iPad and the spy novel out to the hammock, intending to finish the stupid book before checking work emails. Though I'd told them I'd be off the grid for my vacation, I couldn't help occasionally looking in on what was happening in my absence. But first, I had to search what Sam recited, the short poem by "no one." All I had to do was type in "Western wind" and it came up also as "Westron wind" the way Sam had pronounced it. There were several versions with different spellings from before English was regularized. I imagined it made Sam remember his ex-wife and got him thinking about his lonely life ever since. He wanted her back? Was she even alive anymore? "My bed" meaning "their bed," not the one with Hank's hatch above it that I hadn't yet seen? I figured Sam had never let go of the past. He had adopted a sad-looking donkey instead of a cheerful bouncy dog or even a self-sufficient cat. Or two cats like ours to keep each other busy with kitty handball in the bathtub or kitty soccer with crinkled paper on the living room carpet.

I also looked up some of those Wyatt poems and got the depressing gist of them, but they were hard to analyze, at least lying in a hammock on a drowsy cool afternoon. Instead, I went back to the spy's daring escape and how he made it across the Alps to the British command, though I can't say I cared much. World War One seemed a pointless horror show on both sides, not to forget the influenza everyone was coming down with. And I was supposed to be glad the book had a triumphant ending? I grew up with Gramps and Grams O'Dea being none too keen on the Brits.

When the postmistress opened after her late lunch, I went to pick up Robert's card. He reported how Alice and Martha, our cats, were drooping about in the heat because the central air in the building had broken down and he was pretty damn hot himself. "Lucky you're up in the mountains, Griff. Don't come back till fall." He knew I was only staying to Labor Day weekend, but I couldn't be sure how funny he meant to be. Maybe my cards hadn't said enough of how much I missed him. I did miss him very much, yet I was committed to my retreat. I was sticking to our plan. It had nothing to do with not wanting to be with Robert. And I wasn't really in the mountains but more the foothills. On certain hilltops on my runs, though, I did catch sight of a distant peak or two, some to the west but some to the east all the way over into New Hampshire.

Elaine

I didn't know if Sam would want me stopping by again so soon. I even wondered if I wanted to myself. There wasn't much else to do in that quiet backwater, but that was my whole reason for being there, I told myself once again. After catching up on the controversies at work, I was happy not to be in the city. It didn't matter to me anymore whether they put in a rotary at a congested intersection or if the affordable apartments in a new complex were fourteen or sixteen-feet wide. I'd been a strong advocate for sixteen so the renters wouldn't feel squeezed into narrower rooms than the market-rate units. When I paced off my room above the post office, it was only twelve-feet wide and I didn't feel squeezed, but there was only one of me, not a large immigrant family, and I had less than three more weeks to stay there. By September, the board would probably have compromised at fifteen. Was it something about Samuel Fry that caused me to feel less passionate about issues at work?

I mulled it over while I ate my Grape Nuts Flakes and banana and drank my Earl Grey at the counter downstairs. That kitchen was for the postmistress to make her lunches and for BnB guests, by then only me, but the day I arrived two overflow wedding attendees had occupied the larger room and I was told to expect a Connecticut couple on a later weekend for someone's family birthday party. The room with the king-size bed went for sixty a night, still a deal by city standards, no matter what Sam Fry thought.

I kept returning to his various outraged attitudes. Why would I go subject myself to them again? He made me feel somehow ignorant though I'd graduated magna and got A's in most subjects except science. I got an A+ in the creative non-fiction class. My professor said she saw me as a natural writer, even if I didn't know it. That was quite encouraging. Sam put me on edge, especially after I'd been on those long runs with my blood pumping and my brain cleared out. It was usually a form of meditation, but it left me vulnerable to a dose of his cranky attitude.

No, I decided I wouldn't see him that day. Besides, I didn't want him expecting daily visits. Let him talk to Honkety Hank. Let Elaine go bug him instead. Elaine. Maybe that was who I should drop in on instead.

On my run, to stall a decision, I went the long way around, but when I came down the dirt road and passed the fork to Sam's, I did pull to a stop, hands on knees and breathing hard, at Elaine's driveway where the Aztec was standing, its rear door open with two bags of groceries inside. I was still huffing and puffing when she came out the front door leaning on a cane.

"So you're the one!" she called out. "I know all about you." She limped straight to the SUV and picked up a bag, so I sprinted over and offered to help. "Why not. Save me a trip," she said. I hadn't turned on my device. I'm quoting her greeting from memory, but I quickly slipped a hand under the sweaty T-shirt and punched the button. More good sound, I told myself.

Elaine closed the hatch and set off with her cane toward the front door. I followed. "Kitchen's where the living room used to be," she said. "Backwards house. Sunny side's out back, so I switched the rooms. Prefer to paint in the sun. Screw north light." When I set the second bag on the counter, she thanked me and said, "Elaine Greene with a final E. Sam wants me to paint you 'stead of him. Gotta be interested in a face to paint it, though. Not sure about yours yet. Seems kinda unformed. The pale skin reddens up on your runs and the freckles disappear. You're all too smooth." She was looking me over, head to toe. "Not as short as I took ya for, seeing ya run by."

"I'm five-eight."

"It's that baggy shirt and the meaty thighs," she said almost as if I wasn't standing there. Was I unworthy of her brush? I'd never been assessed so particularly. Robert says he likes the whole package. But Elaine was going on: "Been trying to get Sam to sit for me. No deal. I done him anyway." She was putting canned goods and cardboard boxes on the open shelves and the fresh stuff in the fridge. Then she led me past a steep staircase. "Used to sleep upstairs. Too hobbled now." I'd noticed a dark room opposite the kitchen with an unmade brass bed and clothes draped about. "Bathroom's in under there if ya need it." She pointed with her cane at a narrow door behind the kitchen, and we trooped ahead into the wide sunny back room where she immediately began pulling out half a dozen canvases from stacks leaning against the wall and then a pile of pen-and-ink sketches from her work table. Beyond were two easels with some work-in-progress on one, and on the other she started displaying the Sam portraits one by one. "He never seen 'em," she said with a twinkle in her dark eyes.

"I'd recognize him anywhere," I said. She had got his wrinkled brow, the silvery wisps of hair, and those pale eyes, behind glasses or not. Elaine pointed out the liver spots on his cheeks, the short stubble in some portraits, the clean shave in others. One showed his lanky self standing on his porch, another at the split-log fence with a hint of the donkey in the background. "Why don't you show him these?" I asked her.

"You kidding? He'd kill me. Don't ya dare tell him."

I shook my head and put a hand up, like taking an oath.

"All right. I'll go get some iced tea. What's your name anyways?"

"Griffin, Griffin O'Dea."

"Griffin, like the medieval monstrosity. Sam told me."

"It's a family name," I explained. "Then Harry Potter had to go use it. I got kidded a lot in school."

Elaine directed me to a long window seat in the bright sun, so I sat and watched her clunk her way back to the kitchen. Sam had said she was tall despite her stoop, and she was all sharp angles, too, elbows and knees and chin. Her dyed jet-black hair up in a bun on the back of her head could've come off a bear, and her long blue-jean skirt hung loosely from her narrow hips. Like Sam, she was wearing cracked-leather ankle-high boots but no socks I could see.

"I hear the Cobbles got you paying thirty a night," she said when she handed me a tall cold glass of tea with ice and a slice of lemon. "Couldn't even give a monthly discount? Those people! They take us flatlanders for all they can. Those two go back generations in this town. Newcomers they tolerate, but you summer renters!" She blew out her cheeks and blubbered her thin lips.

"You've been here how long, Ms. Greene?"

"Elaine! Not quite so long as Sam. Soon as I move here, he takes an immediate interest, the horny old bastard."

I was startled and probably showed it, so I sipped my tea and waited for whatever was coming next, glad to be recording this.

"Oh, he's a good enough egg," she said. "We worked it out quick. Thinks I'm gay. Solved the whole dilemma. Wasn't any gal a lesbian who wouldn't hop in bed with that old letch? His way of excusing himself." Elaine Greene took a seat beside me with her own glass of tea and started spreading out her sketches on the coffee table. "Caught every characteristic gesture. Sam reciting poems. Sam haranguing. Sam nuzzling Hank. You met Hank?"

"Funny," I said, "when Sam told me Hank was napping, I thought he was referring to another old man."

"His boyfriend!" hooted Elaine. "He got a kick outta that. Best joke he ever pulled. But you're the actual queer one, ain't ya?"

"Right," I said. I could tell from the casual way she said "queer" she meant it in a friendly way.

"Got a boyfriend in the city?"

"Robert."

"See, Sam told me everything. You're up here to get your head together."

"Did he say that?"

"Lots of folks come here to mellow out."

So I said, "I mean, working at City Hall gets stressful. Not that I was falling apart. But I needed a break."

"Too much Robert maybe, if ya catch my drift?" She didn't

give me time to reply. "That Sam sees deep into people, reads 'em good." She stretched one long skinny arm along the windowsill and tapped me on the far shoulder. "A philosopher of sorts. Reads all them poems. Writes 'em too. You know about that."

"He told me you were the only other person who knows."

"No poetry lover myself," said Elaine. "Never could get the stuff. Sam reads 'em aloud. Goes in one ear and out the other. I'm a looker not a listener. What are you?"

I had to think. "I suppose a listener." I wasn't sure about it, though. I knew I liked sounds, if not necessarily words. I liked going to sleep with my recordings of nature plugged into my ears. "But look at all your lilies out there," I said. I'd felt the golden glow off them before I'd even turned around to see what it came from.

"Sam calls me the Lily Maid," said Elaine. "He's always making shit up. Like Honkety. Got a name for you. Calls you the Sweatbox." She ran her palm across the back of my neck. "Redheads get the sweatiest." She wiped her palm on her jean skirt. "No offense. Hard to paint sweat."

"I thought I'd cooled off."

"Two kinds of sweat: heat sweat and nervous sweat."

"I'm not nervous," I said, but when I played back our conversation, my voice did sound a bit shaky.

"Just don't see painting ya, Griffin," she said with a pat on my bare knee. "Bet your boyfriend would like a portrait, huh? Could maybe do a quick pen-and-ink for him."

She stood and went to her high wooden work table and fetched a drawing pad and some pens. She leaned her flat bottom against the table and began scratching on the paper. I didn't know if I should move at all, so I sat in the glow of the lilies behind my back and felt the perspiration dripping into my T-shirt. It wasn't the Pete shirt. It read "Somerville City of Seven Hills" with a depiction of the tower on Prospect Hill where George

Washington first raised the flag of the United Colonies. Somerville is home now. My parents kept changing houses and school districts, which is probably why Robert and I are sticking where we are. His family isn't half as well off as mine, so our condo and his job means even more to him.

When Elaine had put down her pen and closed the pad, she said, "Can work from that. Maybe take more interest in your bland exterior before ya leave town."

Playing back the tape that evening, I noticed how Elaine and Sam each tended to start sentences without a pronoun. She'd say, "Just don't see painting ya" or "Can work from that." Sam did the same. I wondered which one had caught it from the other. Or maybe it's what happened out on dirt roads in Vermont. Those two were seriously entwined, what with all those drawings and paintings of Sam Fry and the way he kept grousing about her bothering him. In Somerville, I pass hundreds of people every day, but in those hills I might not see more than three on a single day and they'd usually be the same ones. You couldn't help getting twisted into other people's lives.

I finished my tea, set the tall glass on the coffee table, and said I'd better get back to my run before I completely dried off.

"Pale skin gets slippery," said Elaine. "Not leathery like Sam's—or mine," she added. "Tell the old man I said howdy."

"However, I think I'll head straight home now."

"Back to that thirty-bucks-a-night room? I seen it. Looks like Van Gogh's bedroom. Without the color. I need sun. You pale faces best stay in the shade if ya know what's good for skin cancer. Sam's had it bad despite being all leather. See, he's pale underneath. Light blue eyes. Not me. I started out all dark." She accompanied me past the steep staircase clunking on her cane.

It had been puzzling me, so I asked, "Where were you living before settling here?"

"A life of wandering. Midwestern, just like Mr. Fry. But no city gal, me. Farm girl, small town Wisconsin, Iowa, Dakotas. Went to college in Vermilion. Me at college? Yes indeed! You New Englanders don't half know what else is out there."

"But how did you end up here?"

"End up? Ain't ended up yet! Let's say I chose to get as far away as I could from some nasty shit. Leave it to your freaky imagination. But now, Griffin, if I'm to call ya by your fancy-pants name, look in on Sam soon and report. The man needs watching. Gets lost in poems and talking to that dumb donkey."

"Yesterday he recited a poem to me," I said, standing by her front door. "Then he said it'd be best not to come in because he wasn't in a nice mood."

"Look out when he's that way, boy. Starts mulling over all his wrongs. Reading gets him all het up. Then it's his damn 'Unfaithfulness' poem. Can't guess why he puts himself through it. I say move on, live now, haven't got time to waste, Samuel Fry, you old beast."

"He's actually sensitive, isn't he," I told Elaine.

"Sam's a sufferer, my friend, him and his pathetic old donkey. They let you know it, too." And she made her own imitation bray I couldn't wait to get home to replay. "Now, Griffin, go on, get outta here!" She gave me a gentle shove through the doorway.

Day Five

It was overcast and cool enough to feel a chill on my legs and arms. The back of my neck hardly got wet before the sweat evaporated. I had decided to see what kind of mood Sam Fry was in but was prepared not to stay long.

No sign of him outside. Honkety Hank wasn't in the meadow, but I'd seen the Isuzu down in the shed and doubted Sam ever went out walking. So I stepped up on the porch and knocked.

"Come on in," came a loud scratchy voice within. "Where you been?"

I peeked in. He was in his armchair with a huge book on his lap, a heavy old dictionary that no one else uses anymore. In getting to know Sam, I was indeed experiencing how things once were. I was sure he wrote those poems with a pen in a spiral notebook, the way I followed writing prompts back in sixth grade.

"Been to see Elaine, I hear," he said. "That dame can't resist stumping up here to bother me with all the latest. As if I cared what's happening! Not going to be around long enough to waste time on all that mess."

He pointed me to the couch, so I took a seat and said, "Oh, you'll be here a long while. You're very spry for almost eighty."

He ignored that. "Want a cold beverage, Sweatbox?"

"I'm actually not so sweaty today. But I'll go get one since you offered. Could I get you one, too?"

"Bring me a Pepsi. Need to wake up."

I noticed Hank's hatch was open, but there was no sign of the animal. I flipped open two cans from the fridge, handed one to Sam, and asked, "Is Hank napping?"

"Naps a lot more of late. Finds himself a shady spot by the back barbed wire. Me, too. Nap a lot more. Hell, allow me to enumerate all my debilities. Varicose veins in both legs, worse on the left, not enough feeling in the feet—gets tricky balancing. Got those liver spots Elaine always got to notice, not to mention skin cancers I had taken off. Little scars. Won't even talk about colonoscopies. You don't have to go through that yet, son. Hemorrhoids, if you'll excuse the expression, softening of the gut muscles, dimming of the eyes—had cataract surgery but can't drive at night, not that I want to. Digestion? Irregular. Once was a well-oiled organism. Damn potent, as well. Miss Greene don't know what she missed, the old lesbian. I'm talking a quarter century ago. She tell you about that? What else? Root canal, tooth implants, receding gums, hard of hearing, cholesterol. Hernia on the right. Not so bad yet. You know how that happens? You strain too hard and some intestine pops through the slit your balls descended from. How's that for male anatomy! Prostate, slow pee, aching joints, hunching spine. So far nothing mortal. Oh, I go to doctors and dentists and ophthalmologists. Got myself the best. Use the VA. I'm entitled. No sense living in pain. Physical pain, I mean. Mental pain, what can you do about that, fella?"

"That's the longest speech I ever heard from you, Sam."

"Didn't I tell you I don't like idle conversation? What did you and Elaine Greene 'converse' about, I'd like to know."

"She told me I was bland or blank or whatever. Anyway, she did a sketch of me to take back to Robert. It's not finished."

"I told her to paint you 'stead of me. Why she'd want to paint my wreck of a carcass I don't know! Thinks it has character, I suppose. You have character, Mr. O'Dea? Let's talk about character."

"Everyone has some kind of character, don't they?"

"Then let me ask you this: what makes one person more interesting than another? Why should you be more intriguing than those Cobbles you rent from?"

"You find me intriguing?" I was flattered but not sure how exactly he meant it. I leaned forward, elbows on knees, and stared across the sunlight at the old man sitting in the chair with shelves of books behind him. "Maybe I'm the one," I offered, "who finds yourself intriguing."

"'Course you do," Sam snapped. "Can't figure me out. Poet or hayseed? Scholar or nutcase? Recluse? Misanthrope? You know what that is?"

"That you don't like people."

"Think so?" He slammed the huge volume shut and, with a hefty lift, managed to set it on the low table by his side.

"You do say people bug you," I told him, "but if you didn't care about them, you wouldn't be so ticked off."

He took to nodding thoughtfully and finally said, "Wise boy."

Right then, I realized we were having what he called a discourse. How was it different from simply talking with Elaine Greene about her opinions and attitudes? "So I'm not as ignorant as you thought, Sam?"

"Never said you were ignorant. Said you didn't know much. Ignorance is not wanting to know. Not knowing is a pre-condition to knowledge."

When I played the tape that evening, I googled "ignorant" and it said "lacking in knowledge" which seems the same thing as not knowing. I decided Sam had a way of making stuff up.

"But, Sam," I told him, "you're the one who doesn't want to know the news, the environment, politics, race relations, immigration, the economy." I was wearing the Pete T-shirt I'd washed in the sink the night before, so it was clean again.

"It's hopeless," Sam said in his calmest voice. He didn't sound angry or despairing, merely matter-of-fact.

I risked going on with: "Because of all the right wingers?"

"The human race, fella! Its own worst enemy. Always has been. Don't see animals being self-destructive. Ask Honkety Hank." He beckoned me toward the kitchen end of the room where the donkey's head had silently protruded through the open hatch. "Go on," Sam urged.

"I'm supposed to talk to Hank?"

"Aw, at least give him a parsnip. In that paper sack on the counter."

I did as Sam said. I even patted the rough hairs on Hank's long nose and tried scratching his giant ears.

"Go on, talk to him."

"Hello there, Hank," I said. Robert and I do talk to our cats, Alice and Martha, so why not talk to this donkey?

"Tell him what you think of Samuel Fry, kid."

"Well, Hank, I'd say you're lucky to have such a devoted friend. He believes animals like you are better than people. Maybe it's true. You're very patient. Did he rescue you from some crummy kiddie park?" I looked back at Sam, who appeared not to be paying attention. "You've got your stable and your meadow and you can look in on your friend Sam when you want company. What's it like in winter? Must get cold."

"Heat lamps above his stall" came from Sam's end of the room.

"And I bet he lets the wood stove blow warmth through your hatches," I said. "What do you spend your time thinking about, Hank? Not just food and weather. I bet you spend time thinking about Sam. Our cats think a lot about Robert and me," I added.

"Inter-species relationships" came from Sam.

"So Mr. Fry's a good man, Hank. He's more sensitive than he acts. I happen to know he writes poems and reads them aloud to you." Here the donkey let out an ee-yaw more shattering than Elaine's imitation. "Can I take his picture?" I asked Sam.

"Ask him."

"He won't answer. I'll just take it." I unclipped my device and stood back by the kitchen table to snap a few. In one, he's looking droopy, another he's twitching his ears, and the third shows his sad profile turning back into his stall. "And now, Sam, how about a photo of you?"

"You'll show it to Elaine and she'll make a painting of it."

"I promise I won't." Before he could say more, I took a few. I'm not sure he even noticed, not being familiar with new technologies. That night, when I zoomed it in, I could almost read the titles of the books behind him. Days later, I took some closeups for future reference:

Poetry of the English Renaissance, Poetry of the Victorian Period, The Works of Geoffrey Chaucer, The Faerie Queene Volumes I and II, The Complete Poetical Works of John Milton, Complete Poetry and Selected Prose of John Donne and Complete Poetry of William Blake, The Poems of Wordsworth, Coleridge's Poetical Works, The Poetical Works of Byron, Complete Poems of Keats and Shelley, The Poems and Plays of Robert Browning, Tennyson's Poems and Plays, Algernon Charles Swinburne Poems & Algernon Charles Swinburne Tragedies.

Below was a shelf of Shakespeare plays in little volumes and more books below that by famous authors like Homer and Virgil and Dante and Goethe and ones I'd never heard of. At the bottom were a few Bibles and Greek plays and whatever. It was enough to have kept him going all these years. I doubt I could make it all the way through even one of those old books.

When I sat down again, I waited quietly for Sam to pick up where we left off. Finally, he said, "We were talking about character." I nodded. "And then you went and spoke to Hank. Anyone can speak to an animal. Idiots speak to them. But you spoke to him as if he was a person. Asked him questions. Wanted to know what he thinks about. However, Mr. O'Dea, you didn't get permission to take his picture, and you damn well didn't get mine, either. Big mistake. Can't have pictures of me floating around. What's that little gadget of yours, anyways?"

"Just my phone." I feared he'd want to inspect it, so I tucked it back under my shirt.

"One of those jobs that does photos and counts how many steps you take and what your heart rate is? Doctor wanted to set me up with one. Told him that's the most appalling crap I ever heard, fixing to trail me about like that. Last thing I want is to know when I'm about to have a heart attack."

"You should at least have one of those beepers, Sam."

"No need. That prying old Elaine'll come stumbling in soon enough and find me. Rather be dead."

"But, Sam—"

"Character!" he practically shouted. My chest clenched and my cheeks started to flush. Sam had a way of suddenly upping the volume. Now he was ranting: "You have any idea what it means to put your whole self together in one piece? Into character? Can't be done at your raw age. Most people never can. They want to do 'this' but end up doing 'that.' Really care about somebody but can't find the time. Should watch what they eat but say gimme more of that chocolate brownie with vanilla on top!"

The sunlight had moved closer to the couch and was heating up my knees. Before it could creep to my face, I leaned back into the shadow and watched Sam, now in dimmer light, across the narrow room. He'd calmed down a bit.

"I was taking stock of my ailments, wasn't I? I do that to keep myself sure who I am. Put myself to sleep reciting the litany."

"But you won't check your blood pressure."

"Take little pills for that, little pills for cholesterol, little vitamins and aspirins. Does a donkey have to think about blood pressure? He knows where he aches, where he itches, when he's tired or hungry. He's himself all the time. Not only talking about the physical. Talking about thoughts."

"Do animals have thoughts, I mean, like memories?" I asked.

"But they're freer than us. We're stuck in our pasts. Don't want Hank's kind of freedom, however," Sam said. "Wouldn't be able to write my great long tedious poem in three, as I like to call 'em, cantos."

"Maybe people are better than animals, after all?"

"Where do you get 'better'? Isn't it better to be free? Something's in us composed of memories. Isn't that worse?"

"Sam," I said, trying to get hold of this conversation or discourse, whatever we were having, "now you're sounding like a professor again."

"Never was a professor. Never was an actor, either, just so you know."

"Maybe someday you'll let on what you actually were."

"Maybe, maybe not. What you want to know for? Wasn't your life! You should start asking what your own self is."

"I don't have as many memories as you do yet, but I guess I have more than Hank," I added to lighten us up.

"Hank, he don't bother with memories when he's awake. Only sleeping. Animals keep the past stored deep inside. Must've seen a dog dreaming, trembling and running the paws and whimpering. Donkeys do a version of that. Fears, desires, impulses, things that happened to them. When Hank's asleep in his straw with the hatch open, I can hear him flustering and go lean out to remind him I'm there, not to be afraid."

"You talk to him like a person, too."

"'Course I do, and what's a person?" Sam asked flat out. "Didn't say 'human being'. A person needn't be human. A person's any living thing with a personality, an individual, a character. Weren't we talking about character, Mr. O'Dea?"

Sam was goofing on words again, but I let it go and said, "But since he can't speak, he can only take it so far."

"Is that so!" Sam twisted his stiff neck around to indicate the bookshelf. "Words," he said. "Thomas Wyatt ain't the half of it. However, good place to start. Why don't you?"

"I find poetry hard to take in."

"Living's hard to take in, young man. Doesn't mean you're not alive."

"Sam, sometimes you're hard to take in!"

He set his Pepsi can on the closed dictionary, lifted off his spectacles, and folded them up beside the red and blue can. Then he put his stiff knobby fingers together as if doing "Here's the church, here's the steeple," and said, "How many times a night do you get up to pee, young fella?"

"I don't usually."

"I get up at least three times, sometimes six. No deep sleep. Always on edge, watchful animal-like sleep. So I was talking about my bodily decline and then went on to the disembodied. Elaine might say 'soul' or 'spirit.' Bullshit! It's simply the mind, the brain, the thing between your ears." He glanced toward the hatch. There Hank was again, ears and all. "He understands my tone of voice. Doesn't need words. Listens to poems for the sounds. Hears the western wind blowing and the small rain raining down. Do you like sounds, Griffin O'Dea?"

"I do, Samuel Fry, I love sounds, I have sounds—" I stopped myself from telling him about my nature recordings that ended up including him.

"I was talking about putting your whole self together. You're too young to do it. What did I know at your age? Not even thirty! Didn't read poems from the English Renaissance. Didn't read poems of the Victorian Period." He tapped the spines of those volumes. "What I read was law books and crime stories to put myself to sleep. Had a wife and later a daughter. She's almost fifty now. Haven't seen either of 'em in thirty years. Never seen the grandsons."

"Then, Sam, how can you ever put your pieces together?" Imagining his loneliness, I'd felt a sharp twist in my stomach.

"You and this Robert of yours going to be together in fifty years?"

"We plan on it."

"Wish I could see it. Could happen. Can't say it won't. Thought Helen and I'd be together all our lives. A piece of me. Gone now, like the old digestion, the joints, the sharp eyes, the unblemished epidermis. How's that for a word? 'Epidermis.' Now you'd best go back to your dirt roads. I'll head in to my desk and do some scribbling while the muse is upon me. 'And may at last my weary age find out the peaceful hermitage, till old experience do attain to something like prophetic strain.' John Milton. Look it up. Now, not to appear rude—"

"Of course not, Sam."

"Aw, I should shut my yap." He was standing now at the closed door to the back room where I'd figured his desk was. "Least you won't remember much of our attempt at a discourse."

"But I'll be trying to remember it," I said, knowing I'd soon be playing back the whole thing, word for word. I was accumulating quite an archive of Samuel Fry.

"Don't you go stopping by Elaine's now. Better she don't hear how I been yammering on at you. Bad enough I talk to Hank. She gives me such shit. What she don't get is how the only way I ever make sense of anything is with pen and paper. She thinks I wallow. Thinks I'm stuck. Has no idea how far beyond all of that my great long poem is taking me. Where do her paintings take her? Captures the moment, she says. The old dyke—excuse me for that, son."

He lifted the inner door's latch, and a bright ray of sunshine poured in from the mysterious back room as he snuck in and shut the door behind him.

I stepped out onto the porch to find a warm wind blowing a new front in. I set off at a comfortable trot and, out of deference to Sam, turned left at the fork and took the long loop back, not to risk coming upon Elaine Greene out in her yard. I began building up quite a sweat again.

Explanations

One reason I'm doing this creative non-fiction project about my month in Vermont is that I took on two major responsibilities before I left. I need to put in writing all that led up to my agreeing to Sam Fry's requests. I'm very glad I made those surreptitious recordings, ashamed and guilty as I still feel for never telling Sam.

I'm not proposing to report everything that went on during August. Robert and I had our daily exchanges of post cards, and we did occasionally talk by phone. Several times, I drove down to a town on the Connecticut River. He and I would catch up on the phone while I did a load at the laundromat before going for groceries or treating myself to lunch at the Nibble Nook. I didn't tell him I could access the post office Wi-Fi where I was staying, so we could've Skyped, but Robert believed, and I did too, that it was important for our relationship to take a break from all our back-and-forth calls and texts, from our nights of streaming stupid shows or playing kitty sports with Alice and Martha, from our constantly interwoven lives. I'd been so agitated by my job that Robert was getting seriously concerned. We'd miss each other, but we'd soon come back to being who each of us was in his own self and get centered again with each other.

I didn't tell Robert much about Samuel Fry. I only listed him along with the landlord Cobbles and the cheery postmistress and the guy at the dump who got on me about my Smart Car and the painter Elaine doing my portrait to bring home to the boyfriend on Labor Day. Sam Fry, I said, was an old recluse in the woods who wrote poems and had a pet donkey. Robert wasn't particularly interested or curious about any of them but glad I had some people to hang with. "And no 'adventures' on the side yet, Griff?" he asked. Not that he'd mind, he assured me. I said he had way more opportunities down in the city than I ever would in the boonies and added, "Not that I'd mind either."

I also told him about the recordings I was making of all the country sounds, wind through the trees, rain on the metal roof, frogs in ponds, birds calling each other, strange underground sounds of water gurgling or creatures burrowing. One night

I caught the hoots of an owl, and in the morning an annoying woodpecker tapping away. And there were plenty of moos from cows and snorts from pigs and sheep bleating and, of course, the donkey's bray. I'd fall asleep with all that in my ears, my meditation tapes. I missed Robert especially at bedtime, though I did regularly release the pressure solo in that little bedroom Elaine said was like Van Gogh's, but without the color. I'd looked it up on the internet and saw a resemblance.

So what I'm writing here leaves out most of how I filled those mornings, afternoons, and evenings. Here, it's only my visits to Sam and the few I made to Elaine Greene that seem relevant. As I said, when I left I'd been given two major responsibilities. Sam gave them to me. This account is helping me understand why I said yes and what I myself had come to mean to old Sam Fry.

Day Six

Summer's heat was back. I might've skipped a run that day, but remembering our last talk, I decided I'd better check on Sam. He'd sounded down on himself, and life, depressed. It didn't seem his poetry writing was helping much. I think Elaine made a good point about not wallowing in the past.

I headed out before the sun was above the treetops. At that hour, the roads were still mostly in shade, and I took a new supershady side road, more of a farm road along a cow pasture. I didn't know where it led. I recorded some nice moos and the distant neighing of a horse. Farther along, I glimpsed something shining through the forest and took a deer path into high grass down to a small pond fringed with cattails.

To catch my breath, I lay down on the bank. Sweat was beading up all over me, so I pulled off my running shoes and dangled my feet in the water. Out from below an underwater rock crept a pair of crayfish. One crawled up and pinched at my toes. Strange sensation. I shook my foot, and off it scuttled. Looking deeper into the clearing pond, I saw what must've been a couple hundred tadpoles. Some had begun to grow little legs. Waterbugs were prinking (good word!) the surface, and a dragonfly was hovering above. Only the tiniest ripples made their way toward me, nothing that would register on my recorder.

I had been concentrating so closely on the tiny scene that I hadn't noticed how hot the sun was. I pulled my Somerville T-shirt over my dripping forehead and considered taking a dip. Did someone own this pond? Was I trespassing? I'd heard a tractor engine far off, but it wasn't coming my way. I yanked down my running shorts, yet I'm too much of a city kid to skinny dip. My light green boxers could pass for a swimsuit, if anyone came along.

I stepped onto the flat crayfish rock and then edged my way onto the sandy bottom, stirring up silt. When I was sweltering sufficiently, I made myself plunge in. I'm not a great swimmer like Robert, but I did paddle about and cooled off, disturbing the pond life, then staggered onto the grassy bank. For half an hour, I let the sun dry me and didn't get sweaty again until I'd suited up and was jogging back along the farm road to the familiar pavement, now shadeless. I took the most direct way to the dirt road past Elaine's (no sign of her SUV) and on to the fork to Sam's.

His porch was half in sunlight. On the shady half sat Sam in his rocker, peering at a book through his reading glasses. He didn't bother to greet me but just said, "In time for a recitation suitable for this weather," and creakily got to his feet. Again, he put his palms out to stop me at the foot of the porch steps. I listened while he, with brief pauses for all the commas, spoke these odd words:

Hot sun, cool fire, tempered with sweet air,
Black shade, fair nurse, shadow my white hair.
Shine sun, burn fire, breathe air and ease me.
Black shade, fair nurse, shroud me and please me.
Shadow, my sweet nurse, keep me from burning.
Make not my glad course reason for mourning.

When I found the poem online, it had extra e's on words like "aire" and "burne," but I've written it the way I heard Sam say it.

"Poetic warning for you, Mr. O'Dea. Put on sun cream and cover up those pasty arms and legs. Should wear a cap. Red hair won't keep out the killer rays." I moved into the shade after he'd taken his seat again. "Not that it's sunburn she's worried about in that little song. She's out there taking her bath bare-ass nekkid. I wonder who might be watching."

"Funny," I said, "because I just took a swim in a pond I came across in the woods."

"Thought you looked slicker than usual," said Sam.

"But who is she?"

"Ah! This song stands at the top of my first canto."

"You wrote it? I liked it."

"What, you think I'm a Renaissance poet? George Peele wrote it. Look it up on your machine. Can't figure what it's about?"

I stood there, afraid I'd once again demonstrated my ignorance, or my not-knowing-something he thought I should know.

"Here's a clue: the title of my first canto is 'David.'"

"David?"

"David, I said David, didn't I?"

"But who is she?"

"Ever read a Bible? All bullshit, of course, but some racy stories in there. First canto's my biblical one. Unfaithfulness? Ring a bell?"

"I was never up on Bible stories," I admitted. "My father is especially against all religion, not only Catholicism. He gets mailings from the Freedom From Religion Foundation that Ron Reagan advertises on TV. You and he might really get along. But are you talking about unfaithfulness to God or being unfaithful in love?"

"Both," Sam said, "but since there's no such thing as a god except in the primitive human brain, that part's only metaphorical. Still, there is such a thing as love. Evolved over millennia. Helped preserve the species. A cooperative impulse. Strong in humans, but you find it in most creatures. Hank has a modicum of it. They say, 'God is love,' but you never heard 'em say, 'Love is god.' Leave all them gods out of it. Unfaithfulness to a god is unfaithfulness to nothing. But in this Bible story, which you evidently are unacquainted with, the human-invented god punishes David for sending a good man off to war so he can get at his widow."

"The one in the bathtub?"

"Bathtub!" Sam hooted. "Suppose you could call it that. You're priceless, kid. Don't you know anything?" He was shaking his book at me. "King David, Mr. O'Dea! King David, the poet, the adulterer!" His shouting called up an echoing bray around the corner from the stable.

"I'm sorry, Sam. I know I'm not well-educated in certain subjects. My mom's sometimes a Unitarian, and my father's almost an atheist—"

"Didn't grow up with that old Jewish bullshit? No Jesus shit, either?"

All I could do was run my fingers through my wet hair to fluff it up to dry and shake my head.

"Forgiven," Sam said in a softer voice. "Don't need to believe to know about it, however. Bet your dad knows. Didn't want to burden you with it? I understand. Maybe best when all the old lies fade away. Aw, come inside now for a cold beverage. I'll pull out my King James and read you about Uriah the Hittite, sent to die in battle."

Sensing a personal aspect in all this, I asked, "Sam, were you in Vietnam?"

"Little old for that, son. Nineteen fifty-seven. Stationed in Kaiserslautern. American base in Germany. Desk job. Got lucky. Hadn't married yet. Just a kid."

"So your poem isn't about your own experiences?"

He'd lurched himself up again, with his book under his arm, and was making his way carefully to the front door. "When I'm writing my poem," he said, "I have to be it. Couldn't write it otherwise."

"So it's partly you?"

"Everything is partly me. See that oak tree? Partly me. You too, Mr. O'Dea!" He'd stopped with his fingers knotted up on the cabin door latch.

"You're still only on the first canto?"

"Look, my friend, I been writing this whole epic poem for thirty years, getting it all down, tuning it up, cutting it back, rearranging, starting fresh. Biblical, Classical, Medieval: three foundations of our pathetic culture. Can't escape it. We're stuck with it."

We both looked up. We'd heard a tapping of wood against stone. Before Sam could lead me inside, up the path came Elaine Greene with her cane. It was only when I got back to my room and googled "Uriah the Hittite" that I learned the famous story I had been so shamefully ignorant of.

Day Six, Part Two

Sam called to her: "Well, if it isn't the bothersome old stick of a neighbor lady!"

"Came from town," said Elaine stumping along. "Parked at the fork. Got something for ya."

"Your running boy's here."

"So I see." She clunked her cane up the steps and paused at the top to breathe deep. Elaine was in overalls this time, with a green-and-blue-paint-stained T-shirt underneath and sandals on her long brown feet. She straightened up to full height then bent to hold onto the porch railing.

"Aw, come on in outta the sun," Sam said.

Elaine poked him on the chest. "Still wearing that stinky ratty sweatshirt on a hot day like this!" She nodded to me like a co-conspirator.

Sam was holding the door open for her. I followed them inside, and he went to get a third chair from the back room. As our eyes adjusted, we took seats around the kitchen table. Sam had produced a pitcher of iced tea, three ice-filled glasses, and a bowl of smoked almonds. "Doctor tells me to eat nuts," he said. "And you, Sweatbox, replenish your salt." He poured out the tea, and we sat a moment in the dim quiet. I was waiting to see how those two would act face-to-face instead of complaining about each other.

But first, Elaine turned to me and asked, "Ain't you stopping by to see me ever?"

"She says 'ain't'," said Sam.

"If 'ain't' was good enough for Queen Victoria, it's good enough for me."

"What do you know about Queen Victoria!"

"I know she said 'ain't.' Proper in those days. Don't talk too good yourself, old fart."

"Don't have to when talking to you, Lily Maid. Save my eloquence for the youngster here."

"See," Elaine began, grabbing my elbow, "he shoulda been a

teacher. Instead, he was a nasty mean lawyer back in Chicago. Bet he got deadbeats off the hook. Didn't ya, Sam?"

"And what did you ever accomplish, old lady?"

"It was a hard life, son," she said to me. "That old fart has no idea. I'm a starving artist, always have been. See how bone-thin I am? Scrimp and save, that's my life. Didn't have his bank account to live off for the past thirty years."

"Lasts me till I'm dead," Sam bragged.

"Probably leave what's left to Hank, won't ya?"

"If I die first. What, you want me to leave it to you?"

"Could do worse," said Elaine. Then to me: "Not that he'd think of leaving it to the grandsons he's never seen, selfish bastard."

"What've they ever done for me?"

Elaine had hooked her cane over the back of the chair and was stretching out to rummage in her overalls pocket. "I got something for ya, Sam. Saw it at the resale shop down in town. Dollar and seventy-five cents."

"Big spender," said Sam. She handed him a small wooden carving. He was turning it over and over in his stiff fingers. "What's this for anyway?"

"Looks like you, don't it?" Sam just snorted, so Elaine said, "Ain't ya gonna thank me?"

"What do I want with this ugly thing?" He held it out for me to see. It was a sort of troll carving with beady eyes and a big round nose and long straight hair hanging all the way to its huge feet. It didn't look at all like Sam.

"Inspiration," Elaine said. "Set it on your desk when you write those damn poems. It'll be watching. Keeping you honest."

"It'll scare the shit outta me," said Sam.

"Just what you need," Elaine said. "It's a muse. I know about muses. How else do I keep myself drawing and painting and deluding myself I'm a great artist?"

"With one of these jobs?"

"With a muse! None of your business, Sam Fry."

He turned the little thing upside down and discovered a yellow and blue label that I later copied down as "Svensk Slöjd." Two dots over the "o".

"What the hell is Svensk Slodged?"

"That's his name," Elaine said.

"I imagine it means 'Made in Sweden,'" said Sam.

"Call him Svensk. Ain't ya gonna thank me?"

Sam weighed the little fellow in his palm and said, "I like him. I'll keep the queer old thing. You come up with strange shit, Lily Maid."

She stood up to pour out more iced tea. My fingers were sticky from the almonds I'd been scarfing down. I did indeed need the salt. Lately, I'd become more aware of my body's requirements. At home in summer, between central air at work and home, I never really noticed salt loss. When I looked over at Elaine returning the pitcher to the fridge, Hank's head was poking through the kitchen hatch.

"Holy crap!" gasped Elaine. "It's like that Fuseli painting of the ghost horse sticking its face between the girl's bed curtains."

"Ah, 'The Nightmare'," said Sam.

That night I found the painting online. Elaine had a point, though the ghost horse's blind eyes were nothing like Hank's warm ones. I had to wonder how those two old folks in their seventies knew so much in common about art and history and everything. Why didn't they get along better? But I suspected most of it was for fun. My parents often jab at each other like that.

"That's all I came for," Elaine announced, unhooking her cane and heading for the door. "Got some purchases in the Aztec to get home. Thanks for the tea."

"Do you need help? I mean, carrying things?" I said.

"Hate to rob Sam of his acolyte."

"Aw, take him away. He's had enough of me for now."

I went over to stroke Hank's nose. He seemed to know me. He rocked his muzzle up and down to get more scratching. Then I tickled his ears. Sam was thoughtfully rolling Svensk around in his hands while I followed Elaine out the door.

It took some effort getting her down the slope. At the fork, I hopped in the passenger seat, crammed next to paper bags of various sizes full of supplies. She backed and filled until we were headed toward her house. In the rear compartment, there was a heavy wooden armchair upholstered in brown leather. She would never have been able to maneuver it by herself. "Found it on the curb for free," she said. "Couldn't pass it by. Need a comfier chair to cuddle up in."

In hauling out the chair into her painting room, I seemed to have punched off the record button because the sound from Day Six stops there. I remember Elaine showed me what had turned out to be not a simple sketch but a yard-high oil painting of me. I looked older than I think of myself as, and tireder and sweaty, but it was definitely me. Given her complaints about money and art, I thought I should offer to buy it. She said she had lots more to do on it, but it looked about done to me. It made me think of how I might seem to others. I didn't appear to be happy, maybe only contemplative. It was how I'd been feeling up in Vermont. Elaine had seen inside me.

I had lots to think about on my run back to my temporary home. Who did I find there but a middle-aged couple from Connecticut staying in the bigger room with the king-size bed. I heard them talking and stepped quietly past into my Van Gogh room. I remembered about the big family birthday party at the Town Hall. I hoped they wouldn't stay up late carousing. I'd become used to the silence around me.

Day Seven, But With Hank

The party goers had come in after eleven when the rest of the village was sound asleep. There was some slamming of doors and chatter about old Uncle Johnny's big seventy-fifth. I heard the wife say, "It's your family, I did my bit," and the husband said, "You were perfect, sweetheart." They sounded like Robert and me after visiting each other's parents, always glad to get back to just ourselves.

In the morning, the guests slept late. I had the kitchen to myself. It was Sunday so the postmistress didn't come in. I hadn't been noticing days of the week, not having my work to order my life. I heard a bell ringing for the nine o'clock service from the Bible Church steeple down the road. It was the only local church. When I stepped outside in my shorts and Tufts jersey, grubby as it was, the landlords across the driveway were getting into their car to head for the Congregational Church in the next town. They raised their eyebrows at all the evangelicals' cars lined up along the road. Church people tend to look down on those in other denominations. My father says they're all equally deluded.

I was happy to have the beautiful cool morning to myself with no such obligations. I figured Sam Fry had none either and felt oddly eager to go see him. I set out on the long way around to avoid passing Elaine's.

At last, pounding down the hill by the decrepit dairy farm with its lone horse and huddled cows, I was full of questions I intended to ask the old man, but when I took the fork and ran up to the lopsided metal shed, I found it empty of the Isuzu. I'd come to think of Sam and his truck and cabin and donkey as permanent fixtures. He certainly hadn't gone to church, but I should've known he'd have to go shopping sometime. The supermarket and hardware store in the town where I'd done my laundry were open seven days. If I waited, he'd be back soon.

As I walked up from stone to stone, I thought of the first day when I didn't yet know what I'd find there. I felt again almost like a trespasser. Even if I found the door unlocked, I wouldn't snoop inside, but Sam surely wouldn't mind my walking around his land without him there. True, I did pull myself up by the window ledge to peer into the inner room I'd never seen. There sat the hairy backside of the wooden troll figure on the desk, no doubt aiming his beady eyes at Sam's empty chair. There lay a spiral notebook and a ballpoint pen on the desk, as I'd imagined.

I let myself down and went to the split-log fence, hesitating before I dared open the gate. Would Honkety Hank resent the intrusion without his master's presence? I avoided a pile of donkey dung and went to look in the stable, but Hank didn't seem to be there. I went in to check his sleeping stall: only straw, no donkey.

Then, I remembered he had a shady spot at the far end of the meadow, out past the solar panels, and trudged up to look. There he was, rubbing his gray old rump against a fence post. He didn't stop when he saw me but eventually took a step in my direction, and I almost feared he might charge. Aside from our cats, I'm not much used to animals. Robert grew up with dogs, but my parents never gave in to my little sister's pleas for a miniature long-haired dachshund, and typical of a bossy big brother, I took our parents' side. Now I think I was jealous of her yearning for something I didn't know I wanted for myself.

Soon, I could tell that Hank had recognized me. He stepped closer and nudged me with his nose. It was remarkable, me alone scratching a donkey's long snout in a sunny meadow. Next, he was leading me to his shady corner and, to my amazement, easing himself down onto the high grass. I'd never seen any big animal in the process of lying down, only those cows at a distance already resting. So I knelt on my own knees and then leaned on an elbow and stretched out my legs, cradling my head on my forearm. We were suddenly two creatures getting comfortable together, despite my being afraid of attracting ticks.

Staring at Hank, I remembered what Sam had said and asked out loud: "Are you a person?" If he heard, he didn't even snuffle, but his left eye stared back at me then shifted away. His barrel chest heaved a relieved breath, and he laid his heavy head right onto the earth. I did the same but kept watching him sideways through a fringe of light green stalks. My bare thighs itched, my elbow itched, but I didn't want to budge. Maybe Hank was sleeping, or maybe he was contemplating his own pleasant sense of peace.

Because donkeys are the most ill-treated of working animals, most don't live much past ten, after doleful years of carrying huge burdens, pulling heavy loads, receiving whiplashes and not enough fodder. At least, that's how it used to be. This beast, however, had been spared and, from what Sam said, had made it to my age, which was his equivalent of Sam's. He might even make it to forty, affirmed the website I'd looked at.

I decided to record his breathing. What could be more meditative than half an hour of soft whooshes from a donkey's nostrils? I set my device as close as I could. Carefully, I then reached over to pat his ribcage, stroking slowly back and forth, and then gently down to the hoof he'd tucked under himself. I wished he'd nuzzle up closer but didn't want to break the spell. What if he died? What would happen to Sam then?

The only sounds on my recording are of Hank's very soft breaths. I didn't speak to him but, instead, thought my questions. Do you love Sam Fry? How does a beast of burden show love? Is it merely a reciprocal arrangement you two have? He feeds and shelters you, and you listen patiently to his poems. Maybe he needs you more than you need him. No, I don't think so. You two need each other. You're both old for your respective species. Sam certainly thinks about his own death and yours, but you don't know about death, do you? You know about discomfort—too hot, too itchy, too sleepy to stand up—but nothing of an end to it all. You don't trouble to make up what Sam would call bullshit about life after death. Life is what you know and don't think it ever ends. You won't know it when it does, though you may suffer. I hope not. Sam will be sure to protect you from pain, let you fall quietly to sleep.

This may not be exactly what my mind talked to Hank about, but it's close. I have tapes of what Sam and Elaine and I said to each other, and of an occasional ee-yaw along with croaking frogs and chirping birds, but I can't have a tape of my own thoughts, let alone anyone else's.

I also remember lying there imagining what that old donkey would say to me, if he had words. Yes, I love Sam Fry. I am coming to love you too, Griff. You're somewhat familiar. You gave me parsnips and scratched my nose and tickled my ears. I recognize your sweaty smells. Watching you and Sam talking from my open hatch is a comfort. And you're quieter than the skinny old woman who riles him up so. Though I sort of love her, too. I am a lucky animal with my meadow and my stall and my two hatches so I can check on Sam. I watch him eating or reading or when he's asleep in his bed. Just to know he's right there.

Something like that might have come from Hank, lying in the grass with me at his side, living each breath. Had he sensed my restlessness? Animals are attuned to moods. Watching him unfold himself to stand was, at first, worrisome, but he did it, and then so did I. He took off at an old person's version of a trot toward his stall. When I caught up, he was standing at the water barrel, and then he went to munch some hay from the trough by the kitchen hatch. He wasn't looking my way. A bit regretfully, I decided to sneak off unnoticed.

At the fork, I took a left to avoid Elaine seeing me. I didn't want human interactions. I ran all the long way around to that farm road and out to the pond. That time I had the nerve to take everything off for a very quick dip. I'd never done so before. After I told Robert about it, he wrote back that he wished he'd been there to take advantage of my vulnerability. I figured he was feeling as sex-deprived as I was after only half a month apart. I hoped the postmistress didn't read those post cards.

When I made it back, still wet from my swim, the Connecticut couple was packing their sedan. I had to hear about Uncle Johnny's great day, with the extended family coming from as far away as Iowa. They were lucky to get that room so cheap. Other guests were mostly down at a resort on a lake paying big bucks. What brought me up there, they wanted to know. I pretended I was having a writer's retreat, so they asked did I have a contract, is it a novel, what's the genre? I said it was more philosophical essays, you might call it a series of discourses on various subjects, maybe for a podcast or blog. I could see they'd lost interest.

Back in my room, I went on transcribing the tapes into my laptop, just the voices, like a play. I would add the local color later, which is what I'm doing now back home in spare moments from my real job.

Day Eight

It was pouring rain, no weather for running. Besides, Robert had warned me against too much exercise. He was all for me getting in shape, but he said bodies need a day to build back after a strenuous workout. I took his advice and hopped in the Smart to drive down to the town on the river and treat myself to breakfast at the Nibble Nook—fried eggs, home fries, bacon and coffee. Oh, and a pancake with local syrup.

Then I called Robert at his office for a quick check in. "And don't you get too trim, Griff," he said. Robert's all nervous muscle and likes some cushioning from me. I told him I was feeling really healthy and not at all stressed now. And I'd have a present for him from the painter woman Elaine Greene. It wasn't merely a sketch but a big oil painting. "She do you in the nude?" he asked. "You wish," I said, "but no, T-shirt and shorts." He always kidded me about not going in for appropriate running attire. "No one wears boxers under plain old gym shorts!" "I prefer hanging loose," I said. He thinks I should at least wear a jock. Robert's had a jockstrap fetish ever since his high school locker room days. I'm too modest, but one exhibitionist in a couple is enough. It's what keeps our relationship going, opposites attracting. Men and women have that already built in.

So I wondered, while driving back into the hills with rain pelting the windshield, why Sam and his wife Helen hadn't seen it through. What was the unfaithfulness that brought it to an end? I assured myself that Robert and I were totally faithful in that we could never imagine splitting up. But being still in our twenties, we do occasionally have what we call "adventures"—safe ones, of course, no strings, and they're never as good as what we do together because we know each other so well, know what to do to make it feel best. A one-shot event can't ever equal that. It's only to let off steam or act out some passing fantasy. We never keep secrets. But is that what Sam Fry could call unfaithfulness? The difference between women and men must completely alter the equation. It always seemed to me that women can't fully understand men's bodies, and men can't fully understand women's. When things go wrong, they both retreat to their genders. But two men have nowhere else to go. And what about people who don't even want to have a single gender? I'd pondered these things before, but driving up those slick twisty roads in the rain, I wondered if I could discuss the issue with Sam. I'd probably get an outraged rant about how I know nothing about anything.

My little car hugs the road and rides high with excellent visibility, so I made it safely to the village post office but didn't stop. I stayed on the pavement till it turned to dirt and then rode right past Elaine's, her shades drawn against the gloomy day, and on to Sam's. I pulled in, blocking the pickup, and leapt quickly up the slippery slope. Somewhat drenched, I made it to the cabin and knocked loud enough to be heard over the rain pounding on the metal roof.

"You fool, running out here in a storm!" Sam growled when he opened the door. "All right, come on in."

"I drove, Sam. Where were you yesterday? I came by and sat in the meadow with Hank."

"So he informed me." I gave a doubtful frown. "Well, not in so many words. Could tell from the way you hadn't locked the gate properly. He might've got out."

"I'm really sorry," I said, dripping on the rubber mat before stepping inside.

"Seldom seen you without knees," Sam said. "Gimme the rain gear." By which he meant my nylon jacket and crusher hat. I was wearing khakis and the one collared shirt I'd brought. "Should dress nice more often, young fella. Show your elders some respect."

"As if you're so fashionable, Sam!"

"Aw, who wants to see me? Even in town. Nobody takes account of old geezers. Expected to be slobs. Bet you need a hot cup of tea."

Soon we were sitting at the familiar table, and Hank was sticking his nose through the hatch. With all of us out of the rain, I felt totally relaxed.

"We needed rain," Sam said. "Wells go dry. Big problem. Only getting worse." He shoved back his chair, went to the bookshelf behind the armchair, and reached up top for a small world globe. "Want to demonstrate something," he said. He rotated it on its spindle and handed it to me.

"It's got out-of-date countries," I said. "Congo Free State?"

"The King of Belgium's personal slave colony," said Sam. "Free State, my ass!"

"It says Persia not Iran. The Ottoman Empire."

"Believe it or not, kid, I wasn't born yet when the world looked like that. Our market town down there, in the eighteen hundreds, had a globe factory. First in the country. Thousands of small pasteboard planets sent out from here across the actual world. Business long gone. So if a hundred years ago the world was so different, try going back a few more centuries when no one even knew the earth was a globe. Then go back a millennium or two. Greeks didn't go beyond their so-called known world. 'Europe, Asia, and Africa' only meant the lands around the Mediterranean. Named Europe after this girl Europa. Got swum across the sea by a bull by the name of Zeus. You heard of him? Greeks named everything for their gods' exploits, their whole damn world. And how about the Trojan War? They could've called it World War One. Want a muffin with your tea?" Sam turned to grab a box off the counter before sitting back down. "Blueberry or corn? Picked 'em up yesterday. Thought I went to church?"

"I know you by now, Sam."

"That portrait painter of yours goes to some oddball Peace and Love church. She's nuts, in case you haven't figured that out."

"I get along with her," I said.

"Not saying you shouldn't. Long as you don't have her dropping in on you unannounced."

I put a blueberry muffin on my saucer. After my huge breakfast, I didn't want to undo all the good I'd done running, but I couldn't hurt Sam's feelings.

"Anyways," he said, "what was the Trojan War about?"

I knew that one. Before I realized what I was saying, I answered, "Helen of Troy," and then it hit me: it was his ex-wife's name. "Oh," I said, "your second canto?"

"Don't lay blame entirely on Helen," Sam said. "Paris had something to do with it. Wasn't her fault for being a beauty."

"So first you wrote a poem about King David. Then you wrote one about Helen of Troy."

"Helen of Sparta, as she was. Euripides sent her away to Egypt and let a ghost Helen run off with Paris. Lots of contradictory versions. Never could get to the bottom of 'em."

I hadn't yet gotten a straight story from Sam Fry, either, so I went ahead and asked outright: "Did your wife Helen have an affair with a man named David?"

"Maybe, maybe not."

"So then your third poem is probably about someone named Samuel?"

"It's only poetry, son." He picked up the globe again and pointed at tiny Greece squeezed among the Ottomans. "Those people thought their little patch of land and sea was everything. Remember the number of galaxies? Humans have yet to absorb what's now known as fact. Most still see our planet the way the ancients saw their piddling little corner of it."

He stood up in his usual bone-creaking way and shuffled in his fuzzy bedroom slippers to the bookshelf and set the globe back on top.

I said, "At least, Hank doesn't worry about any of this."

"What we like about him, right?" Sam asked. He pulled out a small book from the Shakespeare shelf and opened it to a page he knew precisely how to find. In the faint light from the rain-dripping window, he began to read in his actor voice:

"'Let thy song be love. This love will undo us all. O Cupid, Cupid, Cupid!' That was Helen," he explained. "'Love! ay, that it shall, i' faith,' says Pandarus, who starts to sing a dirty little ditty."

Love, love, nothing but love, still love, still more!
For, O, love's bow shoots buck and doe.
The shaft confounds, not that it wounds,
  But tickles still the sore.
These lovers cry, O ha! They die!
Yet that which seems the wound to kill
Doth turn O ha! to Ha, ha, he!
  So dying love lives still!

"Then Helen says, 'In love, i' faith, to the very tip of the nose.' And Paris says, 'He eats nothing but doves, love, and that breeds hot blood, and hot blood begets hot thoughts, and hot thoughts beget hot deeds, and hot deeds is love.' But here comes Pandarus again: 'Is this the generation of love—hot blood, hot thoughts, and hot deeds? Why, they are vipers,' he declares. 'Is love a generation of vipers?'"

Sam shut the book with a snap and stared accusingly at me, or that's how it felt. So I said, "That was kind of nasty."

"It's Shakespeare, son. Not what they teach you in school. Poetry's not all romantic bullshit. Get it?"

"You say 'bullshit' about a lot of things, Sam."

He shelved the little volume in its correct slot and took his seat back at the table to sip his tea awhile. "Lot of bullshit out there, young fella. Don't say I didn't warn you."

"Is this another discourse we're having? You said before that love is god! And now love comes from vipers?"

"It's Pandarus who says it, not me. Love is born in a snake pit! Eat your muffin."

It was odd not having normal conversations. Sam lived so alone that he must not have been used to the way most people socialize. As far as I knew, it was only Elaine Greene he ever saw, and they mostly squabbled. Why had I been drawn into his hermit life? Because I was young and didn't know anything? Was I a stand-in grandson for him? He'd left his whole family behind in Chicago.

I looked between the stove and sink at Hank's long face hanging thoughtfully in the open hatch. Was I no more than another listener? But Sam didn't tease him and nag him and conceal things from him the way he did me. The donkey must've heard the whole story over and over of Helen and David, if that was his name, even if he could only decipher it from the tone of Sam's voice.

I finished the blueberry muffin and promised myself to have a simple can of soup for dinner and a banana for breakfast and get back to my exercise routine if the weather cleared. My muscles tend to lose tone if I'm not careful.

Sam took up the discourse again. "Now I ask you this: given he's talking to Helen and Paris, what's Pandarus after?"

"Who exactly is this Pandarus?"

"You heard of pandering? Got a whole shameful profession named after himself. Arranging liaisons. Know what liaisons are?"

"I guess you mean of a certain kind."

"I hear they're all electronic these days. You familiar with 'em?"

"Not really."

"Oh, yes, Robert Ay-broo, I forgot."

The unfaithfulness subject had come up, but I didn't care to pursue it. I wanted to tell Sam how we'd never break up over some stupid liaison, as he'd call it, but I knew he wouldn't believe me.

"So answer the question. What's this Pandarus fella getting at?"

It was like being back in high school. "Could you read it again?"

The book was over on its shelf, but Sam leaned his head back and went through the whole thing from memory and only left out the line about love "to the very tip of the nose." When he reached the last part, he raised his voice almost in a fury: "Is love a generation of vipers?"

"Whoa, Sam," I said. "I have a feeling this means a lot to you."

"Damn right it does! You think what I read don't mean a lot? Why would I waste my time reading if it didn't? Take your Thomas Wyatt! Or the Coleridge I was reading when you tramped up here the first time. Ancient Mariner! You going to answer my question?"

That night, I googled "Ancient Mariner" and also found *Troilus and Cressida*. I read Coleridge's poem. Sam was an ancient mariner, for sure. But the play was too hard to get through. I did copy out the part he read to me. I decided it wasn't only Sam's wish that his love was in his arms and he was in their bed again. It wasn't mere yearning for what he'd lost. It was anger at human nature. No wonder he preferred his donkey.

But he was awaiting my answer. I had stalled for time, the way I used to in Chemistry class. "I guess, Sam, it's that Helen and Paris are at the infatuation stage when all they want to do is, you know, go to bed, and Pandarus knows it won't last. And all the trouble it's already caused. War, I mean. But I don't understand how love itself is a generation of vipers."

"All in how you look at it, son," said Sam. "Love can go good and love can go bad. Take your pick."

"Sam, I wish I could read your epic poem. Even if it isn't exactly autobiographical, I'd know you better if I read it."

"Why ever would you want to know me better, Griffin?"

It was the first time he'd called me simply Griffin, not Griffin O'Dea, Mr. O'Dea, young fella, son, kid. Suddenly, Sam felt closer to me. I wasn't sure how to answer without sounding too soft-hearted. He wouldn't like that. I set down my teacup on the muffin crumbs in the saucer and said, "To understand more about life?"

"Good answer, even if you put it as a question. See, we're not like the other beasts. We know death's coming, so we made up crap about Heaven to keep us from facing it. And made up Hell to keep us in line. We don't go in and out of heat like the four-footed critters. We're always up for it. Big problem. So we made up shame and guilt and something we call sin. Most of us never grow past these delusions." He turned toward the hatch and raised his voice again, this time warmly: "What do you think, Hank?" The steady animal eyes were staring back at us. "There he is, like Bottom with the ass's head. *Midsummer Night's Dream*."

Bottom sounded familiar. Maybe I'd come upon him when I searched "donkeys" online.

"When we do Shakespeare, it's Hank's best role," said Sam. "But now, young fella, I'm afraid we both need our naps. The rain's let up. Go on down and bother Elaine Greene. She'll appreciate it, lonely old lez, if you'll excuse the expression."

I said good-bye to Hank with a pat to his nose. I wasn't wary of him anymore, even if I was still a bit wary of Sam. I got my rain gear from the hook by the door and left with a smile and a wave. I nearly slid down the squishy slope to my glistening car, dust all washed away. Elaine's shades were still drawn closed. I drove slowly past and back to pavement and finally to my own meager room above the post office.

A Day About Sam

In the morning, I went down to the kitchen and found the postmistress getting coffee for herself and none other than Elaine Greene. "Oh, we know each other," she said when the postmistress introduced us. I wish I had a recording of our conversation. They took the stools, and I hopped on the counter with my mug and the banana I'd allowed myself. No cereal, no toast. The women did most of the talking, about villagers I didn't know and even some about Sam. Elaine said he was off that day to doctors' appointments at the VA down in White River. "He takes good care of himself, don't let him fool you." (With no tape, I'm approximating what she said.) "He grouses about his knees and his varicose veins and his skin cancers and his hernia, but he's in great shape for a man turning eighty. I'm seventy-six," she said, "and I can barely walk without my cane." Which wasn't quite true. The postmistress said she herself was only fifty-one, but she had plenty to complain of, too.

"And look at you," I remember Elaine saying to me, "out there running your life away to keep the boyfriend interested." By then, the postmistress had certainly pried enough into my mail not to be surprised by the mention of Robert. I said it was more for my health, but Elaine said she knew what it was like, trying to hold onto being young. "A losing battle," said the postmistress. And off they went into gossip about other local folks falling apart.

I asked why Sam was seeing doctors, he hadn't mentioned it yesterday, but Elaine didn't exactly know. "Very mysterious, that Samuel Fry," she said. I agreed because I'd never gotten a straight story out of him and asked, somewhat hesitantly, what had happened to his marriage. Both women looked at me as if I'd opened a secret drawer.

"Wouldn't we all like to know!" Elaine said. The postmistress thought his wife found out he had another gal over in Vietnam, but Sam told me, I said, that he was only stationed in Germany well before he even got married. "Either way, he's a vet," the postmistress said, "and he gets to go to the VA." Her own husband got nothing. If she wasn't working for the postal service, they'd be in deep doo-doo. "Deep doo-doo is where I live," I remember Elaine saying.

I wish I had tape of those two. Best I can do is try to recapture their flavor. Mostly, it was all about how rough life was. I said, in comparison to city life, at least they had plenty of open space and nature and not so many people everywhere. Yeah, but the unemployment and the oxycontin epidemic and break ins and long winters—that was their take on it. In the city, you've got hospitals and schools nearby and shops, they told me. People up there had to work three jobs and travel miles between to keep afloat. "You flatlanders!" Elaine said, even though she was from the Midwest and so was Sam. The postmistress was proud to have been born and bred in the county and her family went back eight generations.

I asked again about Sam and his wife Helen. "You mean who cheated on who?" said Elaine with a sly glint in her dark eyes.

The postmistress always figured it was Sam with the devil in him, but Elaine claimed to know it was Helen. "Sam was on the rebound when he got up here," she said. "I know from personal experience, if ya catch my drift." That's not exactly how she put it, but it's one of her phrases.

I was about to mention Sam's "Unfaithfulness" poem but remembered that only Elaine knew about it. I had to be careful. In that village, people talked about each other all the time. In Somerville, Robert and I feel safely anonymous. We only see neighbors in our building coming and going, and we're not on the condo board. We have our own friends, but in a small town you're stuck with whoever happens to live there. You keep your eyes on everyone's business. There's not enough people to blend in. I realized I was part of it now.

At eight-thirty, the postmistress had to go open up. Elaine thanked her for the coffee and told me to buzz up to Van Gogh's bedroom and put on my stylish athletic costume and she'd drive me to her place. She wanted to give me another once-over to touch up the portrait. Then I could run all the way back, if I needed to work up my traditional sweat.

I made a quick change into my Pete T-shirt, remembering to clip on my device, and came down with my post card to Robert, which I tipped into the flap in the lobby. Elaine was in at the counter sending something by priority mail. The tape begins when she came out, full of information for me. "Important documentation. My life's blood. See, I got this long-term grant from some Midwest arts outfit. Didn't know I had such a reputation, did ya? Back home, various states, taught high school kids how to waste time drawing and painting. Moved here, same deal at the regional school down the valley. Subsistence wages. They cut the programs, of course. Then outta the blue this grant lands on me!" We'd made it to the Aztec. She hooked her cane between the seats and hoisted herself up and in. I jumped in the other side, and soon we were tooling along the pavement at an unsafe speed.

"So what were you mailing?" I asked, holding tight to the armrest. I'd noticed Vermonters tended to tailgate out-of-state drivers like me that didn't know all the curves.

"Anyways, as I was saying, I got this grant," said Elaine, one hand on the steering wheel. "Seems an old student moved to Springfield, Illinois. Got on some committee. Said I'd inspired him for life, even though he ended up a lawyer. Point is, I get these regular little checks, not enough to live high on, but pays the bills. All I gotta do is send 'em quarterly reports. Photos of recent work. Next envelope's gonna have you in it. I make up crap about gallery shows. Who's to know the county arts barn ain't some classy joint? Got my drawings on their walls. Sell at farmer's markets, too. Quaintsy landscapes and shit, not my real stuff, not the Sam series. Those I do for me."

"And now you're doing me for Robert."

"Damn generous of me."

At the change to dirt, Elaine gunned it all the more, rattling the undercarriage, kicking up dust clouds. Fortunately, there was never much traffic. When I'm out running, I hear cars way off in plenty of time to move to the side where the Bud Light cans get tossed.

"I wonder why Sam didn't tell me about an appointment at the VA," I said. "He's been expecting me to show up every day almost."

"Keeps ya on your toes. Anyways, he don't mind you the way he minds me. Not that I care. He likes you better."

"He says I bug him."

"'Cause you got under his thick old hide. It's youth. Has a thing against youth, always bitching about the decline of culture, is what he calls it."

"He does like to point out all the things I don't know."

"So sling it right back! What does that old fart not know, for chrissakes?"

"In front of the postmistress, I didn't want to mention his poems."

"Lucy?"

"I wasn't sure of her name."

"Ya gotta credit Lucy. Knows everything. Or thinks she does. Been behind that counter ever since I come here."

"Probably she reads my post cards," I said.

"Nothing too randy, I trust."

"We keep that for sealed envelopes," I joked, though we'd agreed to stick to cards as part of my decompression.

"I do real fine without any of that lovey-dovey shit," Elaine said. "Been on my lonesome since I left Wisconsin. Who needs men!"

I gave a laugh, meant to commiserate, though she knew it wasn't true for me. She was pulling around back of her house where the bed of yellow-orange lilies was glowing in the morning sun.

"Had enough coffee," she announced. "Ready to do some fine work today." She lifted herself out and hobbled to the back door that led into her studio. I followed. Right away, she had me sit where she'd sketched me before. She grabbed my ankle to get my leg in the same position across my knee. "Now look up here," she said. "It's the light on the right cheek and on the hair up top. Less of the red on the hair, little more flush on the cheek."

She was already at work on the other side of her easel. I couldn't see what she was doing, but I sat patiently and listened to her talk.

"So ya want to know about Sam's poems? He'd never let me read 'em. Once, I picked up what was out on the table when he went to give Hank a carrot. I saw scrawls and scribbles and words crossed out and arrows to other words. I did catch the name Helen. By then I knew that was his ex-wife. But he grabs the notebook outta my hand, says none of your business. From what I could see, he was writing poetry, ya know, in lines. Not that I razzed him for it. Told him, as a fellow artist, I could appreciate the creative process. Hell, that's what I taught kids all those years. Make a mess or ya never find out what you're doing! 'Fellow artist, my ass,' says Sam. Not sure if he meant I wasn't the fellow or he wasn't. I'm used to Sam's temper. See right through it mostly. Bet you do, too. Difficult man, for sure. Who ain't difficult some of the time? Me included. Not you, of course, oh no, you're still smooth as silk."

"Robert thinks I can be difficult. I was getting so stressed at work, that's why I'm here. He was worried about me."

"So he sends you outta town."

"To give me a break from the tension. I mean, I was bringing the stress home."

"So he needed a break from you," said Elaine with a wink.

"It's good for both of us."

"Probably having an affair," Elaine said. "Don't shift your pose. Hold it! Sorry, shouldn't be razzing ya. Anyways, I know men."

"I'm not worried about that," I said without turning my head or adjusting my stiffening knees.

"Oh no," Elaine said, looking intently at the light surrounding me and then at the canvas and working away while she went on talking, "you're a sweet kid. Bet Robert is, too. Have a dog?"

"Two cats."

"That'll keep you together. Responsibilities."

"I'm not worried," I said again, as firmly as I could.

"Lucy says ya write each other every damn day."

"We do."

"Youth!" proclaimed Elaine. "Sam takes against youth, but I'm all for it. Taught all those years, loved my pupils, loved the work. There was hope in it. Sam sees stupidity, I see hope. You're right on the edge now. Less stupid, but also less hope. Look out! My thirties did me in."

"That's when you moved up here?"

"Nope. Stuck it out to my forties. Bad news. Finally hung it up. Fresh start, different slice of the country. No one to mess with me. And not old Samuel Arthur Fry, Esquire, on the rebound, if ya catch my drift."

"But you keep doing his portraits."

"Don't move. Almost got ya. Yeah, I keep painting the old codger. Looking close at getting old. Painting you to look close at still almost being young. Done ya a bunch of times."

I leaned forward. I couldn't help it.

"Hold still, buster! One more minute is all." I leaned back into the light. It was heating up my back. "What's that 'Pete' doing on your shirt?"

"Is it in the painting?"

"But ya weren't wearing it the first time. Don't like words in my pictures anyways."

"He's running for president."

"I know that. Don't stand a chance."

"Too young," I said with a smile and then, "Too gay?"

"That, too. All right, ya can move now." I stood and stretched, and she beckoned me to come around and view the results. "Done," she said.

I couldn't tell what was different, but somehow I didn't look as moody as I had before. I looked silkier, to use her word. It must have been the feeling she was wanting to get at. "And there's other ones of me?"

"None for you to see. Ya won't get to see more of you, and Sam won't get to see more of him. Only that arts outfit in Springfield, Illinois. Have to document my latest work to get the dough. Can't only send quaintsy landscapes."

"I hope you won't do as many of me as you've done of Sam."

"Can't say. Fifty years difference, not yet thirty and almost eighty. What am I getting at?"

"And you hide them all away?"

"Up them stairs. Attic's full of 'em. I pull out the quaintsy ones for the farmer's markets. Additional source of income. Also sell my jams and pies. All under the table," she added with another wink.

"Elaine, you really are a serious artist. You shouldn't hide out like this."

"And Sam's a serious poet?"

"Well, he's serious anyway. I couldn't judge his poetry, even if he let me read it."

Elaine had stumped off into the kitchen and called back, "Got something for ya." I didn't think I should follow, so I stood at the easel and studied the portrait more closely. I could see layers in the paint, as though there were other versions of me hidden underneath—older, younger, rougher, smoother, sadder—now I looked happier. Robert would be glad.

Elaine came back with a teapot on a tray with plates of blueberry pie slices. I shouldn't have, but I couldn't not. "Told ya about my pies. Blueberry bushes out back. Didn't see 'em? It's their season. Want ice cream on top?"

"Oh, plain is plenty. Thank you, Elaine. I'll have to run this off."

"Yeah, keep your figure, kid, it don't last. You go either meaty or scrawny like me. Once, I was a diaphanous hippie chick."

"I believe it," I said, because she had the style for it, but I wasn't clear about diaphanous. "I wonder what Sam was like back then."

"Stalwart suburban country club lawyer with a poetry hobby. My guess. Never even seen a photo. Never talks about married life and not much after. That poem's about ancient Greece from what I could see. Could hardly make sense of the scribbles and scrawls."

"Helen of Troy," I said.

"Sam's stuck way back when."

"But he also wrote one about King David in the Bible. He told me to look up the story because, of course, I don't know anything. So now I do."

"Aha!" Elaine exclaimed. "I get it now. His unfaithfulness obsession. Injured husbands. Get off the pity pot, Sam!"

She'd lounged into the new leather chair, and I sat on the window seat again. We were eating our pie and sipping our tea, and I felt we were getting somewhere. "He calls it an epic poem in three cantos," I said. "Biblical, Classical, and Medieval."

"Ya know more than me," said Elaine. "Funny how he tells you things. So you're out running and ya stumble on this cranky old man, and it's like his own self from the past showing up. Wants to teach ya things he didn't know when he was your age. Ain't I clever?"

"Sounds about right."

"What could I ever mean to him? Put the moves on me back when. Ever since, thinks I'm a dyke. Man's gotta do what man's gotta do. That's pure crap, but it's how a man like Sam sees it."

I was embarrassed to say anything. I was undoubtedly blushing while Elaine looked me over with her painter's eyes.

"Okay, Sweatbox, about time for ya to run," she said.

"I'm too full of pie to run now."

"Another slice?"

"I couldn't."

"Then rest a spell. I got work to do." She put the cups and plates on the tray with the blue teapot and, without her cane, started for the kitchen. I got quickly up and took the tray. "Gentlemanly," she said and let me go ahead. "It's a disaster in there. Late night baking." I found a clear spot on the counter to set down the tray. "Just leave it."

"So Sam's not likely to be back yet?" I asked.

"Makes a day of it. Who knows what that man does out on his own. See him tomorrow and he won't let on a damn thing!" Elaine went to open the front door to clue me I should take off. "But you stop by anytime. If I don't feature a visit, I'll say so."

"I appreciate it," I said. "Sam's the same. You two aren't all that different."

Elaine gave me another once-over and said with a nod, "Sharp kid," before closing the door.

I walked off, happy being called a kid. I'd be thirty in a year, but it's all relative. Despite the pie, I did feel lighter and bouncier on my feet as I picked up a jog all the way to that farm road and the pond with the crayfish and tadpoles turning into frogs. I didn't stop to worry about taking off my clothes. The water was so pleasantly cool and tingly with the sunshine sparkling all over. I couldn't help imagining maybe some hunter or farmhand coming upon me swimming there. He'd peer through the cattails like a David. The first time I swam there, I was afraid of being seen, the second time, I did dare to skinny dip, but this time I almost wished someone would come, a man, couldn't quite decide who. After all those days away from home, I knew how I was feeling.

When I climbed back on the bank, I kept envisioning things happening right there in the grass. I let it build and build until I couldn't stop it. Then I splashed back into the pond to wash off. This is a scene I'll delete if I ever put this up online, but I had to write it because seeing myself in a painting was such a new thing for a modest person like me. Robert says I don't think enough of myself, which is why I get so stressed, as if the world is pushing against me instead of me pushing against the world, the way he does.

Day Nine

It had turned cloudy and cool. I had less than two weeks left of my rest cure, as Robert called it. He knew I wasn't truly that badly off, and I knew, even if he had an adventure or two in my absence, that I'd hear about it when I got home and it wouldn't be a problem in the way Elaine had joked—or maybe not joked— and it certainly wouldn't be the big unfaithfulness deal Sam made of his broken marriage. Robert and I do plan to get married, mostly for financial security, but we won't make a show of it, simply go to City Hall with a few friends and my little sister (who lives nearby) and our cats in their carrying case, if they're allowed. Robert might've been imagining me hooking up with some unshaven back-to-the-lander, but my fantasy by the pond was as far as I was likely to go. I could easily hold out for thirteen more days.

Next morning, I didn't feel at all like a run, so I cuddled up in bed with another book from the dump. It was one I was supposed to have read for my creative non-fiction course but never did, and there it was on the sagging shelf among the thrillers and gothics and moldy old bestsellers. It was one guy's personal account of life back in the day, the hippie life Elaine Greene had lived when she was my age. The author sounded like the sort of prick she got screwed over by, but he obviously considered himself totally cool. Maybe back then he was, before the women's movement and LGBTQ rights, but now he only pissed me off. Still, it was fun reading a book where you dislike the main character.

I began to wonder, if I ever got to read Sam's poem, would I start to dislike him? I hoped he'd learned something over the years about his bad behavior. It couldn't all have been Helen's fault, or David's. In Elaine's case, if she had a rival, it wouldn't be a man but another woman. In love triangles, it's either two men fighting over a woman or two women fighting over a man. Is it different if it's three women? Or when it's two men fighting over another man, can't they just call it an adventure and go back home?

I seemed to be having a discourse with my own self. It was cozy thinking these thoughts in my bed under the fuzzy blanket with the brisk wind outside the window and thick clouds covering the sun. Robert wrote that it was sweltering in Somerville. In Vermont, even the warmest days cooled off at night, no air conditioner whirring, only sounds from the woods. I'd recorded that night owl hooting and the birds waking at dawn. I had more time and space up there. After I got home, we should stop scheduling so much. We should take long hikes in the Fells or along the Mystic instead of me jogging the bike path and Robert working out at the gym.

Would I be missing Sam and Elaine? Would they miss me? I almost thought they might, and I might miss them, too. There were so many questions I wanted to ask them, but Elaine had her snappy way of talking and Sam didn't expect to hear all that much from me. Robert would've lectured him right back, but that's Robert. I have always been more of an attentive student.

When I noticed it was getting on toward eleven and all I'd done, after a quick shower and getting myself a coffee downstairs, was to crawl back in bed and read that aggravating book, I decided to pull off the blanket and put on my thick gray socks and hiking boots and go mail the card I wrote last night before I decided what to do next.

I'd visit Sam later on. Since I didn't feel like a run, though the cool air would've been ideal for it, I took the car and drove out past the dump and hung a left toward landscapes new to me, I stopped at some other town's general store for a salami sandwich, chips, and a can of Moxie. The sky was beginning to clear. I found a half-sunny spot beside the road and had myself a picnic. But this isn't meant to be a chronicle of my own doings, except in so far as they relate to the discourses with Sam Fry. I'll simply record that, after a cold north wind had swept most of the clouds to the south, I could almost see Quebec past the far horizon and both the Green and White Mountains to the west and east.

When I drove back through the village and on to Sam's, I was in a new frame of mind. My bouncy mood of the previous day had turned into a calm expansiveness I hadn't felt for months, maybe years. I'd seen things so far off, so unreachable and yet right there, the roofs of little towns emerging from the woods, a road winding up a distant hill. I walked up the slope to Sam's cabin in a weirdly blissful state.

He was out with his donkey. Hank was actually cavorting around the meadow, kicking up his hooves. I'd never seen him do that, almost like dancing. "Weather's got to him," Sam called when I approached the gate. "Senses the season changing. Stirs him up."

Having spotted me, the old gray animal did a quick turn and

galumphed to the fence so I could greet him. While I patted his shaggy head, he relaxed into his familiar contemplative state.

Sam came over, a red plaid woolen coat and knit cap over his sweatshirt and grubby jeans. "Where you been, young fella?"

"And where have you yourself been?" I tossed right back, though I did know.

"When I was away, you didn't even look in on this lonely guy."

"He told you?"

"He communicates the way of watchful animals, when you know how to interpret them."

"I could call that bullshit, Sam," I said, surprised at myself.

"Aw, you don't know bullshit from bullshit!" I could tell he enjoyed me razzing him. I'd picked it up from Elaine. "All right, Hank," he said, "you go rest. Too old to be acting coltish. And you," Sam added, coming through the gate and jabbing his knotty knuckle at me, "I have another poem for you."

"One of your own?" I asked hopefully and followed him onto the porch.

"Mine? Hell, no. Shakespeare again. Makes up for that nasty one you didn't appreciate. Here goes." Turning to face away from the wind, he recited from memory another song, again without singing it. I later found it in *Measure for Measure*, which I'd also never heard of. Coming at me from his old man's voice, it was slightly embarrassing.

Take, O take those lips away,
That so sweetly were forsworn;
And those eyes, the break of day,
Lights that do mislead the morn;
But my kisses bring again, bring again,
Seals of love, but sealed in vain, sealed in vain.

"And that's supposed to make me feel better?" I asked, amazed at how feisty I was being.

"Don't think so? Come on inside. Chillier out here. I'll put on the kettle."

After he'd filled the pot and lit the gas, he went to open Hank's hatch, and soon there stood the donkey, checking us out. "He'll want to hear this, too," said Sam.

I took my traditional chair and waited in silence while he heated up muffins in the toaster oven. He brought out plates, butter and knives, cups and spoons. Sam was a thorough provider. I wondered if he'd always been.

"That little song," he said, "is sung to a young woman who's been abandoned. Despite what happened, she still wants the man that done her wrong. You familiar with the phrase? And you don't find that encouraging?"

"Not really," I said. "But it seems like hoping for what she can't have."

"Ah," said Sam, pouring the mint tea and placing a warm corn muffin on my plate. "Don't credit hopeless desires?"

"They happen, but I don't give them any credit."

"Plain old stupid human nature, then? Can't let it go. Maybe you'll prefer this one then." He leaned back in his chair and recited something else from memory.

Since there's no help, come let us kiss and part;
Nay, I have done, you get no more of me,
And I am glad, yes glad with all my heart
That thus so cleanly I myself can free;
Shake hands forever, cancel all our vows,
And when we meet at any time again,
Be it not seen in either of our brows
That we one jot of former love retain—

"That's Michael Drayton. How rational of him. Clean break? Look up the rest of the sonnet on your machine. Maybe you'll get what I'm driving at."

"You're not going to recite it?"

"Can't quite recall how it goes."

"You don't fool me, Sam. Your head is full of old poems."

"Anyways, son, you go and do some research all by your inno-cent self tonight."

"This discourse thing of yours—" I began, and then Hank let out a sudden ee-yaw, so Sam went to give him an apple from the wooden bowl on the counter. Back at the table, he waited for me to finish my sentence, but I couldn't.

"This discourse, son? It isn't about broken love affairs. Petty stuff, considering the cosmos. This love mess, this unfaithful-ness, faithfulness as well, right? A microcosm! But my kisses bring again, bring again—"

"Kisses are microcosms?" I was aware of hot tea washing the scratchy crumbs of the corn muffin down my throat.

"Christ, that my love was in my arms and I in my bed again. Remember that one? Of course, leave out the 'Christ'."

I was more and more puzzled by what Sam was trying to tell me.

"Our place in the cosmos, my friend, won't remain forever." Sam gave me a wry tilt of his head and a dry thin-lipped smile. "The sun will first grow huge and absorb us and then burn itself out. That's a mere smidgin of the total cosmic activity. Wonder what these poems have to do with all that?"

"You're going to tell me now?"

Sam spread his hands on the table and slapped them against the wood. "No, I am not!" He was staring across, expecting me to answer my own question. Where had my feistiness gone?

"You know," I said at last, "I'm not used to this kind of con-versation—" Sam held up a warning finger. "I mean discourse, nowhere else in my life. I do appreciate it. It's certainly not a waste of time. But sometimes, Sam, you go way beyond me." I was collecting my thoughts, glad I'd have my tape to listen to and try to make more sense of it a second time through. "You'd be surprised," I told him, "I did very well in college, got mostly A's, but you're not being exactly fair, Sam."

"I'm not a professor," he said, "I'm a goad." I thought he'd said "goat" until I played the tape back. And he went on: "You think I'm writing an epic poem about how a woman named Helen once did me wrong with a handsomer, younger man named David, and how after all these years, I still haven't got past it but spend my days stewing over the raw deal I got. Uriah, Menelaus—so how about the last wronged husband?'"

"I can guess! Samuel Taylor Coleridge."

"Mr. O'Dea, when do you suppose Coleridge lived? Didn't I tell you the third canto's medieval? No medieval Samuels. Ever heard of King Arthur?"

"Oh, and you're Samuel Arthur Fry! I remember. The Knights of the Round Table." I couldn't help looking down at the round kitchen table where we were sitting."

"And in the end, what happened to King Arthur?"

"Something about Sir Lancelot?"

"We'll get to that. It's my Epic Poem in Three Cantos. Lots bigger than two men and one woman."

"If only you'd let me read it."

"Possibly when I'm dead."

"You're not sick, Sam? Elaine Greene said you went to the VA yesterday."

"She did, did she? What were you hanging out with her for?"

"The portrait. It was your idea."

"Suppose it was." Sam was leaning back, sipping the last of his tea. I glanced over at Hank to see how he was dealing with all this. He was asleep on his feet. "No, I take good care of myself," Sam said. "Don't worry about me. I've come to terms."

"With what?"

"With terms. You understand the term 'terms'?" He was

pleased at being so clever, the evasive old man. "So go off to your rented room at nine-hundred a month and look up Drayton's sonnet. Don't come back before you got something to say about it. Tea's putting me to sleep."

I drove off slowly past Elaine's little brick house without thinking to stop in. A pick-up had pulled right close behind me to let me know what it thought of Smart Cars with Massachusetts plates. Reaching the pavement, it whizzed around me with a blast of its horn and a "Make America Great Again" sticker on the tailgate.

I checked the post office to see if the mail had come in, but Lucy—I knew her name now—said there was nothing for me. Sometimes the delivery gets backed up a day. Noting my disappointment, she said I'd surely get two cards tomorrow.

I did look up Michael Drayton and found the rest of the poem. It was saying the same thing as Shakespeare, maybe a bit differently, but still despite everything, even at the very end, there's his desperate wish to get it all back.

Now at the last gasp of love's latest breath,
When, his pulse failing, passion speechless lies,
When faith is kneeling by his bed of death,
And innocence is closing up his eyes,
Now if thou would'st, when all have given him over,
From death to life thou might'st him yet recover.

I decided that Sam wasn't so much using a microcosm to contemplate the macrocosm as using the macrocosm to contemplate his own private microcosm. Maybe it came to the same thing. My thoughts were twisting me up. Sam had spent a whole day seeing doctors. He was almost eighty. He could talk about the sun exploding but not about himself. It's easier to talk about the death of the sun, or maybe not so easy anymore, what with us worrying more about the death of the planet than we used to. Tomorrow, I was going to have to make Sam start answering some questions.

Day Ten

Cold but sunny. The wind had died, and it felt like fall, great weather to go for a run. I couldn't skip another day. My joints needed to move. I spent a longer time stretching and put on sweatpants for the first time, then went to mail the card I'd written last night about my trip into the hills and the vast views and how alive I felt, but nothing about not getting a card from home or about Sam and his poems. Robert had no idea how much of my day was organized around that old coot. I'd have to get him to listen to the tapes, the only way to explain the discourses, with a donkey in an open hatch.

Now, in the process of fleshing out and trimming the text so it doesn't get boring, I hear how dumb I sometimes sound. I've come to understand it all a lot better. Robert hasn't quite appreciated that. For him, it's a story of me meeting two eccentric old folks who recited poems and painted my portrait (which he really likes) and who did an incredible job of cheering me up. And he credits himself with facilitating my successful recovery. I do give him credit. We're back to our reassuringly homey routines. The planning office isn't getting me down as much now that I feel better about myself. I've taken a larger view of life, thanks to meeting Elaine and Sam and even Hank. I see his animalness in Alice and Martha, not that cats and donkeys are at all comparable, but looking into Alice's eyes or stroking Martha's fur, I make a connection to another species. I've discovered I need that. I need Robert more now, too, despite his not having the patience to listen to all the tapes. He's glad I have a creative outlet that puts my day job in its proper place. After all, on my side I'm not that interested in what he does at work, handling demanding clients and complicated charts and tables, playing with other people's money. He never stresses out. That's all that matters to me. We've got a good balance going.

So back to the month of August.

Jogging along the pavement, it hit me again, that guilty feeling I sometimes got that I'd never confessed how I was secretly recording Sam. It was too late to tell him now. He knew I had one of those gizmos clipped to my belt. If I explained it was only a camera phone with GPS so I wouldn't get lost, he'd scoff at me for not trusting my own sense of direction. True, I'd started taping Sam only inadvertently, but the second time I'd consciously planned it. I had no idea then what it would turn into. And not only do I feel guilty but also ashamed, dishonest, unworthy of his trust.

So when I made it up the slope, breathing heavily in the cold, and saw Sam kneeling down in his garden looking older and tireder, I hesitated to switch on my device. But I did anyway. I couldn't stop myself. As bad as I felt for being so sneaky, I knew I had to make a record of everything Samuel Arthur Fry said. I knew it would mean more to me each time I played it back.

My stay up there was somehow outside regular time, not part of the real world or my real life. It set different rules. It was about running, thinking, listening, meditating—it all was simply happening, digital record or not. I'd begun to think of it as Donkey Time. Besides, I told myself, if Sam knew what I was up to, beneath his bluster and scorn he might be secretly pleased.

"Keeping the knees toasty, I see," he said.

"It's cold out."

"Late August. Warmer in the sun. Look at Honkety Hank up there. Got a sunny spot." The donkey's gray coat was shining almost white against the still-green grass on the hillside. "Lots to catch up on," Sam said. "Behind on my weeding. Can't entertain you inside today. Take advantage of the crisp air. Invigorates me."

I agreed with a nod but was still panting.

"Tell you what. Your day to talk. Figured out that sonnet?"

I came inside the rabbit fence and squatted beside where Sam was bent over and managed to say, "I think I got it. It's the same deal as the 'kisses bring again' song. It's another depressing one about hopeless desire."

"What you might call self-destructive?" Sam asked.

"And somehow it's connected to the cosmos or whatever?"

"Getting there, son."

"Sam, would you simply tell me about your 'Unfaithfulness' poem? I can't figure you out without some idea of how it's a microcosm."

"It's my life project. Everyone needs a life project. You need one! Life's a hell of a project, Griffin." He turned his head to look at me straight on. He'd called me by my name again, and that time I felt he was challenging me instead of coddling me for my innocence. Then he went back to pulling weeds and plopping them in a bushel basket.

I leaned back on my heels but didn't have anything to say, so I waited.

"You want to know about my tedious poetry?" came his voice up from the soil. "Not gonna let you read it. But, well, come on out now." He pushed himself up with one hand in the dirt and one knee under him until he could stagger upright. I leapt over to steady him. "We'll go out in the meadow. See Hank there? Could be Robert Louis Stevenson's Modestine from his travels. Could be the ass that carried the so-called holy family into Egypt. You're familiar with that charming myth?"

We reached Hank's side, and I scratched his warm back and Sam chucked him under his muzzle. "Are you re-telling myths in your poem, Sam? I mean, does it take place in olden times, like the Bible or the Odyssey?"

"Or the idylls of the king?" he asked. I thought he'd said "idols" but found what he meant when I went online that night. "Nope," he said, "takes place, in so far as any poetry takes place anywhere but in words—it takes place in living memory."

He was standing on the uphill side of Hank, and I was looking across at Sam, lit by the sun while my face was in cold shadow.

As if seeing it all before his eyes, Sam said dreamily: "Bluff above Lake Michigan. Swimming pool. Bathing cabana like a Bedouin tent." Then, he chuckled. "Who needs a pool when you got a Great Lake?"

"That's where David sees Bathsheba, or Bethsabe, however you pronounce it?"

"Later on, she's called Helen. Only three names in my poem. In the pool, she's the Wife. And there's the Husband and a young man named David. Second canto, Helen's got the Husband, of course, and the Lover. That one takes place, if you must put it like that, in a neo-classical mansion with columns and marble steps down to the lake where the Lover moors his yacht. My kind of poetry, stuffed with words, to see, to touch, words you wouldn't know."

"And the third?"

"Oh, the North Woods, Upper Peninsula, Arthur's hunting lodge. Wife and Lover come to find him. Forgiveness? Forget-fulness? *Morte d'Arthur*?" (I looked that one up, too.)

I didn't know how to respond to those questions, but I did say, "Sam, is this about what happened years ago in Chicago?"

"It's a poem, my friend, not an autobiography. Who says any of it, to use your term, 'happened'?"

"But it's about you and your wife Helen and some guy named David with a yacht!"

"You're confusing him with Paris sailing her off to Troy. Naw, it's plain old midwestern Arthur, Helen, and David, the eternal triangle. By the way, my name's Sam."

"Samuel Arthur Fry!"

"No similarity. Right, Hank?" The donkey was leaning down to nibble a stubbly clump of wildflowers and weeds.

"Fine, I'll play along, but at least tell me the plot!"

"No plot, son. Too ordinary to have a plot. A man seduces another man's wife, and the husband dies alone."

"You call it an epic. You say it's actually about the macrocosm, not the other way around." As I said it, I remembered how stupid it had sounded last night after I thought it over.

"Physics tells us that everything in the cosmos is implied in the smallest particles," Sam said in his professorial voice. "Of course, it also works the other way round!"

"Sam," I said, getting serious, "why did you go see doctors yesterday?"

"And I'll be going back on Saturday. Nothing to worry about. Overnight stay for some tests. Was going to ask you to look in on this poor critter," he said, stroking Hank's tangled mane. "Make sure he has water and feed. Could spend time with him, so he don't get lonesome. Could even sleep out here. The Lily Maid might come by, but don't encourage her."

"I will if you explain what you're going in for," I said firmly, already wondering how it would be, sleeping in that mysterious inner room in Sam's own bed, with Hank snuffling above me from the hatch. Or I could sleep on the sagging old couch.

"I'll lock my poem in the desk drawer so you won't be tempted," he said, as if I'd already agreed. "Couldn't decipher my hieroglyphs anyways. Must make a clean copy soon, before it's too late."

"But what are you going in for?" I insisted. "And on a Saturday!"

"Aw, just some sleep study. Sleep after toil, port after stormy seas. Seems foolish to me. You don't need to worry your red head over it."

"That's all you'll tell me?"

"Told you enough. Don't go getting that Greene woman all riled up. Don't want you two conspiring."

"But if she stops by?"

"Make her a cup of tea. I'll bake some cookies. Come tomorrow, I'll give instructions. Day after, I'm off at dawn."

"Are you getting cold, Sam?" I asked because I'd caught him covering a cough with his gnarly hand.

"Making the most of the outdoors. Have to be cooped up this weekend. Doubt I'll sleep at all at the VA."

"Anyway," I said, "let's take a rest on the porch."

His twinkling sunlit eyes shone at me through his old-time spectacles, and he said, "You figure I'm feeble, don't you! Feeble in mind, too, I suppose."

"You're definitely not feeble in mind, Sam. I can't catch up to your mind."

"A man lives in the woods with a donkey, all he's got is his mind. Spends too much time thinking. Aw, what the heck, we'll go set a spell."

I'm still puzzled by Sam's way of talking. Old hillbilly, then college professor, sometimes both in the same sentence. I wondered if his poetry was like that. Elaine was somewhat that way, too, but had probably always talked the same, and not as professorial, though she'd gone to college in South Dakota. (I found out where Vermilion is.) Sam, in his lawyer days, must have talked normally, and if he lived in a neo-classical (not sure what that is) suburban mansion above Lake Michigan, he must've attended snooty cocktail parties and talked shop about business and politics and culture. Had he acquired his country talk from Elaine? There had to be more to their relationship than either let on.

On the porch, Sam in his rocker and me cross-legged on the warm floorboards, kept talking:

G: You won't tell me what's real in your poem and what isn't?

S: It's all real. But it's not real at all. It's words, that's what it is. Beautiful words. Real words. Rich and strange words. That's why it's hard to write.

G: I mean, I took a creative non-fiction writing course in college. I know from my personal essays that you can't get a hundred per cent of real things into words. You paint a word picture. That's what my professor got us doing. It's more universal in meaning, she said, if you use specifics. The universe is made up of specifics, details, close-up things. It's not made up of generalities.

S: Good, young fella. Finally telling me something.

G: It's hard to get a word in when you're running the show, Sam.

S: Comes from having only Hank to talk to.

G: But also Elaine.

S: Aw, she don't listen. Always got a bug up her ass.

G: Sam!

S: She's a good old gal despite.

G: I think so.

S: She's doing your portrait.

G: I can't say it's flattering, but it's me all right.

S: Enough reason she won't do me. Come out like a wrinkly buzzard.

G: Oh, no, you're not vain, Sam!

S: Who I got to be vain for? Hank don't mind. He's an ugly cuss himself. Two bony old wrecks we are.

G: I have to ask you this, Sam. Why do you like talking to me? I'm some ignorant flatlander who's here for one month and I'll be gone, and then what?

S: And queer besides.

G: Is it easier to talk to a gay guy than a straight one? Or not to any kind of woman?

S: Never thought about it. You showed up. Could've been anyone.

G: It's not me specifically?

S: All right, it's you, I guess. You're a good listener.

G: I've always been told so.

S: Hank's the best listener in the world.

G: But you never razz Hank for not knowing things.

S: Because he knows everything already. How animals are. It's all inside, from birth, all he needs to know.

G: Sam, did you live in a neo-classical mansion with a pool and a cabana? Did you have a hunting lodge in the Upper Peninsula? At least, answer me that!

S: Lived in a world where such things were possible.

G: You sure do drive me crazy, Mr. Fry!

S: You'll get over it.

That's an accurate transcript, smoothed out a bit, of what we said to each other on his porch. Because it was frustrating trying to pin down Sam's past, I found myself gradually losing the need to. No doubt that's what he wanted. Did it actually matter? He'd said there wasn't a plot. It was an ordinary story. I thought about me and Robert and our occasional adventures. There was a married man at his gym. Once, when the wife was away with the kids, he had Robert back to his house. Married bi-curious men are the hottest sex, Robert said, not hotter than you, Griff, but as adventures go—something like that. I've had a number of my own, though I wouldn't describe them as hot, and they weren't married. They were more of a "yeah, whatever" kind of thing. I always felt stupid afterwards and couldn't wait to go home and tell Robert about it to clear my head. I was perfectly satisfied knowing we always had each other. That's why I'd been interested to know what had caused Sam to leave his wife and daughter or to cause Helen to leave him for another man or for them both to split for whatever thoughtless reasons. If these triangle stories are what makes for poems and plays and novels and songs, and for history itself, they must be about something larger than just plain sex. Larger than love? Is there something larger? Is love the macrocosm Sam's writing about? Hopeless desire? Self-destruction? Is love a generation of vipers, whatever that means? The line's in the Bible, too. I googled it. Shakespeare stole it, or did whoever translated the Bible steal it from Shakespeare? But all of it's a myth. That's what Sam would say. Everything from the past soon becomes a myth. Even now, transcribing our talk, it's ceased to be objective electronic evidence. Sam Fry up there in Vermont, now in the winter snow (I watch the weather reports), is becoming my own personal myth. As is Elaine, every time I look at my portrait hanging above Robert's desk. As are those roads and hills and distant views, now all in white. I'm back to my day-to-day reality down here, and it's not so bad. If it weren't for the promises I made to Sam before I left, would I still be thinking of my month there as a puzzling dream I'd woken up from, and now it's gone?

That day, our discourse on the porch soon fizzled out. I could see how tired Sam had become, despite his intention to get back to weeding. When I left, he was still sitting in the rocking chair the way I'd seen him on the first day, but without his Coleridge book in his lap. We were both being rotated away from the sunlight. He would soon be all in shadow.

I went the long way around, working up quite a sweat despite the cold air. I didn't take the detour to the tadpole pond but ran straight to the post office and up the stairs to my room to take a hot shower and then lie down with a nature tape in my ears to clear my thoughts of Sam. Then, I remembered the mail had come. I ran down again and inside where, behind the counter, Lucy was holding up two post cards. "What did I tell you!" she said. I was sure she'd read them.

Day Eleven

That Friday I didn't stay long. Sam was preoccupied. He said he was busy copying his first canto cleanly into another notebook. At least, he'd got that much right for now. And he was packing a bag for what he called his sleep study, but I had a suspicion it was something more serious. He seemed too jittery for it to be nothing to worry about.

I don't need to transcribe all the logistics regarding my stay in the cabin to look after Hank. Sam explained how to light the wood stove if it got cold, how to operate the toaster oven (a very complicated high-end one), where to put out the compost, and he opened the fridge and cupboards to display the food supply. Sam was a vegetarian, but I could eat whatever I wanted. He left me some of his stuffed peppers I could heat up, and in the bread box was an apple pie Elaine had foisted on him.

Sam had a dozen instructions for donkey care, including the vet to call in an emergency. Because he had no phone, it meant going to the Lily Maid's and using hers. "So you depend on that bothersome woman for some things," I said.

"Least she could do!" What a bluffer the old man was.

I was finally allowed in the inner room. There was his desk with Svensk, the wooden troll, and a spiral notebook open to a page of tidily printed lines. He closed it quick, stuck it in the desk drawer, and turned the key, which he tucked in his jeans pocket and said, "Forbidden!"

I inspected the narrow bathroom behind the kitchen wall and

the bed, no wider than Van Gogh's, and he showed me how to open and latch Hank's hatch. "He'll look in on you," Sam said, "and you won't be me, but he'll recognize your sweat." He chuckled to himself. "Can't help recalling how you thought Hank was the man I slept with!" And he told me he'd put on clean sheets and a pillowcase and then led me outside and around the cabin to find Hank in his stall, quietly munching hay. I learned how much feed to put out and how to fill the water barrel. "Most important," Sam said, "spend a good long time talking to him. What he expects. Quiet steady voice. Take a book off the shelf, read him anything. Don't have to know what it means. Open to a page and read. Might learn something yourself."

Before I left, Sam said he had one more poem for me. He'd read me the one called "Bethsabe Bathing" and acted out that scene from Shakespeare. "Epigraphs," he said. "You know what they are?"

"Epigrams?"

"Epi-graphs, what you put at the top of your first page. Someone else's words. Gets you going. Here's what I got for canto number three." Of course, he knew it by heart. We were back out on the porch. He was standing in the doorway, and I was under the roof because rain was beginning to fall.

O golden hair, with which I used to play
Not knowing! O imperial-moulded form,
And beauty such as never woman wore,
Until it came a kingdom's curse with thee —
I cannot touch thy lips, they are not mine,
But Lancelot's: nay, they never were the King's.
I cannot take thy hand; that too is flesh,
And in the flesh thou hast sinn'd; and mine own flesh,
Here looking down on thine polluted, cries
"I loathe thee:" yet not less, O Guinevere,
For I was ever virgin save for thee,

My love thro' flesh hath wrought into my life
So far, that my doom is, I love thee still.
Let no man dream but that I love thee still.

"Then, Tennyson turns all Christian on us. You don't need no superstitious bullshit to be forgiving or forgiven for everybody's hopeless desires. We're all plain folks here on our obscure little planet."

"There it is again," I said, "your whole thing about holding on to the very end."

"Is that what it is?"

"Isn't it?"

"One way of looking at it," said Sam. "Is it a good thing or is it what I might call self-destructive? Seem to remember I once said how no animal goes around acting self-destructive. Leave it to humans, holding onto the same old mistakes to the very end."

"Love's a mistake especially when it's hopeless?"

"Figure it out, fella. Don't have no answer myself." Now the rain was picking up. "You better run home before the storm hits. Bet that old gal will drive you, if you stop in. Don't make nothing of my tests, you hear? As for tomorrow, Hank'll be fine till noon. No need to rush over."

I took off at a run down the hill and was soaked when I got to Elaine's. I ran around to knock on the back door. She was at her easel and looked up annoyed but beckoned me inside.

"Dripping all over my floor. Don't move. I'll grab a towel. Hell, this place is a disaster anyways." She steadied herself on the work table, flipped a paint-spattered towel off a hook on the wall, and tossed it across.

"I was up at Sam's. He was too busy and sent me down to bug you instead."

"About time," said Elaine. "You prefer visiting that old crank than a respectable woman like me."

"No, but he expects me. He doesn't get out much."

"But he's off tomorrow for two days, and you'll be donkey sitting."

"You weren't supposed to know."

"Intrigue, lots of intrigue in that man. I know all about his doings. Check on him most evenings. One time may find him dead on the floor. Doesn't believe in phones. Makes it hard on the rest of us. Lucy that knows everyone's business, those Cobbles that think they run the town, we're all caught up in what's going on with Samuel Fry. Why we bother I can't tell ya."

I'd thoroughly dried my dripping head and sopped up the puddles on the floor. "I think," I began hesitantly, "I think you and Sam are better friends than you admit."

"You can have him. He's too much for me."

"But I'll be gone soon, and you'll be stuck with him,"

"Griffin, ya look too damn worn down. What's all this running for? Getting almost skinny. Your Robert's gotta have something to hold onto."

"You said I had meaty thighs."

"Nothing wrong with a little meat, says this scrawny old dame. I'm serious, ya don't look as healthy. What ya been eating? Better raid Sam's larder and fatten yourself back up."

"He's got one of your pies."

"And ice cream in the freezer compartment. And I happen to know he made his famous stuffed peppers."

"You know all about him, don't you!"

"Ain't ya gonna sit down, now you're dry?"

So I did, and she gave me a cup of hot tea and soon was feeding me a warmed-up slice of blueberry pie with vanilla ice cream melting all over it. She was right. I hadn't been eating enough. Freeze-dried soups and microwaved noodle dishes weren't keeping me going. At home, Robert's the cook and I wash dishes, take out the trash, do the vacuuming and scrub the bathroom. I'm not domestically creative. Robert chooses our décor and decides where to hang prints and photos. But he does deal with the kitty litter. When I lived alone in a studio apartment after graduation, it was pretty minimal. Elaine lived in an untidy mess, but hermit Sam's cabin was always clean and organized, everything in its place.

I wasn't going to ask Elaine for a ride but figured if I hung around long enough she'd offer, which she did. We didn't talk more about Sam. Mostly she wanted to hear about urban planning and concluded it'd given me a nervous breakdown. I said it wasn't quite that bad. She had her own definite opinions on what was wrong with cities.

When we pulled up outside the post office, she said, "Warning ya, I'll buzz up to look in tomorrow. Talking only to a donkey could half-turn ya into a Sam. That sleep study of his? Fact is, he never makes it through a night. Up working on his poems. Should take to drink like me. Do my best work on a night cap after eleven. Who says artists need daylight?"

"But are you concerned about his health?"

"Sam's? No use in that. He does what he does. Could be at death's door and wouldn't show it. I don't ask. Keep an eye on him, though. Now, boy, jump out and check your mail."

I thanked her, she bombed off, and I ran into the post office where Lucy had, not a card, but a sealed envelope for me. We weren't going to write letters. Our plan was the daily cards and the occasional phone call when I got a signal. For Lucy's sake, I pretended to be thrilled, but I was anxious.

Upstairs, in the gray light from the storm, I slit open the envelope and read Robert's eighth-grade cursive with relief. Most of what he wrote isn't relevant to these discourses, but a few sentences touch on the triangular theme that Sam Fry was obsessed with. After Robert said how much he couldn't wait for me to return, he wrote: "It's weird how with you away, Griff, I don't have a single adventure to report. It's not the same without you to come home to. I'd feel like crap coming home alone, like back in the day before we got together. But you can have all the adventures you want up there. I want you feeling better no matter what it takes. I mean it. I love you so much."

With the rain pouring down in windy torrents, splattering the windowpane behind my head, I soon fell into a comfortable snooze with Elaine's pie and ice cream gurgling pleasantly inside me.

Donkey Time

It was a one-sided discourse with me doing all the talking. Or was it a discourse in another language, Hank taking it all in and sending it back through his sad eyes, his snuffles, and the rare ee-yaw? There's something great about feeling that an animal particularly likes you.

I'd filled my backpack with toiletries and clothes for every weather. I'd given up reading that annoying hippie memoir. It was so sexist and homophobic, though he wouldn't have recognized it at the time. Maybe that was my professor's point in assigning it, to show how attitudes change. Instead, I decided I should read a classic to broaden myself, so I studied the dump's recycling shelf and, between the thrillers and mysteries, I noticed a thick water-stained hardback of *The Magic Mountain* by Thomas Mann. I'd certainly heard of it, and even though I didn't know what it was about, it seemed appropriate to read in the mountains, or the foothills of the mountains. Thumbing through, I found there was a young man named Hans at a TB sanatorium in Switzerland back before World War One. I could try reading it to the donkey, if he didn't like the poetry from Sam's books.

I pulled my little car into the lopsided metal shed from which the Isuzu had departed at dawn. The sky was clearing, but the trees were still dripping, and the slope to Sam's was slippery. I found the cabin unlocked and a note on the round table with all the instructions he'd given me yesterday, spelled out in neat print. I felt awkward, standing alone in Sam's home, as if I wasn't supposed to be there. Right away, I went out to find Hank.

At first, I couldn't. He wasn't in his shady spot or behind the solar panels or anywhere in the stable, but then there he was, over the lip at the top end of the meadow, lying behind some baby pine trees. I approached slowly, whistled softly to alert him, and back came a loud ee-yaw. I peeked through the green branches and our eyes met. Then I came around and patted him on the top of his head between the long ears. He stretched himself and laid his head back in the weeds.

I had decided not to tape our two days together. I wanted to live in irretrievable donkey time, even if Elaine did come and interrupt us. So I can't transcribe all I said to Hank, but again I can give the gist of it. It was somewhat like talking to a psychoanalyst, though I never have. But Hank's animalness appeared to understand the essence of all I told him. It wasn't like talking to Alice and Martha. They have each other and are either romping or purring self-satisfiedly or catnapping. If cats meditate, they don't let you in, whereas Hank seemed to want me to join him.

We had many one-sided conversations, if not discourses, some up in the meadow, some in the stable, others when I was at the kitchen table and he was at the hatch, and several when I lay in bed awake in the dark with Hank breathing softly not far above me. It isn't the subject of this project, so I won't go into all the things I said aloud to that friendly old creature, but I can sum them up. I told him about my childhood, how we moved from suburb to suburb. I told him that my little sister had a mostly beneficial influence on my life despite the dachshund incident, and about my parents' differing takes on religion (None At All versus Vaguely Spiritual) or politics (Libertarian versus Socially Responsible). I don't have my mom's spiritual side, but I do think my work for the city is about making things better for everyone, if the bureaucracy would only let us. I got the feeling Hank liked me for that. And I told him about Robert's letter, how I'd been afraid to open it in case he had something bad to confess or was having second thoughts on our relationship. That was because of Sam's thing about unfaithfulness and of Elaine's talk about nasty men, and how they both saw me as not knowing enough and how I was in for a shock when my life caught up with human nature.

I did do as Sam suggested. I took his *Poetry of the English Renaissance* off the shelf and read bits aloud to Hank while we stood in the sun of the meadow and again with the book open on the kitchen table and Hank listening from the hatch. I looked up Sir Thomas Wyatt and found "Like to these immeasurable mountains" and the others Sam had referred to. I didn't completely understand them, but out loud they somehow made more sense than from simply being read online. Then I got to the one that began: "My galley chargëd with forgetfulness." It had two dots over the "e" to give "charged" two syllables. It was a very depressing poem, filled with pain and despair. Reading it to trusting Hank seemed wrong of me.

I also looked up Michael Drayton. The poem that came after the one about kissing and parting was even more hopeless. He offers a truce to his love, but all he gets back is hatred. He must have done something unforgivable to her. So I put the book away and found the dark blue volume of Tennyson. It took time to find the bit Sam was using for his third canto. I read past it to the stuff about Christ and had to agree with Sam. If King Arthur thought he'd end up in heaven with Guinevere, he was going to be majorly disappointed. Not that, being dead, he'd ever know. I guess I do take after my father when it comes to religion.

So reading poems to Hank wasn't what I felt like doing. Over in his shady spot when it turned hot again, I did read him the opening pages of *The Magic Mountain*, and though it wasn't the easiest reading I'd ever done, I liked it. It reminded me of driving my Smart Car up from Somerville for my month of recovery, without my job but to get my health back.

True, Elaine did come stumbling up the hill at five o'clock, which she called "cocktail hour." She brought a bottle of gin and a bottle of tonic and a lime because, after the rain, it felt like summer again. I've never been much of a drinker, only a Corona when we go to our neighborhood Mexican place, but I let Elaine mix up two ice-filled glasses with lime slices in each. We sat out on the porch steps in the last of the sun. I admit the drink had a relaxing effect, which I needed with Elaine going on about the rotten behavior of the men in her old life. Sam, too, she said, but she'd sidestepped him in plenty of time.

She questioned me about Robert. She was convinced, with me away, he was "out on the town," as she put it. I told her Robert was a workaholic. When he wasn't at his desk catching up on clients, he was zoned out on the couch watching stupid TV with me. "But you're not sitting there beside him right now," she told me. And I hadn't said anything about Robert going to the gym.

I can't really quote Elaine, but she did keep pushing her theory that you can never tell what men are up to. The more attentive they are, the more they're covering up. I reminded her that I was also a man, and she said, "So you should know! Except," she added, leaning back on her elbows and giving me that familiar once-over, "you're all there, aren't you? With Griffin O'Dea, what you see is what you get. Am I right?" I gave her a casual shrug and said, thanks to the gin, "Maybe, maybe not." "Can't fool me," she said and went inside to pour herself a second glass. I was only halfway through mine. I think that's how it went.

Elaine didn't stay long after her second, but she did show up the next morning when I was out in the stable giving Hank his breakfast. I heard her yelling from the meadow, then she came stomping in on her cane. She had just heard from Sam at the VA. They wanted him to stay another night. He claimed they couldn't get proper readings because he was such a disagreeably "uncooperative mugwump." Elaine was sure there was lots more to it than that. On the phone, Sam could get away with more than when she could look him straight in the eye. But he'd wanted to know if, for Hank's sake, I could stay another night. Of course, I could. I wanted to. I had finally calmed down about staying alone in Sam's cabin and being responsible for an aging donkey. Even Svensk's beady stare helped me sleep. But like Elaine, I had seriously begun to wonder what was really wrong with Sam.

Because I didn't tape any of this, my chronology is a bit confused: when I read what to Hank, when we had our naps, and on which visit Elaine said what. It was either the first or second cocktail hour or that morning after Sam's call that she asked me flat out what really was the reason for this month-long retreat of mine. When she was painting me, she had seen below my pale freckly skin, she said, below the patches of red sunburn and the occasional blush under my crop of reddish hair. She'd seen "fragility." It must've been on that second night, when she'd come back to finish off the bottle before the tonic went flat. That time I did allow her to refresh my glass, though it wasn't even half empty.

It was definitely the second night, because instead of warning me about "the proclivities of the male gender," as she put it, she went sentimental on me, even a tad tearful, and blubbered on about me, Griffin, having surely had a form of a nervous breakdown, even if I wouldn't admit it. The more she talked about it, the more I figured she was talking about her own life, if not of her own nervous breakdown then of someone else's. As if the only reason I could've come up to those hills was the same reason she had done it many years ago, and then stayed and stayed forever! I asked her what specifically had caused her to leave South Dakota or wherever she had come from, but she joked it away ("too flat, too Republican") and turned it back on me: "You had an anxiety attack, right? Panic?" "If so, it was a mild one," I said. She said I was as bad as Sam, keeping it all under. "Men!" she sniffed.

So after she left, I downed another stuffed pepper and then talked long into the night, with me in the bed and Hank up behind me like a psychoanalyst. It helped. I told him all my fears and worries and desires and, also, my blessings because I'd had plenty of those, too.

A Day Without Discourse

Sam didn't drive himself home until Monday afternoon. I'd moved my Smart Car out of the shed so he could pull in. I heard his loud tailpipe coming up the bumpy road and went jumping down the hill to greet him. I flipped my device on for the first time since I'd been there.

This is what we said:

"Welcome home, Sam. We got worried when you had to stay an extra night."

"We?"

"Elaine and me. I mean, you called her and she came to tell me."

"With her bottle of gin."

"That was the night before."

"She get you loose-lipped?"

"No, Sam, I didn't say a thing about your poems."

He had lifted himself down from the pickup and was nudging me out of his way as I backed from the shed. He snatched up his overnight bag in the truck bed, and I said:

"I'm glad to see you look okay."

"Didn't sleep a wink. All these wires attached and machines humming and blinking. Gotta get to my nap. You go on home. How was Hank?"

"Great. I loved being with him."

"That's donkeys for you."

I would've offered to carry his bag, because he was walking with his left leg stiff, but I knew better. Sam had to do what he had to do for himself.

"I'll come up and get you settled first."

"Naw, go on home. You got your Tin Lizzie, I see. Liked the stuffed peppers?"

"Delicious. I loved staying here."

"Even with her poking herself in?"

"We got along fine."

At the foot of the hill, he stopped and said in his most uncurmudgeonly voice, "Thank you, son. Appreciate what you done. Don't trouble about old Sam. They been trying for years to pin down what's wrong with me. Truth is, I been left figuring it out all my life. Don't need no answer, though."

"Now you're being folksy again, Sam. Where's the professor?"

"Poet, you mean? Still here. What do you think poets are? Words come out when they feel like it. You go home now." He stuck out his rough hand, and I shook it. He had quite a grip. "Come see me and Hank tomorrow morning. We'll be expecting."

Then he turned and took his slow way from stone step to stone step. I watched until he made it to the top.

I drove to Elaine's to let her know Sam was safely home, but she already knew. We agreed he was as secretive as ever. When he'd stopped out front and she'd called from her front door, all he said was, "Fit as a fiddle!" "Like hell," said Elaine.

Since I had my car, she wanted me to take the portrait right then. She'd wrapped it in brown paper and tied it up with string. I wasn't to peek before presenting it to Robert.

I drove on, past recently mowed fields, dotted with plastic-coated bales like giant marshmallows. When I stopped at the post office, Lucy wondered where I'd been these days, no Smart Car out front, though I suspect she knew. "Donkey sitting," I said, and she knowingly responded, "Ah!" She was holding up two cards for me and another envelope. I realized I hadn't sent a card since Friday morning. I'd better get one quick in the mail before five.

Upstairs, I read Robert's cards first, his usual jokes about my becoming a survivalist or a tree-hugger or playing banjo on some front porch. But I opened the letter with the same apprehensiveness I'd felt about the previous one. I'll quote some of it, leaving out the sexy part:

"Griff! I just need you home. I don't want you driving in Labor Day traffic. Why not come a couple days early? We need the long weekend together before going back to work. I've been working too hard. Last weekend, I thought about renting a car and driving up to surprise you, but I didn't want to break your spell. It's been too weird here without you in my daily life! I hate it! So do Alice and Martha. They pace around yowling and messing with my stuff. Don't you feel funny about our long time apart? Now you're back to your old calm self again, it's time to come home and we can make up for lost time, if you know what I mean . . ."

Elaine would've said, "If ya catch my drift."

Day Twelve

Early Tuesday morning, I drove down the valley to do laundry and had a long talk with Robert before he left for the office. I apologized for the missing daily card, but I sent one last night, and I'd send another tomorrow. The call counted for today's. I told him how much his letter meant and agreed to come home early before the holiday traffic. I kidded that he obviously wasn't sure how much longer he could wait before going off with some married man. But my Vermont adventures, I said, were only in his imagination. Had he thought I'd been having an anxiety attack or a minor nervous breakdown? Because the fact was, I'd just consulted with a therapist. Then I confessed it was with a donkey. All he said was, "Oh, Griff! You really are crazy." We hung up after some intense words of affection.

Driving back into the foothills, I told myself how lucky I was to be with someone not caught up in paranoid jealousies. I couldn't understand why Sam Fry had been so obsessed all those years or why Elaine Greene had totally given up on love. Desires are only one part of love, and sometimes they go off in different directions. I love Robert and I know he loves me. We can't help desires, hopeless or otherwise, but love is a bigger thing than that.

Back at the post office, I went to the hammock with a noodle bowl and read more of Thomas Mann under the trees. The book was growing more difficult. I peeked ahead and saw whole pages written in French! How was I supposed to read that?

I went up to put on my running clothes, waited long enough for Sam to have done his morning chores, then took off at an easy jog. I wouldn't be seeing those sights much longer. The trees would be turning, the fields would go brown. I'd miss all that space between houses, the trim brick capes and shabby farmhouses. Instead, I'd be running out the converted rail line to Arlington with the bikers and baby strollers and dog walkers past condo complexes.

I tried not to think about having deceived Sam with my underground tapes. Maybe his voice was simply for myself, the way the nature sounds were. It wouldn't help me fall asleep, but on my walk to work, I could re-play Sam in my ears to set me up for another day. Adding visual and interpretive details, the way I'm doing now, helps me retrieve the whole experience. I can picture his world again. I had these thoughts as I jogged onto the dirt road past Elaine's and slowed down up the dead end to Sam's.

He was on the porch in his rocking chair awaiting me. He didn't chide me in his usual grumpy way but announced: "Today I'm not going to assail you with any poetry. Hank heard enough this morning for both of you. Go inside and bring out a kitchen chair and set a spell, as we old woodchucks say on our front porches."

Having retrieved my usual chair, I put it down opposite Sam. Looking into his pale blue eyes, I was afraid he was going to give me some bad news about his health.

"Warm enough to reveal the knees again, I see," he said. "Don't want to show my old elephant knees. Ain't exposed any old flesh 'cept my claws and this ugly mug, not for years. Watch that sunburn, fella. Skin cancer. Speaking from experience."

"Are you feeling okay, Sam?"

"Much as ever. Living with it all."

To stall for time I asked, "Is Hank in the meadow?"

"We'll visit him in due course. For now, I got some things to tell you." It sounded ominous. He noticed my worry and added, "Because you'll be going home before I turn eighty without having absorbed all my words of wisdom."

"I wouldn't want to miss any."

"Aw, they go in one ear and out the other."

"Actually not, Sam. I remember them," I said without admitting how true that was. Maybe after all, he wasn't about to tell me he was on his last legs. In the porch shade, he looked softer than when he was out in the bright sun. His baggy old faded jeans hung loose off him, and his sweatshirt—how few of those did he own?—was as grungy as ever, but he seemed comfortable.

"We talked about the cosmos, didn't we?"

I nodded. "The millions of galaxies and all that."

"And we talked about what makes animals better than us so-called highest mammals?"

"I guess so."

"And I told you more than I should've about my epic work and even recited the three epigraphs?"

"But none of your own poem, Sam. Before you locked that notebook in the desk drawer, I saw how neatly you'd written it out."

"So it does exist? Not merely an old man's delusion?"

"It exists, the page I saw anyway."

"Drawn any conclusions about what you'd call the plot and I'd call the shape of it?"

I had to think a few seconds, not to say the wrong thing. "Well, on the surface at least," I risked answering, "you've got three triangles. The unfaithfulness theme. But it's a microcosm of something bigger that I can't quite understand."

"Stick to the triangles, son," Sam continued in his professorial voice. "The wives are beautiful and lusty. The lovers are handsome and daring. What about the husbands? Not recorded how handsome or lusty they were! Nice trusting fellas, but not exactly Michelangelo statues. Unlovable? Except in the platonic sense? You familiar with the term?"

"As in not sexual."

"Not even passionate!" Sam said, raising his voice. His expression hardened. I saw blood rising up his neck to his craggy hollow cheeks. "What about passion, young man? You know how passion feels?"

"I think so," I said. "I mean, it's in how you define it."

"So what's so great about sex, my boy?" I didn't know how to answer, so Sam went on: "Rhetorical question. If you don't know, not for me to enlighten you." I would've protested, but he was going on: "Here, take a different tack. Now if Sam Fry was king, I can assure you, he'd be an ardent Utopian Socialist. Utopian?"

"I know what it is."

"And you got some primitive notion of Socialism. It'll have to do. In the world this King Sam rules, there's no god with a capital G and no lower-case gods either, no saints, no sinners, only plain folks like us. All work's rewarded with the same hourly wage, doctors to ditch diggers. No one's more valued than anyone else. Everyone's equally necessary to the whole operation. Get it? The way animals do things. But we near-sighted humans, oh, we've evolved beyond the species that get only what they need. Until, of course, we slaughter them. And ourselves? We always want more, more than we need, more! We will not be regulated! Down with Utopian Socialism! Away with Natural Equilibrium! There's too many of us, we have too much, know too much."

"But, Sam," I said with more ideas than I could get into one sentence, "you want me to know more things!"

He held up a knobby finger, as if to put me on pause, and said one word: "Equilibrium."

I took my elbows off what Elaine called my meaty thighs and leaned back in my chair. I drew a frustrated breath and glared puzzledly at serene Sam. He had a way of looking pleased with himself at the most intense moments.

"The sun," he began calmly, "will expand beyond the safe distance that sustains us. But no need to look so far ahead. We're unbalanced right now. Let's call it being unfaithful."

"To the planet?"

"The planet will survive us by eons. Don't worry about the planet, son. It's had many configurations. Ever heard of Gondwanaland?"

"A country in Africa?"

"Never mind," said Sam. I could see the fun he was having at my expense, but it didn't throw me off. I was used to him and could always check things later online. "No, Griffin, no concern for the planet. I wasn't going to give you a poem today, but here's an obscure bit of Victorian verse by one Sydney Grundy. Not much as poetry, but it encapsulates—how's that for a word—it encapsulates my sincere and comforting belief." He stuck his hands out and grabbed the rocker's arms, then threw his head back as far as it would go and proclaimed in his most actor-like voice:

Brief is all life;
Its storm and strife
   Time stills,
And thro' this dream
The nameless scheme
   Fulfils;
Until one day
   Thro' space is hurled
   A vacant world,
Silent and grey.

"Don't bother looking for it on your machine. Won't find it." But actually, I did. Everything is out there somewhere, if you try. "Aw, hell, I'm an old crank," he said. "I'll be gone. Suppose your boy Pete there on the shirt's gonna save us?"

"I know he can't win, but someone had better."

"Now, don't get me wrong," Sam said. "Certain individual humans can be wonderful. Look at you, Griffin O'Dea. You're wonderful in your hopeful innocent way. A kindly friend to a donkey. No complaints about you."

"Thanks for that, Sam."

"Meant it. You put up with me. I knew, when you showed up, I could trust you'd see past my cussedness. But why are you here at all? Something wrong with that Robert of yours? I know your sort has its own ways, but if my wife sent me on vacation, I'd sure know she was up to some hanky-panky."

"Sam, why did you take it so hard? Whatever happened to you, I don't even know, but—"

"Ever virgin save for thee, as Lord Tennyson puts it. Damn, wasn't gonna quote poetry."

"Virgin?" Why did I even ask?

"Let's say, married too young. Outta the army and into the stew. Too many wild oats trapped inside."

I didn't want to hear about Sam's sex life or lack of it. Nonetheless I had to ask, "So you were the unfaithful one?"

"She first, then me. My poem's not my life, you know. Poem's loads bigger."

"And there was a David?"

"Young lawyer in the firm. Hence vain deluding joys!"

"But King Arthur wasn't ever unfaithful?"

"No, conveniently he died. I still had years to live. Went out on the town. Then to hell with it, came up here. But you didn't answer me why you came."

"To take off the stress of working at City Hall. Robert thought I was acting sort of strange. Not like myself. It's hard to get anything good done in a city."

"There you have it," said Sam, "first inkling of what I been telling you."

"But we don't stop trying."

"Something else going on here," he said. He was scratching at his stubbly chin. He took off his spectacles and gave me a hard stare. "Something inside you, son, loss of faith—"

It was that connection he kept making between love and the end of the solar system. To me, it made no sense.

Sam leaned back and out of the blue said, "Uriah the Hittite? Killed on the front line. Menelaus of Sparta? Started a world war. And Arthur of the Round Table? Wife and best pal loved each other the way neither ever loved him. Talking about my poem, you understand. The king all alone in his hunting lodge—" Sam shut his eyes, as if seeing it in the dark behind his eyelids, and said softly, "Folks too damn big for their britches—" His eyes snapped open. "See, I like mixing dictions. You know what I mean by dictions?"

"It's what you do, Sam. I never know which voice comes next."

"I am of imaginations all compact. Keeps me from sounding hifalutin."

"But I still don't get what hopeless desire has to do with this. It's just sad. It's wishing for what you can't have, that's all."

"All?" Sam practically barked at me. "You bet it's all. 'All' is the correct term. It's everything! What's war? More land! What's capitalism? More stuff! Religion? More control! Some big prick in the sky telling us what to do with our lowly lives! Most horrifying concept ever invented by man. And I do mean 'man.' Man in god's image? Hell no, god in dad's image! Hebrew dad-god's a mean old cuss, don't want his sons spilling their seed. No wonder King David was such a horny bastard! As for Christian dad-god, him and his love triangle? Turns himself into a ghost to get a virgin pregnant, and poor old Joseph has to take care of her and the baby that's somebody else's. Somebody else's! Know what that's like, son? And amazingly, that baby's also dad-god himself! Talk about incest! Who believes this shit? At least, Zeus didn't make a religion out of all his bad behavior."

"You're a pagan, Sam?"

"Aw, what do you know about pagans! They got their own

bullshit. I believe in the factual universe, all we can yet know of it. See what's already happening over there?" He angled a crooked finger at the treetops with the first yellowing leaves, some almost orange, a few blowing off in the light breeze. Far off up the hill, we heard Hank braying.

"He wants us," I said to change the subject.

"Give us a minute, son. You'll come here tomorrow morning one last time."

"I'm not leaving until Thursday afternoon."

"But come tomorrow morning. One more discourse, then I'm gonna shut my trap. Tomorrow."

"I'm still confused about what you've been trying to tell me, Sam."

"Because you don't have to consider the end of things."

"But you've got years still. You're not even eighty."

"Next month," he said with a sly smile on his thin lips.

"And in ten years, you'll be ninety. Think of it that way."

"Don't much matter. I am as I am. Live simple, day after day. Read and write. Feed my donkey. Nice plot of land away from people. Not counting the Lily Maid. Me and my private property. Safe. Selfish old retired lawyer? Why not give everyone seven acres and a donkey? Heard something like that somewheres. Or was it a mule and bit more land? Never happened." He was chuckling to himself, as if I wasn't still sitting across from him.

I'd begun to wonder if Samuel Arthur Fry, Esquire, wasn't a little crazy. I only saw him if he wanted me there to sound off to. When he sat alone by himself or with Hank, he'd be spouting poetry or making apocalyptic prophecies or grousing about every bothersome thing like a madman. I couldn't be sure he cared about me for myself. He'd said I bugged him. Maybe that was why he was confiding in me with all that made him grumpy old Sam and no one else. But he did say individuals could be wonderful. He'd said I was wonderful. No one but Robert ever said that to me, not even my mom.

"So!" came roaring from the other chair. "Come!" He pulled himself up by the rocker's arms, knees cracking, and I followed carefully down the steps that could've used a railing. Someday he's going to take a tumble, I told myself. On our way to the meadow, he walked stiffly, slowly. I kept pace beside him. He started telling me about Hurricane Irene: "Water pouring from the mountains down the narrow valleys, brooks all rising, crossed the roads, nearly reached the painter lady's front stoop. Glad to be up here on this hill. Water runs off front and off the other side of the meadow. It's my own peak we're on, Hank and me." He stopped at the gate and rested a hand on the latch. The old donkey was loping down to meet us. "Hello, Honkety. Coming to spend time with you. No more poems. Got a parsnip in my pocket."

Sam dug out a big yellowish one from the side of his jeans. He started stroking Hank's muzzle while the old gray donkey stood placidly in the sunlight. I ran my fingers along the cross on his back, up and over and down. I hoped this was what Sam's life was indeed mostly made up of: caring for his animal, for his land, for his books, even grudgingly for Elaine Greene, and for one brief summer month for me.

Day Thirteen

I woke up in the narrow bed I'd been sleeping in for nearly four weeks and felt the cool morning air through the two inches of open window. I reached over and pushed it farther up. The trees were tossing in a wind from the west. I remembered the first poem Sam recited for me and thought how I, too, wished my love was in my arms and us in our queen-size bed again.

I wrote my final card, nothing but a large XOXO. There were three more of the blank ready-stamped ones Robert had sent me off with, as part of my rest cure regimen, but I wouldn't need them now. After a shower and breakfast, I went outside and ran into Mrs. Cobble at the post box. I told her I'd be leaving before the weekend. She raised an eyebrow and said she'd have to ask Mr. Cobble but she doubted they could give me any rebate because I'd taken the room through the holiday and it was too late to find someone to pay the higher weekend rate. I apologized, and she traipsed back into her house. Normally, I wouldn't use a word like "traipsed," but I've been relying on the thesaurus function to keep from overusing words. Spellcheck has been crucial, and even the grammar program helps, though it doesn't always get what I'm trying to convey.

I couldn't decide whether to run or drive to go see Sam. It was still early, so I took my book out to the hammock and tried to read, but it was hard going. I flipped to the end and saw that, after Hans got his health back, he came down from the mountain and soon it was World War One. The wind kept picking up, so I went upstairs for my jacket and left the book on the bedside table. The next guest would be surprised to discover that the fat black book wasn't a Bible.

I was angsty about seeing Sam. He'd made it clear he didn't want me coming on Thursday. It might be sadder for him to say good-bye than it'd be for me, and he wanted to get it over with. Or was I giving myself too much importance?

I figured it wouldn't hurt to go running in the sharp wind. I zipped up my nylon jacket over my Somerville T-shirt, and my sweatpants would keep my knees warm, as Elaine might say. Sam, too. They both kept making remarks about my knees. What is so noticeable about knees? They must represent something to older people.

I took the longest possible route, all the way up the higher road, past the farmhouse with its peeling paint and saggy porches and the huddled cows and lonely pale old horse grazing. I sped down the long hill to the fork, then slowed my pace and turned up to the bumpy dead end where I'd first recorded the trees rustling and bending and when I'd forgotten to turn off my device, which is how this whole history got started.

I wasn't quite ready to see Sam Fry. I propped myself on the back bumper of the Isuzu to collect my thoughts. I imagined going home and seeing Robert and the cats, the one would hug me tight and the other two would stick up their tails and ignore me the rest of the day. Sitting in Sam's shed, I tried to take in every detail, everything including the ruts in the road and the scraggly grass down the middle.

At last, slowly, I climbed the slope by each stepping stone and past the withering vegetable patch. No one on the porch, no donkey at the split-log fence. The sounds of my running shoes on the creaky wooden steps registered on the tape. I knocked twice. It took seventeen seconds, as the recording shows, before Sam opened and said, pointing first to a darkish cloud and then to the swaying treetops, "I came like Water, and like Wind I go."

Then we took our seats at the table, and he said, "Persian poet. What you'd call Iranian. Filtered through the English language of the Victorian period. Look it up."

Hank appeared at the open hatch to greet me. I got up and went to him and said, "Hank, I'm counting on your Democrats to kick the shit out of the election next year."

"He's sure been known to kick," said Sam. "Got some fine bruises. By the way," he went on after I sat down, "you heard of peripheral neuropathy? Start going numb from the extremities.

Sign of more to come. What, you ran all the way again? Whatever are you gonna do in your City of Seven Hills, run up and down 'em?"

"There's a bike path," I said, "an old railroad line."

Sam had gotten up to make us coffee in his Keurig machine, fancier than the one we have at home. "Bought this job in West Lebanon, cross the river, no sales tax in New Hampshire. Giving up on tea for September, back to the hard stuff. You?"

"Sure." I noticed three black discs, old records, stacked on the counter next to the wooden bowl of apples. "Vinyl!" I said.

"Shellac, son. Goes around seventy-eight times a minute. You wouldn't know. Only things left from the Forties. Shoulda taken 'em to the dump but couldn't chuck 'em. Relics of my childhood. Breakable." Carefully, he passed them over to me.

On top was "The Donkey Serenade" from *The Firefly* by Rudolph Friml, sung by Frank Parker, tenor. I read it aloud, but I had to google "Friml" to remember how to spell it.

"Even as a boy, I knew I'd have a donkey someday," Sam said.

Then came "The Little King of Yvetot." I'd read about that king when I searched "donkeys" online. "Kiddie record," said Sam. Last was the one he'd told me about, "Honkety Hank and his Hootnanny Automobile." I've since also listened to the other two on YouTube, and they're both pretty cheesy.

Sam said, "Don't have a player no more. Never hear these songs again." I got the sense he preferred leaving them in his memory.

He took a coffee cake out of the oven and handed me a thick slice with a plate and fork and a steaming cup of coffee and a milk pitcher warmed on top of the stove. I could tell that Sam was about to say something serious.

"I have two big favors to ask before you leave, Griffin O'Dea."

"Certainly," I said.

"A matter of trust."

"I'm honored."

"Don't know why I trust you, but I do. Easier to trust the young. Your brains not as cluttered as old folks' brains. Forget things day to day."

"My mom makes lists to remember," I said, "and she's only sixty-three."

"Bless her heart, as Elaine Greene would say. But, son, I know how you use those electronic gizmos. Seen the one hanging off your belt. Blinks sometimes. But what I want is your address, by which I mean your good old-fashioned postal address. Here, write it down." He snatched a pad and pencil with a grocery list already begun on it. "At the bottom. Write it out clearly."

So I did. "You going to write me, Sam? I'll write you back, care of the village post office."

"No need to. I'll only write you but one time, for which I need to know where you live. Somerville, seven hills, like Rome. Rome declined and fell, you know. See, if I have time to get to it and have copied out clean my long tedious poem, here's what I'm asking: can you type it into one of your magic machines and make it so it gets onto that famous internet of yours? Who knows but what some fool may read it in the future and learn something. That is, if he can make it past page one. Lot to ask of you."

"I'd love to, Sam. I'd finally get to read it myself. And there's sites where you can post writings for free. Nothing ever goes away."

"A great delusion, son, but cherish it awhile."

"Sam," I said, "don't you ever miss talking to other intellectual types? I mean, with your poems and books and all your philosophical ideas, don't you want to talk to people more like yourself? Because you could buy a computer and find poetry groups or philosophical discussions online, and why don't you even have a phone! You've got that top-of-the-line coffee maker."

"Need my coffee. Don't need more talk. Talk to Hank, and a

few words to the snoopy postmistress, and there's old Elaine, can't forget her. That's plenty. And I talked to you, didn't I?"

"Well, I'm going to write you letters, if only to say hi."

"Aw, don't bother."

"But your eightieth birthday's coming up. At least, I can send a birthday card."

"Birthdays don't mean much anymore, son. No, you write Miss Greene. The old bag will appreciate it."

"Oh, Sam," I sighed with nothing more I could think to say.

"As for those three cantos, assuming I live to fix them up, I confess I'm no Thomas Wyatt, mine own Griffin O'Dea." (He definitely said "mine own", which I interpreted as affectionate.) "And I'm not even Algernon Charles Swinburne over there." He gestured to the bookshelves. "Be damn lucky if I was one iota as fine. 'Laus Veneris.' Look it up."

"You're fine enough for me, Sam Fry."

"Aw, what do you know!" he grumped, what I now took to be defensiveness. Soon, he resumed a gentler voice and was serious again. "One more favor to ask."

"Anything, Sam."

"You're acquainted with that critter over there?"

"We're close friends now."

"What if one day the Lily Maid comes and finds me stone dead on the floor, and there's Hank in the hatch with his mournful face hanging down, wondering what he's to do. That gal don't know squat about handling a donkey."

"But I would?"

"What I'm asking is, if I die first, that you arrange—"

"You're not going to die."

"'Course I am, so are you. So's Hank. But if you should some-how manage still to be alive, young fella, and he is too, when I'm a goner, and you get a letter from my executor—I do have one—you will be instructed to arrange to have that old beast transported to a rescue farm for donkeys down in your Commonwealth of Massachusetts. Executor can't do it. He's back in Illinois."

"I wish I could take care of Hank myself."

"In the City of Seven Hills? But you go visit him often at his retirement community. Bring him parsnips and apples. Promise?"

"Yes, I promise to do both, post the poem and arrange for Hank. I hope the poem comes first and that, if anyone has to die before the other, it'll be Hank because he wouldn't do well without you. Sorry, Hank, but—"

"He understands. What's death to animals? They don't waste time thinking about it." Sam had stretched out his gnarly old hands on the table and was beginning to push himself up.

"The coffee cake was great," I said.

"Go say good-bye to the donkey. I'll be at the cabin door. Ah, one more line from the Iranian: 'Came out by the same door as in I went.' Go read the whole thing. It's meant for young men like you."

It was very upsetting, giving Hank's big old head a hug. I had to do it, but I wasn't sure he liked it. Afterwards, he shook his whole neck and turned away into his stall. My own eyes had tears in them.

I walked slowly over to Sam, but he was gazing out the door and didn't see me wiping my cheeks. "One more thing," he said. "Not a favor, a big deep secret. Promise?" I nodded. "May change what you think of me, me who doesn't even know his grandsons, left 'em all behind. First, I have to ask you something. How do you think that painter lady down the road manages to keep body and what she calls 'soul' together?"

"She actually told me," I said. "She got a lifelong arts grant for her paintings."

"True, she did. And who sends her the dough?"

"Some arts organization in—Illinois?"

"My executor sends it! She thinks he's a judge of art!" Sam laughed with his head thrown back as far as his stiff old neck would go. "She has to send photographs of her work. He sends them on to me. That woman's been doing versions of my sagging carcass for almost a quarter century." Sam was even more pleased with himself than when I thought Hank was his boyfriend.

"Wait a second," I said. "You're the arts organization?"

"True story. Have plenty money. Principal reverts to Donkey Rescue when she dies. She'll outlast me, tough old bird. Am I a saint or what?"

"I've always thought you were a lot nicer than you act. I don't know about saint, though."

"No saints, no sinners, remember? No gods, just near-sighted humans. We'll leave the earth to the animals. Endangered ones will be long gone. Leave it to octopuses and clams."

"This was our final discourse, Sam?"

He held out his hand for a shake. I held it in mine for a few extra seconds and with my other gave his bony shoulder a squeeze.

"I don't want to leave," I said, but part of me wanted to run off and not look behind.

"Then I'll give you one last song. I can't sing it, but you'll hear the music in the words. Step down a ways. I'll say it from up here." I took the steps slowly and made my stand on the yellowing grass. "My other most favorite poem. I once told you I have two."

"You did."

"It doesn't have an author, either. It's another poem all on its own. Here goes." This is the most beautiful recording I made that summer:

The silver swan, who living had no note,
When death approached, unlocked her silent throat.
Leaning her breast against the reedy shore

Thus sung her first and last, and sung no more.
"Farewell, all joys; Oh death, come close my eyes;
More geese than swans now live, more fools than wise."

Sam made a modest bow and disappeared into his cabin before I could settle one last look on him. I waved at the closed door then went off cautiously down the slope.

The Day After

With the discourses and the donkey in the past, I will simply summarize what else I taped that's relevant to the themes of this project of mine.

Two main occurrences. The first began in the post office kitchen, where I was having my noodle soup and toast. I was washing up when in came the postmistress on her lunch break and, with her, my portrait painter, laughing loudly about something they refused to reveal. I would've gone on upstairs, but they insisted I stay. They made enough coffee for the three of us, and Elaine produced a paper bag of her own raspberry turnovers, which she warmed up in the oven. "Fattening you up for your sweetie," she said. What with Sam's coffee cake, it seemed I was living mostly on pastries and caffeine.

We took our picnic out back in the noon sun. Elaine and Lucy dragged over two rusty lawn chairs, and I sat sideways in the hammock and listened to the village gossip that included speculation on Samuel Fry's health. All I chose to contribute was that he'd seemed pretty chipper that morning. I actually said "chipper," not sure where it came from. I guess I'd picked up some Vermont vocabulary.

They wanted to know why I was leaving early, was anything wrong at home, did I think Robert might be having an affair—the whole "ordinary" story Sam took for a microcosm. I protested and they said I protested too much. "Look at him, he's blushing," Lucy said, and Elaine went on about how she tried and tried to give my reddening cheeks the right shade with her paints and pastels. When I asked why she was doing more of me, the two women had a good laugh, nudging each other, and I had the terrible thought that Elaine was drawing me in the nude, as Robert had joked, not that she had any idea what I'd look like with no clothes on. Maybe I was being paranoid—or narcissistic?

After Lucy went to re-open the post office—I'd told her I wasn't expecting any cards after whatever might come today (which turned out to be from Alice and Martha: "Yowl meow, mew mew yowl, purrs from the girls")—anyway, when Elaine and I were sitting outside by ourselves, she went off into her theories again about men and love, and I had to tell her things had maybe changed since her day, that it was more possible now for men to be all kinds of different men, and for women to be all kinds of different women, and even some people in between to be whatever. She said that might well be true as far as she knew, but there were still chemical impulses involved. "Men will always want more. Then they'll go off to get even more somewheres else."

It began to sound sort of like Sam's argument about human nature. You can't escape the horrible things people do to each other, despite all those individuals he admitted were wonderful, including me. Finally, I had to ask Elaine if, for some reason, she was trying to make trouble between me and Robert Abreu. She said she was sorry, it wasn't that, but she didn't want me to be hurt, that's all. How long had I been with him? I said we met in college but didn't get together till five years ago. "Five years!" she said, as if it was nothing. "But I've known him a third of my life," I said. "We were nineteen and had other boyfriends in college and after, but somehow we knew that one day—or at least I did."

Then, Elaine took a kindlier line. "No, you'll both be together one way or another," she assured me. "There's different rules, different expectations, I get it," she said, "just be honest with each other," and I told her we always were. "Him, too?" "Yes," I said. "You sure?" "Yes, Elaine, I'm sure." "Then, that's true love," she conceded but added, "What the fuck do I know! Couldn't find true love in an Iowa haystack." I'm glad I'd secretly turned my device on to capture all that.

I did ask her how she truly felt about Sam Fry. They acted so cranky around each other, but she said she'd given him Svensk, hadn't she? Early birthday present. More to come. I remembered how, when I slept in Sam's bed and looked over at that hideous little carved thing with the huge feet and floor-length hair, I'd pondered the strange bond between those two old hermits out on those dirt roads, every mile trod by my running shoes, up and down and around all month long.

Soon, Elaine and I were back to arguing about city life versus life in the foothills. She didn't know how I stood it down there, all crowded and jangled and rushing about. Was I actually looking forward to being back? Yes, I was. "Not just for your honey pie?" "No." "For your work?" "Yes, to my surprise, I am. I've sort of missed it." "Because you're still young," she said.

Then she had to drive off to the stores to stock up. "Won't be seeing each other again," she said. I was sad about that. We stood up and she gave me an embarrassingly intense hug against her angular self. I followed her to the Aztec, parked outside next to my Smart. "Write me care of the PO," she said. And I have, several short chummy letters asking for news, especially of Sam, and to let her know how much Robert loves the portrait. She wrote back one time, enclosing a sketch of Hank. It's above my desk at City Hall. I'm sure she'll let me know if anything happens at Sam's, to either of them up there on their hillside.

The second occurrence of my last full day in the village won't take long to report. That afternoon, I took one more slow jog the other way from Sam's and ran out the dusty farm road to the tadpole pond. It was too cool for a swim, and whatever pond life there was must've gone down into the silt. Still, I wanted to try recording sounds I could barely make out. The pond had an outlet that gave off a soothing gurgle as water spilled over into a narrow rivulet. In the breeze, the stalks of the dying cattails and the reeds along the bank made silvery whooshes, as if brushing their stiff old hair. I heard quarrelsome crows, or ravens—not sure of the difference—cawing from a dead tree past the opposite shore. As I lay there in the yellow grass, I dipped my fingers in the water and made splashes for my device to pick up. "Ploop, plop, plip" is how they sound. I often replay that bit.

But when I was somewhat lost in that meditative miniature soundscape, I heard a crunching on the ground behind me—a deer, a moose, a bear? Those crunches are on the tape, too. I can even hear my quick intake of air to hold my breath. And then a voice:

"This is private property, just so's ya know." I whipped my head around. "Oh, you're the one with the toy car from Mass," said a man in a green-and-black camo jacket and wool cap. "What're ya doing out here?" It was the guy from the dump.

"I was taping some nature sounds, sort of a hobby," I said, getting to my feet. I held out my device to show him. "I didn't mean to trespass."

"Don't matter. But see, we own this land," he said, pointing a jacketed arm past one end of the pond off into the woods. "Private hunting for me and my buddies. Runs all along the road and way up to there." He pointed at the top of a far ridge. "Season's coming. Gotta check out the place. Gonna take a swim before September hits."

"I guess it's getting colder. I should be heading on, anyway."

"Going back to Mass?"

"Actually tomorrow."

"So the dump ain't gonna be seeing that Death Trap anymore," he said with a slow shake of his head, to show what he thought of my car. He tossed his wool cap into the long grass.

"No, but it's sure been great up here." I didn't know what else to say. I heard myself give a nervous chuckle.

"That car handle the interstate?"

"Sure, it's made by Mercedes." I hoped that might impress him.

"Mercedes, huh?" He had taken off his camo jacket and was starting to unbutton his work shirt. I decided I'd better get out of there. Though he was kind of hot in an unshaven woodsy way. Longish dirty dark hair. Once more, I told myself to get going. But wouldn't I always regret not staying at least long enough to see him dive naked into his pond? I couldn't make out if he was looking at me suspiciously.

"Welcome to swim if ya want," he said and leaned over to untie his boots.

"Naw," I said, to sound more local. But I supposed the water wasn't all that cold. I could maybe take one final swim. I'd keep my boxers on, but that might seem wussy. Then I began thinking how, later that night, I'd be lying in Van Gogh's bed for the last time, and I'd be looking forward to going back home and telling Robert everything.

I punched off my device and tucked it away in my jacket pocket. That's where the digital record of my month in Vermont comes to a stop.

Playful and Thoughtful

In memory of James Samuel Davis

My own great-grandfather Albert, as a schoolboy,
kept a copy book from which I have transcribed
one of his essays along with an admonition by
my great-great-grandfather Erastus to his son.

J.S.

September

They'd had an affair once years ago, then gone on to other lives, but they'd kept in touch, even become friends, and long after those other lives had turned into sweet memories, here they were, now quite old, sitting on a stone bench on a rocky headland above the Atlantic, talking and looking out to sea.

One of them was playful, the other thoughtful. They always found much to mull over, humorously, regretfully, with the noon sun sparkling off the rippling waves. Below the cliff, an occasional lobster boat went putt-putting past into the harbor. Both old men had grown up by the Great Lakes—Michigan, Superior—and if the ocean smelled different, their eyes recognized in it a lost youth: same far flat horizon, same rolling waves, the same but also not, much as they felt about each other.

One was William, one was Benjamin, Willy and Benjy to each other, both just now into their eighties. They sometimes asked themselves how long should life last anyway if they so easily might have died back in those bad, or were they also better, days?

Now they had each come to live far from home in that small town on the coast, one first, the other much later. Benjy had migrated to Boston with his life's love and stayed on, up the shore, as a widower. Willy had worked well into his seventies but at retirement wanted a complete change from his life in Chicago. Benjy wrote him about a small fisherman's cottage for sale, perfect for Willy's minimal domesticity. It sat a few blocks up the hill from his own top-floor rental above the diner on the main street.

They'd made it cozily through Willy's first winter there, right into the long season of the pandemic and considered themselves a virus-free unit: entered no one else's quarters, sat inside no restaurant, only got supplies curbside or took take-out lunches to picnic on the grass by the mill pond or to eat leaning against the seawall at the beach. Often they'd treat themselves to ice cream cones handed out from under a plastic shield. In town they dutifully wore double-lined glasses-fogging masks and had as much trouble identifying familiar faces as others had in recognizing the two of them, an anonymity almost as if a return to the closet, no longer quite their own individual selves except to one another. Soon the cold weather would again bundle them up even more.

Today out on that headland, perched on their usual bench ("In Memory of Ruth Brown—Artist—1893-1994" chiseled into the polished granite), they were maskless, breathing free, their sunglasses filtering the sharp glare and their brimmed caps keeping their heads of thinning gray hair, not trimmed for months, from fluffing up in the wind off the water.

"It's increasingly difficult to fill my days," Benjy remarked. "I can read for only so long before eyestrain blurs the page. I can only listen so long to music with those clunky headphones squashing my earlobes. I can't spend all morning tidying up the place—"

"But you do," interjected Willy.

"—or check the tides from my picture window. And we can't go for a hike every day. And it's trickier on the trails, even with my poles for balance. And when the snow falls—"

"I can still hop around," said Willy, one year older but less cautious. Up in the woods, he was apt to take a tumble then quickly stagger to his feet, brushing himself off with a hoot of a laugh before striding on. Benjy would follow, careful of slippery leaves underfoot and protruding tree roots or sharp edges of stones, worrying that his boyfriend of years long ago might one day be out on his own and end up lying on some untraveled path with a broken leg and no one to rescue him.

Benjy, being the thoughtful one, was always conjecturing what might happen, what could go awry. Because he had suffered the death of his other self, as he'd known Tom to be, he should have decided the worst had already come to pass, yet now even small things threatened him. Despite being of a vulnerable age, it wasn't the virus that haunted Benjy. He and Tom had escaped that other terrifying virus, and because he and Willy were being so careful, he figured they would escape this one now. It wasn't even the nation's angry underbelly that this political year had revealed. No, Benjy's worries came down to descending a steep stair, forgetting a name, confusing historical events, being unsure which Mozart piano concerto he was listening to (the D minor or the C minor), or punching the wrong number when calling his sister back in Ontonagon.

And he worried that Willy's casualness could turn to disaster. Mere physical decline was the least of it. Benjy himself was methodical about finances, about writing or calling his friends and relatives. He kept a calendar for birthdays and medical checkups, a drawer of clearly labeled files for insurance policies and documents disposing of his assets, while Willy's little writing desk in the corner of his living room was piled with receipts, circulars, and unopened envelopes, and his wall calendar in the kitchen was stuck back in February. Willy's bed up the stairs was generally left unmade, his cat's litter box overflowed on the bathroom floor, and the cat herself lay lazily on the couch with outspread claws shredding the upholstery. Willy claimed he didn't have time to organize his life, which simply meant he didn't feel the need to. Still, he wasn't a hoarder because he didn't have enough to hoard. What little there was he left to the slapdash last minute: "Where did my keys go?" "My wallet has disappeared!" To Willy, objects had lives of their own. In Benjy's case, they were scrupulously under control: years of correspondence archived in chronological order in his lower file drawer, books and CDs alphabetized, towels and washcloths in trim stacks by size. Although he and Willy would happily tolerate each other's ways, they could never have shared a dwelling, even back in the distant year of their affair.

On that sunny breezy day resting on the centenarian artist's memorial bench, they began considering which cafe to patronize for lunch on what might be one of the last days when tables would be set up outside at a proper distance. Then soundlessly, from left and right, three large dog heads poked around their knees, sniffing and panting, followed by tails wagging from wriggling behinds. A female voice called out, "They're friendly!" Willy was a cat person now, but he'd gone through many dogs over the years. Benjy, however, appreciated animals best at a remove and had not yet warmed to Willy's calico.

"I call 'em Blackie, Brownie, and Goldie though their owners gave 'em actual names," continued the cheerful voice. When the young woman stepped around front, her shadow fell across the old men on the bench. She appeared to be in her late twenties and was sloppily wrapped in tattered jeans and a baggy sweatshirt. Her dogs went prancing over the broad slabs of granite toward the cliff side. "Watch it, guys!" she shouted, so they romped right back, nuzzled her hip pockets, then ran off into some underbrush to do their business.

"Sharon," the young woman announced, a black mask covering her nose and mouth. Quickly, Willy and Benjy pulled out their gray ones and hooked them over their ears.

"William," said Benjy pointing to his friend, "and Benjamin'" as he patted his own Icelandic sweater.

"Great to know you guys," said this chatty Sharon, silhouetted by the bright sun. "I noticed you two around town. You probably saw me with one pack of pups or another. It's what I do." Her long streaky blond hair blew about catching the light. "Better haul out the poop bags," she said digging into her back pocket as she hustled off. Willy and Benjy exchanged crinkly-eyed glances, smiling beneath their masks.

Sharon soon returned with two heavily-laden fluorescent-green plastic bags knotted up and dangling from one hand and the brown dog on a leash from the other. "This one doesn't go," she explained, "until she's home in her own front yard. Dogs feel differently about where they'll do it. Pee, not an issue, they'll leave their calling cards anywhere, but poo's more of a private thing. The other two, they'll back right up against a bush and squat, looking totally embarrassed if I'm watching. But this one here's gotta be home. She's somewhat insecure. I'm working on her."

The men were nodding and producing muffled um's and hmp's to show they were listening.

"People don't realize," Sharon went on, "how, just like us, dogs have personal issues. I walk so many of 'em, it's been a learning curve, figuring each one out, like I'm a kindergarten teacher."

"Absolutely," said Willy.

Sharon was standing off to one side now, so they could make out her wide brown eyes and the Patriots logo on her sweatshirt. "Are you guys teachers?" she asked. "Or, I mean, were you teachers? I'm assuming you're retired."

"Just last year," declared Willy with pride. "I'm younger than I look."

"You're eighty-one," whispered Benjy.

Sharon must have heard him because she said, "Oh, and I was taking you for just past sixty-five. You know, Social Security and that."

"See," said Willy giving his friend an elbow jab.

"Now you, your name's Benjamin, right? You can't be that old."

"Younger by one measly year he is," said Willy.

"Well, anyway, you're both well-preserved. Teachers stay young because of the kids. But you weren't? I could take you for being fisherman, you know, the sorts of sweaters those guys wear."

"No," said Willy, "Ben wasn't sociable enough to be a teacher, and I never much liked kids. I'm an old newspaperman, and Ben was a backroom librarian, purchaser and cataloguer, never came out to the circulation desk."

"Reference desk sometimes," Benjy reminded his old pal.

"Well, I been walking dogs here for two years now. It took a year to build up the clientele, but in this town word spreads. Covid actually helped. You'd think they'd want to get out with their dogs, but no they're sitting home all day with laptops or whatever, working remotely. What do they have a dog for in the first place? I don't understand most people. And there's the elders, no offense, who got too feeble to walk their snippy little yappy mutts. I never take those ones off leash out here or up in the woods like these three bruisers."

Willy and Benjy were letting her go on, though it was spoiling their seaside meditations. Finally, Willy attempted to engage Sharon in an actual conversation. "Will you get more business when winter comes?"

"For sure. Everyone gets even lazier. Maybe it's fear of Covid, I don't know. See, I come from farm country up in New Hampshire. We know winter, we know outdoor work. I bet back in the day down here, with fishermen and quarrymen, they were hardier. What's with these millennials and retirees, no offense, but how can locals make a living anymore? I take it from the way you talk you aren't locals."

"We are now," said Willy.

"Of course, I liked my own small town, but no jobs up there. I followed my boyfriend Fitz. He switched from repairing farm equipment to boats. He's a mechanic. But I'm not gonna be trapped in a garage or a boatyard shop. I need to be outside. I got the dog walking idea, so I don't mind it down here. I mean, where else do you get woods and beaches and cute souvenir shops? End of the month they'll open the beaches for dogs again. Last winter before Covid we had the best sandy playdates at low tide, two dozen dogs sometimes. Now we'll have to mask up and leash and stay six feet away. Dogs don't get it. What's the new deal on their beloved beach? But the thing about dogs is they adapt better than humans. They forget and move on."

"I have a cat," said Willy.

"Yeah, and we have two cats," Sharon said. "Fitz's cats really. We can't have a dog in the apartment, but I'm a dog person, so this is how I get my fix. Fitz and I, we're working it out. Not always easy when you follow someone for his job."

Then Willy said, "Ben followed his boyfriend out here, too."

"Oh, so you know what I mean," said Sharon turning to quiet Benjy, who was shaking his head. "But this isn't him?" she added, pointing at Willy.

"No, no, we'd be a terrible couple," Willy said.

"Fitz and I probably are as well, but what're you gonna do?" She inquired no further. "Oh, I realize I gotta have these guys back by one." She was corralling Blackie and Goldie and clipping them on leashes. Brownie was doing "Sit" expecting a treat. "Oh, all right, you guys." Out from her hip pocket she drew three dog biscuits. "I better go toss these bags. I hope they didn't stink too much for you. There's a barrel down the path. Great talking to you guys. Enjoy the rest of your day." She was being tugged away by three leashes in one hand, the poop bags swinging off the other.

The men removed their masks and held their sunglasses up to burn off the steam. "We sure learned about her life," said Willy.

"All you had to do was ask and off she went," said Benjy.

"And it didn't even have to be us. She was ready to talk to

anyone. It's the virus. We're all inside ourselves too much. This Fitz fellow must be a patient soul if that was a sample." His benchmate was tightening his lips with something on his mind. "What's the matter, Benjy?"

"Why did you have to mention why I came out east?"

"You mean the boyfriend thing? It barely registered. She's of the generation that's heard it all."

"But what if she'd asked about him, and I'd have to say he died? Then she'd have to say she was so sorry for me, and it'd be awkward."

"No, she'd probably have free-associated to some old dog she'd lost back in New Hampshire."

"That wouldn't have been any better."

"But you do so well talking about Tom. We keep thinking about him and talking, what is it, over four years later? Other people can't bear to bring up a death, but you're always glad to talk about him."

"I am, with you. You're one of the few people left who knew him."

"And Tom's the whole reason I'm here, Benjy, because if Tom hadn't been transferred to Boston twenty years ago—"

"Twenty-eight."

"Oh shit, is it? But I wouldn't have come out to visit those times and thought Boston was so small-towny after Chicago and we'd driven up to all those beaches, and I'd gotten to appreciate the area—I owe being here now to Tom."

"What if he was still alive?"

"What do you mean? All the more reason I would've moved. You two were part of my self-appointed family, and I knew you weren't coming back to Illinois. I'd been ready for a while to get away from my old life. And then when I finally split from delightful Nick—"

"But if I wasn't alone?"

"I was alone myself, wasn't I? And you sent me the ad for my homey little cottage."

"It was just a thought," said Benjy, eyes staring out to sea. He was remembering Lake Michigan, and then the vision took him farther north to the Superior shore when he was small, sitting beside his baby sister Becky in the sand, seventy-five years ago.

October

Willy had returned to his gray-shingled cottage after a robust morning tramp with Benjy in the autumn woods. They had both used their poles, though when they'd met at the corner, his cautious friend made Willy go back and get his. Now, Benjy had headed home to catch up on his correspondence, and Willy unlocked his door to find Elizabeth, the calico cat, meowing about with a twitching tail and slipping into the kitchen in hopes of more chicken liver. Willy obliged then set down his keys somewhere he would soon forget and trudged upstairs for his slippers. He searched under the bed, on the closet floor, by the bathtub, and came downstairs again to find one on the armchair with fresh tooth marks and the other nowhere. He pulled off his dusty hiking boots and took a seat in his socks, puzzling awhile. Elizabeth was more like a dog than most cats, he told himself. Then, "Behind there!" he exclaimed and rose to lean over the back of the couch where the other slipper wasn't in view, nor was it when he knelt down hoping to spot it between the sagging springs and dust bunnies.

"Elizabeth?" he inquired. She had finished her lunch and now peered out from the kitchen in utter indifference, so Willy sat back in his armchair, pulled the one slipper onto his left foot, and picked up the morning Globe from the end table. The horrors of the impending election absorbed his thoughts for half an hour. His old pal Benjy didn't enjoy speculating on the political future because it sent him into a state of melancholy, whereas Willy needed his daily dose of polls and op-eds to keep sane.

He had never been such a recluse in Chicago. This was all new to him. Benjy had four years of practice living alone up here, of being alone, but even with Tom he had been simply one half of a rather self-contained pair, happiest staying at home on Saturday nights when Willy had to be out making a fun party of it whether with Nick or some other fellow or with someone new. After those two stay-at-homes had moved away to Boston and he didn't have them to drop in on, his night-crawling only got livelier. But when Tom died a thousand miles away, it hit Willy hard. He realized he'd been unconsciously thinking of those two as some form of an anchor.

Glancing around his living room, Willy told himself, as he did almost every day, that this was indeed his home. Four years ago, he couldn't have conceived of being happy there, but somehow the notion of leaving Chicago behind had kept growing inside, and now this seaside town was enough for him. There were plenty of summer tourists, even in the year of lockdown, day-trippers out of the city to breathe the salt air and order lobster rolls from the window of the fishing shack. A year ago the town was open until New Year's, but now with the pandemic, shops were shutting up earlier. Willy decided he didn't actually mind. What else could he do anywhere else? There he sat with Elizabeth on his lap and read the news after that brisk walk in the yellow-and-orange woods with his best remaining friend. That they had had such a rollicking affair in their youth seldom even crossed Willy's mind now.

"Oh, Elizabeth," he said with a sigh, "do you miss the old place with your wide windowsill for bird-watching? I'll put on the bird video, if you want." The cat merely purred, producing a gentle vibrato against Willy's left thigh.

Meanwhile down the hill, Benjy was at his desk in the hexagonal turret room over the street that looked across rooftops to the Unitarian Church with its shiny copper-clad steeple. When struck by the sun, the glare shot right through the glass and flashed onto the stationery Benjy was filling with what little news he could muster for his sister Becky. Next, he would write her sons and daughter, or rather her daughter and her two son's wives because he doubted the boys, in their fifties, took much interest in their old uncle's monotonous daily life. His nieces-in-law were two lovely women, one in Madison, one in Iowa City, moms hovering about their recent college grads entering adult life in such a fraught period. The youngest girl, still at U. of I., was scarcely coping with the unfairness of her lot. Benjy decided to write her a separate note to offer supportive admiration from her great uncle Benjamin.

The desk fit perfectly into the angles of his six-sided lookout. Benjy loved writing letters using his fountain pen with the refillable cartridges. It was satisfyingly more personal than talking on the phone or those even-more-detached Skype or Zoom calls they roped him into. Instead of either a distant face on a screen or a far-off voice echoing into his ear, here his correspondent was right before him, between his fingers holding the pleasingly fat pen. He conjured Becky up in the words he was inking onto the crisp notepaper, though she would have preferred he use electronics. But she patiently allowed her brother his quirks, printed out her own emails, and posted them from the actual Ontonagon instead of from elusive cyberspace. Becky always closed with a wish that he hadn't moved so far away. The pandemic had made her fear they might never see each other again in the flesh. Benjy kept reassuring her that they surely would, though he wasn't convinced of it himself.

It was an hour later, after he had sealed up, addressed, and stamped the last envelope, that the Congregational Church, out of sight up the street, clanged its noon bell. The more considerate Unitarians never disturbed the peace except late on Sunday mornings, but Benjy was glad for today's reminder that he was to meet again with Willy at the Beachfront Cafe for take-out. They would find a bench atop the seawall and, for a second time that day, keep each other company.

Willy, too, had heard the church bell. He whooshed Elizabeth off his lap, folded the newspaper, full as it was of grim hospital statistics in the Midwest and agonizingly tight polling data from the swing states, and removed his left slipper to go in search of his town shoes. Beside the toppled-over hiking boots by the front door he found the other slipper. Why hadn't he noticed it when he deposited the boots? Such puzzles were becoming all too familiar. Then he recalled he must have left his town shoes at the back door by the washer-dryer, and to his mental relief there they were. Now it was a matter of the keys. Benjy claimed it was unnecessary to lock up every time he left the house, but Chicago was too rooted in Willy for him to adopt small-town trustfulness. And yet in most other ways he was quite the devil-may-care fellow.

On his third floor, Benjy had simply pulled his door closed behind him with a loose click. He did, however, descend the two flights holding fast to the railing and watching his rubber-soled deck shoes take each squeaky wooden step. He emerged onto the walkway alongside the building and at the sidewalk checked his bin, found nothing, and went to the corner postbox to tip in his several envelopes.

The main street was free of strolling shoppers because most stores had shut down and those that stayed open allowed only two customers at a time, but a few vigorous masked walkers were giving their limbs their daily workout. They preferred smooth sidewalks to the unsure footing up in the woods. There wasn't a line at the Beachfront, but Benjy decided to wait for Willy, who was predictably late.

At last, he came scampering down through the old cemetery as if all those gravestones were no reminders of mortality. One day he'll stumble over a foot marker, thought Benjy, and pitch himself onto one of the ragged slate slabs engraved with a sinister little angel and garlands of willow. But Willy was soon on level ground, adjusting his mask back over nose and chin.

"Ordered?" he asked.

"I was waiting for you."

"I'm only going to get worse," said Willy.

"But I have plenty of thoughts to keep me entertained."

"While my brain is largely an empty shell. As much as I fill it with information, it somehow doesn't stick anymore, and yet I keep putting more in that I'll forget all the sooner."

"I'm going to have a BLT with avocado and Muenster cheese melted on rye," Benjy announced to the unfamiliar girl behind the lifted-up window. "And a Diet Pepsi."

"And you, sir?"

"Give me a minute to think," Willy said. "What soups today?"

"Hungarian veg and the clam chowder."

"I'll take a small cup of chowder and, hmm—" He was going over the laminated list of options posted on the window frame.

"I'll just put in his order first," said the girl.

"Don't look now," warned Benjy, "but that dog walker is across the street with three jittery little toy dogs."

"We won't let her spoil our quiet lunch," Willy assured him. When the girl showed up again behind the glass, he said, "I guess I'll also have a spanakopita, warmed up."

"And to drink?"

"I'll sneak a sip off his," said Willy with a wink.

For the girl's benefit, Benjy gave a perturbed shake of his long-suffering head to indicate what he had to endure. The girl didn't pick up the cue the way the older lady always did but blandly offered, "A cup of water?" To Benjy, kids seemed a different species. Their vocabulary lacked easy humor, at least when engaging with old folks. They shied away from all that encroaching decrepitude, a condition they couldn't imagine ever reaching. Benjy had to remind himself he'd once felt that way, too.

But Willy was taking the opportunity to pursue a chat. "So water's free? Some places they charge. They ship it all the way from the Fiji Islands, as if we didn't have enough water here. The world's getting—"

"I'll go put in your order." The girl dropped the window and disappeared.

"—unreal," Willy concluded. "Which way's the dog lady?" he whispered before turning around to check.

"She's gone down to the beach."

"Then let's take our lunch to the mill pond."

When they had each paid and left two dollars apiece in the tip jar, they carried their sacks into the park and found a bench by the water where a returned pair of mallards paddled about leaving a gently shimmering wake that mirrored the golden leaves above. The two men gave simultaneous sighs of contentment then pulled out the compostable cardboard containers and too many brown paper napkins. Willy lifted the lid off his soup cup and dug around in the sack for the plastic spoon he feared she'd forgotten to supply. But he found it, pocketed the packet of oyster crackers for later, and took a first slurp. Benjy was holding his gooey sandwich, a current favorite he ordered several times a week despite Willy's objection to bacon. It wasn't for health reasons, Benjy knew, but Willy had a deep fellow feeling for pigs and cows and sheep. If he'd been born up in Michigan instead of in a comfortable suburb, he might not have come to such a sentimental resolution. At least clams and other sea creatures, as well as feathered ones, didn't tug at his heartstrings the way four-footers did.

Benjy was concerned that his friend didn't get enough protein. "That's an odd combination, chowder and pastry," he said.

"Clams and spinach, what's wrong with that? I could say the same of your avocado and cheese."

"Mmm—and bacon!" said Benjy.

Food had never been an issue in the long-ago days of their affair. They'd been skinny young men still inventing themselves, even Benjy who hadn't yet settled into any orderly domestic pattern. Back in the Sixties they had to feel their way to some accommodation between what was considered adulthood and their own unpresentable private inclinations. This would be hard to convey to the kids of today. Presumably, that dog-walking woman had experienced an entirely different set of social norms.

The two old men on the bench didn't have much to say to each other while they ate, just the occasional contented murmur or chuckle when Willy flicked an oyster cracker to the ducks. Because Benjy had been writing to his sister, he found himself remembering how anomalous he used to feel visiting his home town when Becky already had her first son and there was a daughter on the way and he'd slept in his unchanged childhood bedroom at their parents' house. He used to envy Willy, who could train up for a suburban afternoon with his own folks and it didn't have to be such a big deal. They saw him as an eccentric bohemian but had further unspoken suspicions while Benjy's relatives suspected nothing.

Willy's memories had drifted back to the day they had met in the stacks at Northwestern where neophyte librarian Benjy was reading shelves. There stood that shy young man in a crisp button-down shirt and pressed khakis somewhat near-sightedly running his eyes along the spines of old bindings and occasionally rearranging them. Willy decided to ignore the catalog numbers he'd jotted on a scrap of paper so he could ask for help and maybe sense if the handsome well-groomed fellow might be interested in a gangly hippie in grubby jeans. Despite the tidy exterior, something wistful in the eyes seemed encouraging.

So Willy had chattered on about his search for lesser-known plays by Ibsen and Shaw so the theater troupe he worked for might attract some critical attention from the big Chicago papers. "You like theater?" Willy had asked, figuring it could be a tip-off. Benjy admitted he mostly preferred picturing books in his head because he did a lot of reading and live theater never matched his imagination. "Then you haven't seen us!" Willy remembered saying. Benjy had dutifully located the sets of Ibsens and Shaws, and Chekhovs as well, and loaded him up with the more obscure volumes, and then Willy had dared to suggest they get a cup of coffee later so he could pick the librarian's well-read brain, thinking more of his body than his mind.

"She's coming," whispered Benjy, interrupting Willy's memory of the Evanston coffee shop. They both cautiously turned to look down the path at three tiny dogs straining at the leashes connected to their walker. She hadn't yet spotted the picnickers on the bench. The men turned quickly to face the pond again and held their breath until they could hear Sharon's enthusiastic voice greeting someone else over on the bridge where the pond spilled itself into the stream and rushed on to the ocean.

"Phew," breathed Benjy, but Willy vaguely regretted an opportunity to enliven the afternoon with a self-absorbed chatterbox the age the two of them had been back when they met.

"What are you up to the rest of the day?" he asked. "Watching the tides?"

"A bit of that," said Benjy. "Some Haydn quartets to cheer me up, reading a travel book called *No Place Like Home*. I found it at the used book store when we could still go browsing."

On their return up the main street, they stopped themselves from grousing too much and reminded each other how lucky they were to have enough money, enough health, the sea, the little town, the woods, and at their age a long, long friendship.

Back upstairs on the window seat below the plate-glass expanse looking out to the waves, Benjy settled in for the afternoon with his book and his music. He kept a notebook and pen handy to jot down memorable passages from whatever he was reading. With the Adagio of the B-flat quartet, opus 76, number 4, pouring from his heavy headphones, he came upon words attributed to Queen Marie of Rumania that he immediately copied out for future consideration: "I think life is like a puzzle, of which one finds, little by little, the separate pieces. I believe that I have found nearly all the pieces, now. But I can't tell you what they are, you must find them for yourself. For no two pieces are alike." And then Haydn launched into the buoyant minuet.

In the gray cottage, Willy with Elizabeth again on his lap held his iPad in one hand while he caught up on yesterday's YouTube postings. Whether it was Reverend Al or the divine Rachel or the heartening comedy of adorable Trevor, wry Stephen, or the Jimmies, they all kept Willy from feeling lonesome. And when evening fell, he would feel especially intimate witnessing his familiar PBS friends in their own homes in front of bookcases, paintings, and potted plants: Lisa with her cat asleep on the sectional sofa and Yamiche in her tastefully spare apartment or that other Nick, bright-eyed while calmly accounting for the whole world out there. Would these people mean anything to historians in the future? Perhaps not, but they were wiser and witticr than the figures history would be required to study. For Willy now, they were comforting replacements for all those people back in Chicago he could no longer hang out with, if they were alive at all. Monday through Friday at six, with a glass of wine, supper on a tray, the big screen warmly shining from across the living room, Judy and her pals would do for Willy what blurry pages and pinching headphones did for Benjy. And there would be more YouTube into the night, devolving as it generally did into videos of a more prurient nature, re-enacting the gambols of Willy's younger years.

Oh hell, he told himself, he'd made enough vegetarian chili for two. He'd call Benjy and have him come by for dinner, but only after the news so he wouldn't have to suffer through the day's disasters. Then they could find some dumb seventies movie to stream and bring back younger times. And Benjy could pick up some Italian bread at the pizza shop on the way over.

November

It wasn't every day that old Benjy and old Willy got together. (They often had to remind themselves that they were what everyone else saw as old.) After the election, his political agonies still had Willy in such a distraught condition that Benjy couldn't spend all that much time with him for fear of catching the infection. Yes, they were both rejoicing in the outcome, but the contest wasn't over. Benjy kept fearing that the worst hadn't yet happened. Willy preferred to reassert his faith in democracy and not panic.

Willy had always believed in moving forward. Their lively affair, half a century ago, had been instigated in the library stacks by his ill-dressed self cheerfully approaching Benjamin, who hadn't known quite what to make of this hippie with his man-on-the-street job reporting for an alternative weekly and his sideline stage-managing gig. How did such a free spirit make enough money to survive? Later, Benjy realized that, even when relaxed, Willy operated constantly at a high pitch, which his slow-poke of a new boyfriend (now nicknamed Pokey, after Gumby's horse) could never achieve in the most energetic of moods.

Benjy's preoccupation throughout life had been patiently trying to dissect the vast variations in tempo that regulated human behavior, his own adagio, he'd say, against Willy's vivace. Sometimes now, at eighty-one, Willy could manage a leisurely andante, but allegro was still merely his fall-back speed. Benjy liked to think in musical terms. Every day he listened to a few of the CDs he and Tom had methodically collected over their years together. Growing up in the far north, he had not been exposed to much beyond the short pieces ("To a wild rose" and the Raindrop prelude) that his sister practiced for her old-lady piano teacher. Becky hadn't touched the piano in years, so in their adult lives it was her brother, through Tom, who had become the musical one, though all he could play was the phonograph and its recent digital upgrades. He had, again through Tom, assembled quite a library of trios and quartets, symphonies and concertos, mostly of the German and Austrian sort, and they regularly went to concerts in Chicago and later in Boston. The two of them used to spend hours cuddling up with books and recordings, but recently Benjy had found himself less able to appreciate words and music simultaneously. While he read, his mind would drift into the music, then soon the words on the page would be pulling him away from the melodies and harmonies. Perhaps all the things he thought he had time for had become, in older age, things he must now pay closer attention to.

Ever since the day Benjy jotted down the thoughts of Queen Marie of Rumania, he had only found himself capable of reading in utter silence or following the contours of music only with his eyes closed. Then his mind could take in the lines, the interweavings, the rises and falls in pitch and volume, the contrasts of velocity. The queen had reminded him to begin putting in place his own particular puzzle pieces. There were so many, but music was certainly a primary one and prose was another. After all, sentences were like melodies, and paragraphs provided harmonic undercurrents. To experience them fully, he could not hold in the other half of his brain mismatched actual music against the rhythms and pitches of prose. It was even sometimes bothersome that the sounding of waves on the beach beneath his window were counting out their own measures of time. He had to remind himself that his resting place by the sea was yet another puzzle piece and he'd freely chosen it.

So after his lunch of microwaved lentil soup and leftover Greek salad from the pizza place, he had settled onto his window seat to read, or more precisely to re-read (after fifty years) a play Willy's troupe had selected from the pile of books Benjy had located for him in the university library. Willy had availed himself of the new Xerox machine at the newspaper office to make copies for the rather large cast. He, a man who never kept much of anything, had given his own to Benjy. It was all marked up with abridgments and stage directions, and because Benjy never threw away anything of sentimental value, there it was all these years later held in his veiny wrinkled hands, Ibsen's *Love's Comedy*. He was slightly afraid, given the subject matter, that it might hit a raw nerve. But what was reading for if not to make you face some things you didn't know you should.

That same afternoon, Willy was working off some tension by taking a vigorous solo hike up in the woods at a pace he knew Benjy couldn't keep up with. Sometimes, he simply had to get moving. Walking fast, without those damn poles, had a way of taking his mind off the political situation and hurling him back to his earlier days when he'd be rushing around the city from one interview or meeting to another.

Instead of counting sidewalk cracks, he now took note of every impressive boulder, every squishy dip where runoff collected, every fork in the trail so he would recognize the turning on the way back and not get lost. The woods had the effect of confusing his sense of direction with all the ups and downs and turns and twists. You could imagine you were going west but the path by subtle shifts right and left pretty soon had you headed east. That day, with no sun shining behind the heavy November clouds, Willy couldn't count on it to show him the way.

He was getting a bit winded, nothing to stop him from plunging ahead, but he did allow himself a short respite on a flat-topped lone erratic, a glacial deposit beside the leafy trail. He checked his jacket pocket for his mask, in case another hiker came along, but walking up in the hills he could mostly breathe the fresh air without endangering himself or others. He seldom encountered anyone, but when he did they both pulled up their masks and stepped aside with a cheery remark about how warm the day was or that they'd heard the wind would pick up and bring on a storm so they were taking their exercise early. Such a couple, looking older than he was, had passed by, plunking their trekking poles on what to them clearly seemed a treacherous trail. Benjy had given Willy a pair for his last birthday, but he tended to leave them hanging from a hook by the back door unless they were walking together, and even then as often as not he'd slap his forehead and curse himself for forgetting them.

Now Willy sat and listened to the faint rustling of the beech leaves, the last to fall. He was gazing downhill toward the low swampland, choked with briars and phragmites, where in the spring Benjy had pointed out clumps of frog's eggs floating in the mucky water. Willy missed the bird songs of those May mornings and the elusive lady slippers on the forest floor. In Chicago, his only experience of pure nature had been contemplating the vast unpopulated expanse of Lake Michigan from a breakwater by the beach. Now he had come to take considerable comfort from the solitude of the woods that crowned the hills above his new town. Never before had he given himself over to so much land with so few people on it. It had been difficult at first. He'd envied Benjy's placidity as being better suited to their time in life. When they went walking together, Willy couldn't refrain from a running commentary or else he'd be forging ahead of his slowpoke friend. It was only when he was all by himself that he could bear to sit still and watch and hear without saying or thinking anything at all.

He felt his breath coming more easily, his heartbeat slowing down. That must be how Benjy always felt, but did he ever experience the joys of enthusiasm? A faint memory of their long ago nights in bed together flashed into Willy's mind, but those exuberant sessions seemed now somehow incestuous, discomfiting to recall. Instead, he concentrated on the emotionless bare branches stretching up around him into the cloudy air.

Suddenly, a large brown dog, unleashed, came galumphing along the trail and sniffed right up to him. "Catherine!" called a male voice. "Don't bother the gentleman."

Willy asked, in a burst of recognition, "Isn't this Brownie?" and quickly hooked up his mask.

"Brownie?" A tall young man (young, as in his forties) came along at a jog, pepper-and-salt curls falling to his tinted eyeglasses above a broad black mask bearing, in sky blue, the word "Science." Nevertheless, Willy imagined a handsome face and a robust body encased as it was in a tight-fitting jacket and clinging stretch pants of the sort ski-racers wear. "Sorry, she gets way ahead," he said with a gasp as he slowed to a halt.

"Isn't she Brownie? I've met her before."

"She's Catherine," said the man.

"But doesn't she go out walking sometimes with a woman named Sharon?"

"Oh, of course, yes, Sharon—she gives all the dogs names. I forgot. She's quite a character. You know Sharon?"

"I see her about town, usually with three at a time."

"I'm Maxim," said the man.

"William," Willy said. The dog was sniffing at his pocket where he'd stashed a bar of peanut brittle for later. "May she have a snack?"

"Oh, better not. She's been putting on pounds."

"Isn't she the one who won't poop in the woods?"

"Very fastidious is Catherine," said the heavy-breathing Maxim. "Yes, and it's always in the same corner of our yard, which makes it easy to clean up. You might say she's somewhat compulsive."

Willy decided to stand up, but it took extra shoves from both hands, an operation he could have accomplished hands-free a mere five years ago. The two men now faced each other some ten feet apart. Maxim took off his fogged-up glasses revealing sharp pale blue eyes focused on Willy. If only this encounter had occurred in my fifties, the older man thought, but he would savor it anyway for what it was worth.

"Sharon takes her out in the mornings so we can get some work done," the man said, no longer panting. "My wife and I are working from home these days, but by afternoon, Catherine's set to go again and so am I. Have to burn some energy. I'm not used to all this confinement."

"I've been getting used to it," said Willy and added, "at my age."

"But isn't it great having all these trails? We're new here. My wife and I moved up from Somerville just when Covid struck. The kids had finished college. I used to run along the Mystic, but it wasn't nearly as challenging as this. You talk about age? Listen, at mine, too, I've got to work at keeping in shape."

In years past, Willy would have said something like "You sure look in shape to me" with a glance at the young man's supple thighs, but instead he said, "Your wife's working from home, too?"

"It's great. We used to have to drive separate ways to our jobs, but now we just retreat to our studies, which are the kids' bedrooms when they come visit. True, it's not always easy being together twenty-four-seven. Getting out of the house used to have its good points. See, I monitor and coordinate research projects at a chem lab. She's doing medical insurance claims. Now it's all online. The occasional Zoom conference is all we see of other people."

He was shifting from fluorescent running shoe to running shoe, but his breath was coming more regularly, puffing his black mask in and out. Willy wore a dumb-looking cloth one from the drug store that he washed, three in rotation. It got so damp from his breath and dripping nose.

"I don't want to keep you from your exercise," Willy said. Meanwhile, the dog was sniffing around in the fallen leaves and branches, absorbed in her fascinating world of smells.

"Oh, it's good talking to a live human being," said Maxim. "We don't see anyone else. One kid's in Manhattan, the other's in DC and we worry they're not being careful enough, but I have to trust them. They're supposedly adults now. Do you have kids—or grandkids?"

"I could've had great-grandchildren by now if I'd started early enough," Willy joked, "but no, I'm a single old gent, all my loves behind me."

"Well, you're here. It's a nice town, isn't it?"

Willy pondered a moment and decided, what the hell, he'd say it: "They were all men, actually."

"Oh," said Maxim and then, "Good for you."

"Yes, it was good." Willy smiled beneath his gray mask where the other man couldn't see it. "Here, Brownie, I mean Catherine," he called, and she ran over expecting maybe a biscuit but seemed sufficiently pleased with pats under her chin and strokes along her spine from Willy's dog-loving hands.

"So you've lived all your life here?" the forty-something asked.

"No, I'm like you, an escapee, but from the faraway Midwest. This New England still seems a strange fantasy to me." He stuck his hands in his jacket pockets because his fingers were getting cold. He really ought to begin the return hike, but Maxim was lingering, shifting about and rubbing his big thick-fingered hands together.

"So what brought you here? I mean, my wife and I knew about it from day trips, you know, the beach, lobster rolls, typical tourist stuff, but after we got the nest emptied, we thought why not? Perfect timing, given the pandemic. It was cheaper to buy here than what we sold our Somerville house for. What about you?"

"An old friend of mine lost his spouse. He was out here and found me a place he knew I'd like, a shabby little cottage. I was alone, too. My last partner and I split some years back. He was a younger man about your age, well, in his fifties—"

"I'm forty-seven. I'm getting there."

"It's all young to me. Anyway, I'm here now for the duration."

Catherine had sidled up to scratch a paw on Maxim's right calf. "All right, girl, still up for it? She's almost nine. She's a rescue from Georgia. Great dog."

"Well, get running, you two. Maxim, wasn't it?"

"Maxim. And William?"

"That's me. You'll probably catch up to me on your way back."

"I think we'll try the whole loop today, though. Lately, I'm so restless."

Willy took a quick glance at the man's tight pants and imagined the bulge there slightly distended. He'd always found middle-aged married men to be somewhat intrigued by what maybe they'd been missing all these years. He anticipated regaling Benjy with a fancifully elaborated version of this meeting in the depths of the woods. Benjy would say, "You're incorrigible," and Willy would retort, "Oh, Benjy, it's us men, we can't help it, and you can't either—you keep it to yourself is all."

He told Maxim, as they turned aside from each other, "I like your mask."

"Science? It's what it's all about, right?"

"Indeed it is," Willy said and unhooked his own mask from his ears as he took off at a renewed clip in the opposite direction.

December

Benjy was to go up to Willy's that night for supper (vegetarian, of course), so for lunch he'd opened a can of tuna to supply his daily protein, with Triscuits and sliced cheddar on the side and a hot cup of tea. There had been only one snowfall so far, and it had lingered just a few days, so now the winter ground was bare again and he and Willy had been taking their usual walks in the woods, if not every day.

They had celebrated, so to speak, their Thanksgiving together with prepared take-out turkey dinners after Benjy made it through the family Zoom call with Becky and her progeny, all confined in their various Midwestern houses while viewing old Uncle Benjamin in what to them was his somewhat mythical aerie above the far Atlantic. He'd aimed the camera eye to show the plunging waves, but Becky said (in her Zoom rectangle) that it didn't look any different from Superior in a storm. She lived now in a development outside Ontonagon, once a stretch of pine woods where they'd played in childhood nearly three-quarters of a century ago.

Now in Christmas-shopping season, Benjy in his mask had darted in and out of the few remaining stores and chosen easily-mailed lobster-themed T-shirts for the grand nieces and nephews, fuzzy pullovers with Boston sports logos for the middle generation, and linen place mats and napkins stitched with sailboats and anchors for Becky—presents requiring no special thought because it was no longer possible to browse through all the options and choose the perfect gift for each distinct relative. No one would mind. They might not even much notice, though most would email a thank you by New Year's. He'd told them not to bother sending him anything because he was trying to get rid of stuff. Becky said she'd be sending the Oregon pears she ordered online every year "and you can get rid of them down your throat, Ben!" He did love his sister. They hadn't seen each other since she'd flown east for Tom's memorial service, a real kindness of hers, but she'd never seen his widower's retreat nor had he seen her new place in the development.

Benjy pitied Willy's lack of family, all dead or estranged, and his Chicago set all dispersed or dead except for a few younger ones: Nick and his friends, with whom he did keep up online. Willy claimed the break with Nick was perfectly amicable. It had simply been time to go their separate ways. Willy had soon been onto something else of a temporary sort, but eventually, when sex was no longer quite such a motivating factor, he'd made his big move east and this one might, after all, prove permanent.

In his twenties, Benjy had done his own share of bouncing around. After two years at Northern Michigan in nearby Marquette, he'd transferred to Michigan State where he discovered a small underground bunch of boys like him, and there were even more when he went on for a library degree. And then he'd risked Chicago, or at least Evanston, for his first real job. Some years later, Willy had introduced him to the North Side theater scene, an unexpected world for a rather inexperienced young man from the UP to find himself in. Willy never seemed to notice. He pulled Benjy along with him for a year or so—wasn't it more like eighteen months before it finally fell apart? They'd never moved in together but had regular sleepovers in one bed or another, despite one of Willy's ex-boyfriends living downstairs or Benjy's unsuspecting female neighbor in the studio apartment next to his.

This had all come back to him a month ago, reading that Ibsen play: the Romantic Searcher versus the Steady Mate, somewhat satirical of each but the characters real enough to seem all too familiar now. I was meant to be a steady mate, Benjy told himself as he took his usual place on the window seat and looked out to sea. He had his headphones in hand and now reached to the shelf above to locate the button on the CD player, stretched the phones over his ears, and soon was enveloped in Schubert's Tenth Symphony, another of the ones he hadn't lived to finish, though not the more famous Eighth. Benjy began pondering all that was unfinished about himself and Tom, what they might still have been doing, even now, old blokes in their eighties. He imagined Tom there with him and the music not confined to his ears, out loud but not too much so for their neighbors. They would be watching the tide coming in and up almost to the seawall and later retreating far out again, uncovering seaweed and pebbles on the flat wet stretch of sand. Benjy had a warm but melancholy sensation in his arms, even after four long years of getting used to tides.

For Willy, this month of December was proving particularly agonizing, what with ongoing federal lawsuits and proliferating conspiracies afoot. Elizabeth was clearly attuned to his agitated mood and had been avoiding his lap, as if she knew he'd be nervously popping up again to get himself a snack as soon as she settled in. She was lying at the far end of the couch, staring suspiciously at him in his armchair, the newspaper flopping up and down before his eyes. He'd peer across at her and growl, "What!" and then, "Elizabeth, cool it" or "Yeah, yeah, I know, sorry, girl."

When he had gleaned all he could bear from the paper, he joined her for a mid-afternoon nap, their latest routine, something he'd never been capable of indulging in before now. He unfolded the afghan, black and red and green with moth holes here and there, that his grandmother had knitted for him when he went down to Champaign-Urbana. It was among the most treasured items in his possession. Elizabeth considered it her personal nest but allowed Willy to spread it over them both, as long as he lay on his side against the back cushions so she could stretch herself out at full length.

Willy had certainly dozed, forgetting politics and old love affairs and even his cat, but she was the first thing that crept back into his consciousness when he awoke. For no obvious reason, the next thought that invaded him—perhaps from an unregistered dream—was of Don, the boyfriend-on-the-side before he and Benjy broke up. "Boyfriend" is a glorified term, he told himself. It still bothered him that Benjy hadn't fought back the way Willy surely would have. "Why should I be recalling that awful mess?" he asked the cat, who only meowed. Because Benjy's coming for dinner? But we see each other practically every day, so why now?

Elizabeth was purring close to Willy's chest. He cuddled her gently, not to get scratched. Young men had no idea back then what they were doing. Sex was simply so much fun, even for those who thought they had to fall in love first to get it. How many times had he argued this out with Benjy? That earnest boy from the North Woods had his chummy parents and his adoring sister, all so unlike Willy's own strait-laced Republican mother and father and his two bossy big brothers, all now long dead.

He stretched with a loud yawn that sent Elizabeth leaping off the couch and meowing at the kitchen doorway. "Not time for supper yet," Willy said, but then, "Oh, crap, I forgot, Benjy's got to be fed as well." The cat stared up at his nonsensical words. He often talked to her about other than feline issues. The sky had darkened. The news ladies would be on soon. Willy stomped upstairs to the bathroom to splash his sleepy face and get himself going. He wondered why he felt the need of a fresh flannel shirt. It wasn't that he had to look good for Benjy but more that he didn't like seeing himself as an untidy old man. Untidiness was for his youthful years of freedom and irresponsibility. Back then, Benjy's uptightness had been what Willy eventually couldn't handle. The years of therapy that finally led Benjy to his Tom, as far as Willy could tell, hadn't changed him much, but Tom was a born caretaker.

After Willy had scraped out the last of the liver paste into Elizabeth's bowl and angled the TV toward the kitchen so he could watch Judy deliver the news summary, he dumped from various paper containers, some carrots, onions, broccoli and cauliflower heads, string beans, and little red potatoes and started chopping. Soon, Lisa was broadcasting from her dreary basement with those narrow windows near the ceiling and—which he always looked for—her black-and-white cat curled up on the sectional sofa. Willy was concerned that Lisa was even skinnier than she used to be. The strain of reporting on the seditiously contested election was getting to her, too. But Yamiche seemed to be thriving. She had spirit, that woman, unflustered and righteous, slinging it straight back at the evil clown in the White House. Willy recalled when there had not been a single female reporter on TV aside from the weather gal—let alone a Black one, let alone one named Yamiche.

Chop, chop, chop, heat up the wok, olive oil, zatar—that Lebanese mixture he wouldn't disclose to Benjy, who marveled how Willy could concoct meals so tasty that he didn't even miss the meat.

Now came charming TV-Nick with the international report. Germany was doing so much better than us, and so was New Zealand, of course. Willy had read that Grenada wasn't letting anyone in or out—Grenada, the island where Reagan got to show how big and tough he was. "What an asshole!" Willy told Elizabeth, the sole resident carnivore, who was rubbing back and forth against his socks, lobbying for more liver.

Benjy would arrive at seven when the TV would be off and the little table would have been pulled out from the wall so two, instead of one, could sit around it—placemats, silverware, candles lit, plates warm from the oven, and then the prompt knock on the door.

When Willy turned the lock to let Benjy in, he was handed a softening carton of Coffee Heath Frozen Yogurt that went straight to the freezer. After so many years, what would those two old friends still have to talk about, given that Benjy didn't want to discuss the depressing state of politics and pandemic and Willy had little interest in much else right then. They certainly didn't need any more reminiscing about youthful bad behavior or any reassessment of their creeping loss of agility or short-term memory. Nonetheless, between bites they managed to keep the chat coming.

During dessert, Benjy went off on the symphonies that Franz Schubert had left unfinished. "He died at thirty-one having already composed some six-hundred songs. Imagine that, Willy!" Benjy said.

"I doubt I've even heard six-hundred songs, pop or otherwise, in my whole eighty-one-plus years," said Willy. They were both wiping their lips of coffee-and-cream smears and sitting up in the opposing straight chairs pushed back from the table, neither yet ready to suggest the more comfortable couch and armchair.

"You've heard the famous Unfinished Symphony—DAA-dum, da-DEE-daDA—" Benjy went on, as he often did about a topic that held little interest for Willy. "But he never got around to orchestrating his Seventh or properly finishing the Tenth, either. Somehow the Ninth got finished amid the others. I spent the afternoon playing them all. It's a set Tom ordered for my seventy-fifth birthday, his last present before he died. The Academy of Saint-Martin-in-the-Fields."

"The what?"

"That's the orchestra, a nice name, it sounds Schubertian."

"You and Tom always loved the same things," Willy noted wistfully.

"Most of them he taught me to love. I hadn't grown up with them the way he had. Willy, do you ever think about leaving things unfinished? When we met we were just beginning. But now—oh, and Tom had cut out a review from the *New Yorker* that explained how Schubert himself had labeled one further fragment in D major as his Seventh Symphony, which makes the Seventh the Eighth and the famous Unfinished the Ninth, so the big one in C major that he did finish becomes the Tenth, and the last one would have to be the Eleventh."

"Benjy, what are you going on about!"

"Sorry. It's my inner librarian. This afternoon, though, it was the Andante of the last one that got me feeling rather melancholy."

"Your familiar word."

"I know. I'm seldom ever filled with your sort of joy."

"I'm not so joyful lately. I do obsess over the soon-to-be-gone creep in the White House."

"You shouldn't. First thing in the morning, I read the headlines online to get them over with and not get too depressed."

"Lucky you," said Willy. Elizabeth had leapt onto his lap and was eyeing the empty bowls, ready for licking, so he set his on the floor and she hopped down.

"Should I let her have mine?" Benjy asked.

"She'll love you for it. Not that you want to be loved by a cat."

"I like Elizabeth," Benjy claimed, "but she's a one-man cat and that's fine with me."

"Tell me," Willy said, leaning his elbows on the table, "you and sister Rebecca, you're both widowed now. Do you ever compare notes? Hey, let's get more comfortable. Bring your tea. I'll take my armchair."

When they resettled, Benjy said, "But Dennis died decades ago. She's been on her own since the kids were little. I had all those years with Tom. I wouldn't want to compare our losses."

"She could've remarried."

"That's what you would've done, Willy."

"I never would've married at all. But I'm happy to say none of my old boyfriends has died yet that I know of."

"Because they were all younger than you."

"Yes, but Don, not to bring up that mess, was older, just barely. Anyway, he's alive in Vancouver. He sends a Christmas card every year. Who could forget him as one of the Hindu demigods in that Shaw play? I got him the part. You have to admit he had a gorgeous torso, all bronzed for the show."

"Oh, Willy."

"Sorry, but he's on my mind because I was somehow dreaming of him in my nap this afternoon. It's cool how dreams have no relation to time. People reappear at whatever age. And people who couldn't possibly have known each other show up together. And I'm always much younger. Hell, I know it was a rough time for you. I shouldn't have mentioned him."

"Water over the dam," said Benjy. "But I wonder if we're coming to think of our pasts as still happening, even when we're awake. Maybe decline is a process of mixing up time, past and present, of seeing our lives simultaneously as a whole thing."

"Especially when Don appears bare-chested in the stage lights in a dream."

"Willy, it's been fifty years."

"Don't I know it!"

Elizabeth had come to sit at the far end of the couch on the folded afghan and was now staring at Benjy, annoyed he was still visiting.

"That's her spot," Willy said. "My grandmother knitted it or crocheted it or whatever she did. And my radical pals at the university loved it: black, red, and green, Marcus Garvey colors. If she'd only known, the old bigot. I grew up in such a narrow-minded suburb and got out in good time or I might've been sucked in forever. We were on the cusp, you know, we war babies, between generations. We had to find our own way, making it up as we went."

"My family would have had no idea either who Marcus Garvey was," Benjy said. "With us it wasn't Black people, it was Indians and Canucks."

"You've got some Canuck in you, though, right?"

"For all I know some Ojibway, too. And we've both got a minimal amount of Neanderthal, if it comes to that."

"I don't care who my ancestors were," said Willy. "I'm an Armchair Marxist. It's Class, not Race, comrade. That Shaw play was a Socialist's version of Judgment Day. You're redeemed if you've been useful. If not, no hellfire, you simply disappear. Don played one of the useless ones. Ah, the good old days of underground theater. Whatever happened to the late Sixties?"

"That Don What's-his-name was definitely useless," said Benjy.

"He got the part based on torso, of course. Nothing had happened between us yet. He was with Teddy downstairs. I got you doing props by then. Remember? You used to watch from the wings. And you helped haul the ropes for the Angel of the Apocalypse flapping down and then back up again. What a wacky play! We pulled it off, though. Those years, innocent as they were—but exciting." Willy was leaning his head back as if he could see the curtain going up. Raising it had also been one of Benjy's backstage tasks.

"I'm unsure how useful either of us has been." The thought came quietly from Benjy on the near end of the couch.

Willy stretched himself closer. "But we haven't exploited anyone," he noted. "We've done honest work, buying good books with public money and organizing them, reporting on events for a progressive little rag, not making too much money, either of us, but enough to get along. Of course, you did have Tom, insuring people's property at maybe too high a fee, but still. Maybe we haven't produced the next generation, but we've paid our taxes for it and who needs more kids anyway? We're useful because we've used up less than most." He patted the arms of his chair and hauled himself out to go heat the kettle for tea. "Milk or lemon this time?"

Benjy called from across the room, "Honey."

"I never know."

"Milk in the morning, lemon at lunch, honey after supper."

"I can't keep track of your systems," Willy said and added, "I couldn't keep track of my own, if I had any. Are we losing our minds?"

"No," Benjy said definitively, eyed suspiciously by the cat. "If anything, we're living much more inside our minds."

"Oh dear," said Willy from the kitchen.

Benjy felt he needed to argue his point but didn't feel like standing up, so he leaned forward on his elbows and spoke more loudly: "But that may be why nobody gets any wiser. We die off with whatever wisdom we've gained kept inside us and leave it for the next crop to find it again on their own. Books do preserve some of it, I guess," he added in a softer voice.

"Marx proposed breaking that hopeless cycle of yours," said Willy, clattering cups and saucers and hunting in the cupboards for the honey bear.

"And a lot of luck he had with that, Willy, old friend."

"The last time you were here, did you put the honey bear back in the wrong place?" Now Willy was frantically opening drawers. "I can't find it anywhere. You're the only one who uses that cheap honey. I have my special comb-honey jar, but I'm not wasting it in your tea."

"You can skip the honey, William."

"Oh lord, there it is on the windowsill!" That seemed to rouse Elizabeth, who slipped off the afghan and padded silently across the rag rug to take a seat in the kitchen doorway.

January

One sunny afternoon Benjy came across something in Samuel Butler's *Note-Books* that he was now copying out. It didn't apply to his own family life, but he thought Willy might appreciate it: "I believe that more unhappiness comes from this source than from any other—I mean the attempt to prolong the family connection unduly and to make people hang together artificially who would never naturally do so." Benjy paused his pen, decided to skip the next sentence with an ellipsis, then wrote on: "And old people do not really like it much better than the young."

Maybe this will help Willy feel better about neglecting his blood ties, Benjy told himself. His old friend always bemoaned his disadvantages when it came to family. He had nothing at all to do with his two deceased brothers' progeny, while Benjy had nothing but fond feelings for his own kin, geographically distant as they were. Sadly, his niece Carol was divorced, and her son had favored his dad and gone off with him to Washington State, so that was another loss, but Becky and her kids had entirely accepted, even welcomed, his own relationship with Tom. They called them Uncle Ben and Uncle Tom, oblivious of those two racial stereotypes, and besides, Tom was as pale as any white man could be. Becky's husband had been killed in Vietnam before Benjy came out to the family, and though she wished Dennis had lived to know his brother-in-law's partner Tom, Benjy was just as glad he never had to test the army man's degree of welcome.

Widowhood caused Becky to love her three kids all the more, and she never turned bitter. To supplement the military pension, she often took two part-time jobs at once: waitress in various eateries, clerk in a series of small shops. Benjy admired her deeply though all they still had in common was their happy Ontonagon childhoods. Her kids had Ontonagon childhoods of their own, mostly fatherless though happy. Then, her sons dispersed and produced a boy and a girl each, and after her divorce daughter Carol moved only as far away as Houghton.

Willy claimed no heirs, which made his casual approach to finances entirely guilt-free. He must have come to Samuel Butler's conclusion himself, but it wouldn't hurt for Benjy to validate it with the quotation. Willy's disposition was naturally cheerful whereas Benjy was withdrawn and meditative, not so much pessimistic as cautious and careful. At eighty-one, Willy would take stairs two at a time going up and grip no railing going down. The steep stairs in his cottage had no railing and no carpet to keep him from slipping. Benjy was glad to live on one floor even if it took two flights to reach it.

His thoughts had moved a long way from Butler's *Note-Books*, so he set the volume aside, folded up the notepaper with his relatively legible script, stuck it in his breast pocket, and decided to go where his thoughts had led him, down those stairs for a walk on yet another snowless January day in his seaside town.

As he descended he heard the couple downstairs on their way back up, and they all converged on the landing outside Apartment Two.

"Afternoon, Ben!" chirped masked Milly (in common areas one was expected to wear a mask). She was a short and perky middle-aged woman peeking out between a bright yellow scarf and a turquoise knit hat.

Benjy hastily pulled his mask straps over his ears. "Hi, Milly, hi, Jack, beautiful day."

She had stepped closer to their door, not to crowd the floor space. Jack squeezed up next to her. "We've sure lucked out all month," he said, also fully swathed but in grays and browns and only an inch or two taller than his small wife.

All three smiled their concealed smiles, counting on the squinting of eyes to convey amusement. People had been learning how to read each other in new ways.

"Have you recovered?" Milly asked. "I mean from the Insurrection?"

"We're both still in shock," said Jack.

"Me too, me too," Benjy said. "I'd been watching that morning but shut it off till my friend Will called to say they'd broken into the Capitol, and I said it wasn't possible but I turned it back on and there it was."

"We had it on all day," said Milly. "You don't hear ours through the floor, do you?"

"Oh no, hardly at all."

"That day we had all three sets on, the little one in my sewing room, Jack's in the breakfast nook, and the big living room screen."

"I didn't hear a thing, but mine was on by then, too."

"I was practically screaming," said Milly.

"What upsets us most," Jack said in a more earnest tone, "is to discover how many hateful Americans we share the country with. I always knew they were there, but I figured it was only a few percent. How naive I was!"

"Me too," said Benjy.

"Jack believes it's smartphones that brought them out," said his wife. They were such a tight little couple. They agreed on everything, did everything together, and Benjy had seldom seen one without the other. He assumed they were happily retired but from what he had no notion. And they'd never mentioned offspring. They'd been there when he moved in and knew no more of his life upstairs than he did of theirs below. He had only once explained that his partner Tom had died and the move up from Boston was to give himself a fresh start, a positive way of putting it so they wouldn't have to utter more than a polite expression of condolence. "And this town's perfect for you," Milly had added. "So many folks here are turning over new leaves." Her sentiment had stuck with him these past four years.

If that was the extent of their intimacy, it had taken the Insurrection to confide anything further. Heretofore, Benjy had been uncertain of their political persuasion. Because he regularly heard loud sporting events through his kitchen floor, he'd imagined Jack, at least, might be some sort of Republican. It was a stupid prejudice, traceable to embarrassing experiences in high school gym classes.

"I'm pleased to see we're on the same page," said Jack. "In this fussy little town you never know who's on what side. It's loosening maybe, with more of us types moving in. Not clear, though, if we're pricing out young families. I hardly know what's right anymore." He was sticking his key in the lock, and soon the two short people had bundled themselves inside with "At least we can enjoy the sun and sea" from him and "Keep the faith!" from her.

Benjy called "Nice talking to you" before their door closed.

Out on the sidewalk, he saw three little dogs' heads protruding from the diner's recessed entryway. Their leashes were wrapped around the post that held the "Take Out Only" sign. Suddenly, from behind him, Sharon popped out of the exit door with a paper sack. "Hey, William!" she said twisting the leashes free.

"No, Benjamin, Ben. You're Sharon."

"Sorry, I can't tell you two guys apart in your masks." That morning hers was shocking pink. "You're the one who followed the boyfriend, right? So what happened to him?"

"He was somewhat older. We were living in Boston when he died, and I moved up here to get a fresh start."

"That's what Fitz says is why we moved here, too."

"Your dogs have shrunk," Benjy joked.

"Huh? Oh, I get it. No, these are Stinky, Yippy, and Pokey. Not their real names."

"I myself was once called Pokey," Benjy said, "after Gumby's horse."

"Gumby? That's a good one. I like that."

"You know Gumby?"

"Some cartoon from back in the day? I don't watch TV much. Who's got time? It's all news lately anyways."

"It sure is," Benjy said.

"I don't follow it, no offense," Sharon said as the dogs kept leaping up, their small paws patting at her jeans. It was obvious which one was Yippy. "All right, you guys, here's your illegal treats, one third of a doughnut each. It's the butter-crunch kind they like best and so do I, one for me and the other I was going to take Fitz at the boat yard, but he'll never know. You want it? They make 'em fresh every morning."

"No thanks, I'm good." (A convenient phrase he'd recently picked up.)

"I haven't seen you two guys around for weeks. Well, it's winter, but no snow. Great for these mini dogs but the biggies, man, they miss carrying on in the deep snow. Blackie's like a porpoise diving in and out. I haven't walked Brownie for a while because her dad takes her on his runs, what with the frozen ground and no ice. But I picked up a few new mutts for late in the day. It's always word of mouth. Which way you heading?"

"I'm going over to William's."

"So you guys don't live together. Oh, I forgot, you're the one with the boyfriend, well, not anymore. Sorry. The other of you lives by himself as well? Why don't you go in on a place?"

"We're too set in our ways," said Benjy, aiming toward the

other side of the street and hoping Sharon was on her way to the beach.

"Well, say hey to him for me. I guess I'll let these buggers divide Fitz's doughnut. He won't know the diff and I'm not shlepping it all the way to the boat yard in this onshore wind." As the dogs pulled her along, she kept talking, but Benjy couldn't make out what she was going on about, probably only for the dogs' ears.

He made his way up the side street past the Unitarians to his friend's cottage. The shingles needed paint. Some random patches of blue still clung to the bare wood. Through the front window he could see Elizabeth perched on the back of the couch, looking out for birds at the feeder hanging off an iron crook outside. Benjy noted that Willy hadn't yet refilled it since he'd reminded him to.

Willy had folded the newspaper when he heard the knock and heaved himself out of his armchair. Elizabeth thought it meant lunch and bounded past his feet, but he caught himself from stumbling over her on his way to the front door. "I wasn't expecting you," he told his friend, who was removing his mask before stepping in to shed his puffy blue parka. "It's windy. Close the door so Elizabeth doesn't sneak past."

"I would've called," Benjy apologized.

"Because, who knows, I might've been, shall we say, entertaining some young man."

"Unlikely," said Benjy.

"You never know, you never know." The week before, Willy had indeed entertained that jogging dog owner Maxim, but outdoors and at a proper distance, having bumped into him running dogless down the hill. He had decided not to tell Benjy, who would only accuse him of harboring unrealizable desires. But even the opportunity once again to contemplate those tightly-wrapped thighs had been enough to bring joy into a dreary day.

184 | JONATHAN STRONG

"I copied down a bit of wisdom for you," Benjy said, holding out the notepaper, which Willy unfolded and read twice through. "I thought it might justify your lack of family feeling."

"Want some tea?"

Benjy nodded, awaiting his friend's response to Samuel Butler.

"Milk or honey? I forget."

"Lemon."

"Squoze from a plastic lemon?"

"Fine."

The kettle only needed a booster on the burner because Willy's cup was still better than lukewarm. Benjy settled on the non-cat end of the couch, and soon Willy brought him the usual souvenir mug (Barack Obama—44th President of the USA), refreshed his own cup from the kettle, and hopped it back to the kitchen before resuming his seat. "The old people," he repeated, "do not really like it much better than the young. That's for sure! My two brothers' kids—the oldest must be almost seventy—I've lost track of them, and who even knows who their kids are, or even the great-grandkids! As soon as our parents were out of the picture, my brothers gave up on me entirely and I on them."

"So you've said."

"And," Willy exclaimed raising an accusatory finger, "though Mother and Father never exactly chucked me out—I mean I got my third of what was left, paltry as it was—but they sure hadn't wanted me visiting when they had fancy friends over. 'What will the Whittemores think!' All because I once brought home a pretty little chum in a fluffy pink sweater! Or in the summer when I showed up in raggedy cut-offs and bare feet."

"I've heard all this before, Willy, which is why I thought you'd appreciate that bit of wisdom."

"Butler's the man who wrote *The Way of All Flesh*? Ooh, my tea's too hot."

"By the way," Benjy said, "I had a rare encounter with the

downstairs couple. It turns out we're on the same page politically. These days you never can tell. And then outside, I ran into Sharon with those three little dogs again. One of them's Pokey. I said that was my old nickname. She didn't seem too familiar with Gumby cartoons."

"You didn't tell her Gumby was me."

"No, but you were quite flexible back then."

"Back then! Oh well. Here, I'll go stick your wisdom on the fridge. What did that dog woman have to say for herself?"

"She doesn't listen to the news. Who has time, she says. She went rattling on to the dogs and me interchangeably. At first, she thought I was you."

Elizabeth had nestled onto the afghan, and Benjy was uncomfortably aware of her eyes investigating him sipping from his Obama mug.

"You can't tell who anyone is," Willy said taking his seat again. "This town, it's like a masked ball without the dancing." He blew on his brimming cup of tea then took a brief sip. "At least when they're on camera at home you can see my news ladies' faces. Out on the street they have to mask up. I was watching Amna. Judy was asking her how it was outside the Capitol that day. She said she was surrounded by thugs yelling "Scum!" and "Fake news!" Usually she's safe at home with her six volumes of Churchill's *Second World War* on the table behind her."

"You love your PBS gals."

"They're my home team," Willy said. "But it's Nick I most look forward to, except lately he's been growing a stupid beard. Covid effect. It's got some gray in it."

"Nick, eh? Not to be confused with another Nick."

"He's the only Nick I've got in my life now. Want a doughnut? I got them from the diner but didn't want to disturb your early morning with a knock. I was up at six. No, not hungry?"

Elizabeth had stretched, gently meowed, and was making her

silent way across the cushion separating her from Benjy. "Umm, Willy?"

"She's warming up to you."

"I'm not so sure." But now the cat was rubbing her neck against Benjy's flannel pants leg and seemed about to slip onto his lap, which in fact she suddenly did, then she snuggled down with a purr.

"That's a first!" said Willy.

"What do I do?"

"She's an animal like us. She recognizes a fellow creature. You should be flattered." Benjy carefully lifted his mug and took a slow sip and breathed out steam. "See, not so bad,"

"But I've been sort of tense in general," Benjy confessed. "Until Inauguration Day comes off, I can't be sure of anything, and even then, who knows? Last night I got thinking about that photo of Johnson signing the Civil Rights Act, wasn't that it, with King standing beside him? And remember how, in the State of the Union, Johnson had said, 'And we shall overcome,' and somehow that day marked the beginning of my adult life. What was I, twenty-four? Way before I knew you. Anyway, I felt America was going to be all right, not immediately, of course, and the war was ramping up, but I believed in something good. Before that, I'd just been muddling along, a dumb young white boy from the UP in the big city. But now since last week? It's as if my trusting grown-up years have come to an end and suddenly I'm an old man."

"That didn't happen when Tom died?" Willy quietly asked.

"Somehow, no, it didn't."

"Wasn't he five years older? And now it's been five more years and you're catching up to him."

"I'm glad Tom died before he had to see what happened last week. Obama was still his president."

"I didn't realize you were taking it so hard, Benjy. I thought

I was the obsessed one. I thought you were hiding away with your books and records." Willy set his cup on the end table and gave his friend a hard look.

Benjy had ventured to rest his free hand on his lap near the cat, who hadn't stirred and whose contented purr could be heard by Willy five feet away. "Reading and listening do help a lot," Benjy said. "They take me out of myself." And he set his mug down, too.

"Is it too cold for a walk?" Willy asked.

"I can't move with this cat here."

"Pst, pst, Elizabeth, liver treats!" Willy stood up, and his cat sprang off Benjy's lap leaving tiny pricks from her hind claws.

"Woods or sea?" came from the kitchen.

"You can't sit still, can you, Willy! Maybe a short hike in the woods would do me good, though." Benjy got up to retrieve his puffy parka from the hook by the front door. "Don't forget your poles," he called.

February

The hinged top of Willy's little writing desk, piled as it was with circulars, torn-out magazine articles, pleas for money, and as-yet-unpaid bills would reveal, when lifted, his stash of notes from former lovers, outdated user's manuals, newspaper clippings and a packet of theater programs, and underneath it all the ancient copy book from his great-grandfather's high school years before the Civil War. It was one of the few items Willy had retrieved from his parents' house, a memento his older brothers had no interest in. He'd read it through at the time but largely forgotten what that boy in rural Ohio had penned so neatly on those stiff pages and proudly orated to his schoolmates at the Athenian Society. The pages, bound in limp flaking leather, had remained in Willy's writing desk through numerous relocations about the North Side of Chicago, and when it came time for his final move, he had jockeyed the rickety little desk, its contents unexamined, into the rental truck and conveyed it eastward to the ocean's shore. The venerable family relic still rested under the lift-up lid of his desk in the corner by the kitchen doorway in Willy's shingled cottage.

Now, on a snowy winter morning, having read the papers while Elizabeth perched on the back of the couch to watch a red cardinal at the outside feeder, what popped into Willy's mind was an image of that long-neglected bit of his own heritage. Benjy was always puzzled by his friend's lack of familial sentiments. True, Willy had nothing comparable to those kindly parents on the remote Upper Peninsula, the lumberman—he'd never been sure if Benjy's dad simply worked in a lumber yard or had been an actual lumberjack—and the elementary schoolteacher dedicated to her pupils, and nothing at all as companionable as the younger sister and her brood with their loyal embrace of Tom and their continuing attachment to their far-off next of kin. Willy's parents had been, at best, indifferent if not outright dismissive, and his brothers saw him as the foolish self-indulgent brat who at first embarrassed them and eventually outraged their conventional sensibilities. At no one moment was Willy thrown out of his suburban tribe, yet he was incrementally pushed aside, ignored, and at last made irrelevant. The big brothers had been born on the wrong side of the generational divide, while Willy was just young enough—coeval with Bob Dylan, after all—to move into the New Age and leave his upbringing behind.

But perhaps, he thought now, having slipped his great-grandfather Albert's copy book out of the desk and resumed the armchair, perhaps he had something to show Benjy of a more congenial blood tie beyond the intervening decades. Benjy was always digging up wisdom to pass on, and Willy had a vague memory of having been moved by the remarkably well-phrased writings of his remote ancestor, tales of hunting squirrels and ducks, of boating on Ohio rivers and streams, of whacking down a hornet's nest, and wasn't the final entry a lengthy account of young Albert's part in a prisoner swap of a thousand men in Confederate gray for a thousand Union men in blue? It might interest his depressed old pal or at least divert him. Willy was concerned that Benjy's mood had remained low, even after they'd gotten their first inoculations at the town's health board. Benjy's sense of having suddenly become an old man troubled Willy, who refused to cast himself in that light. Oddly, Benjy had none of the aches and stiffnesses that he himself complained of—no, it was Tom's death, surfacing again in his consciousness, and not the events of January Sixth, disillusioning as they were. Now with the ex-president's acquittal and the new administration's thin majorities, Benjy had been grumbling how glad he was to be old, not to have much more time to witness the course of history. Funny, thought Willy, for a man who had for years worked in Boston as an archivist at the Massachusetts Historical Society! Benjy loved and studied history. He was fascinated by all its origins and outcomes. But history is left unfinished for each of us when we die. Still, up to that final moment, wouldn't he want to follow its every turn? I should've seen this coming, Willy decided, when Benjy stopped watching the News Hour.

And yet he was convinced that his old friend (by now his oldest friend) had been struck five years ago with a truly essential loss, his whole life with Tom, a loss Willy had difficulty even conceiving. Sister Rebecca—Becky, as she told him to call her when she flew east for the memorial—said it was her first visit, in fact her first visit to her brother's world since the time years ago when she'd nervously driven down to Chicago to see Ben as an extra in the party scene of that Chekhov play. She had met Willy then, briefly, as one of the troupe though apparently he was no one special, but she'd hugged him and said she'd heard so much about him and was grateful Ben had a friend who brought him out of his shell. It had pleased Willy but also unsettled him that his latest boyfriend might be depending on the relationship more than he did. Anyway, bare-chested Don came into the picture soon enough.

Over the years that followed, Benjy would take a bus up north for summer vacations, and with Tom they made a road trip of it. Willy, by then a rather occasional friend linked more by youthful memories than common daily events, did envy Tom's experience of in-laws, not that he wanted any for himself, but Tom obviously loved Benjy's family, and his own was equally fond of Benjy as Benjy was of them. Willy asked himself why he was sitting there dwelling on families. He looked out with Elizabeth at the bright red bird at the feeder, but the memories kept coming.

His own flight from Chicago for the memorial had landed minutes after Becky's from Detroit. Benjy was there to taxi them together to his apartment on the back side of Beacon Hill, suddenly bereft of one half of its couple, the solider half, the insurance man. What Willy recalled most vividly of that sad weekend wasn't the formal gathering, held at a grand old Boston men's club hosted by Tom's firm, but his quiet talk with Becky about her brother and how she worried over his being alone now and wished he could come home to Michigan and live with her. Willy knew it wasn't likely, but he promised to make the case to his old friend. She'd said it was so kind of him to fly all that way and how much he'd meant to Ben when he first came to Chicago. She still couldn't believe that he'd got her shy brother out on that stage! "Well, Becky," Willy remembered saying, "our shoestring operation needed bodies." Back then, Willy had always called her brother Benjamin, except privately in bed when they were Pokey and Gumby. "Time, time, years, years," he said aloud, and Elizabeth switched her gaze to stare quizzically at him. "Hey, girl," he continued, "do you think I should let Benjy read my great-grandfather Albert's high school copy book? He used to work transcribing diaries and letters at the Historical Society. He loves that old stuff."

Elizabeth held her stare. It was nice having someone to talk to, a fellow creature in the house. Willy had warned himself not to fall into the habit, but every now and then he liked hearing his own voice putting words to thoughts. The cat seemed to like it, too. And he'd even talk to the unresponsive people on TV and YouTube as did probably every other old coot alone at home. At the memorial, he remembered, they'd played a tape of Tom's disembodied voice. It had given Willy the shivers. And there had been a gallery of photos and a loop of videos you could look at. Other people found it comforting, he supposed. "It wouldn't do for you, Elizabeth," he told his cat. "Only smell would bring someone back to you. You will outlive me and be left with nothing but my scent on cushions and slippers and your afghan."

He decided he'd better shut up, but the thoughts persisted. We think of the past, he told himself, as something three-dimensional as if it's still real. But it's only a thought. It's gone for good. That's actually a relief, Willy decided. He wouldn't want to experience bits of his life again, even its best moments. He wondered if Benjy thought of it that way, being such a brooder over things.

The cat stretched herself down off the back of the couch and made her silent way across the cushions to the armrest from which she jumped in a graceful arc onto Willy's lap. She sniffed the leather-bound copy book before curling up with a purr.

Willy opened to the page entitled "Indians Wrongs." He mentally supplied the missing apostrophe. In his final years at the now defunct alternative weekly, his role as reporter had devolved to copy editor because he was by far the oldest guy on staff and could spell and punctuate and tighten up the young folks' redundancies. As he read what young Albert had written at age sixteen, he smiled at the occasional misspellings (*Europian*, *steadaly*) while being once again impressed by the eloquence of a country schoolboy in those days. And he began to feel redeemed by this single one of his forebears who had expressed such progressive views, even if he had supplied only one-eighth of Willy's genes. His heritage wasn't entirely grounded in the closet racism and class disdain of the suburban Fifties. Wouldn't Benjy be amazed!

But who knew what young Albert had grown into. Had he lost his passion for justice the way so many idealists do? After the Civil War, he had trained as a doctor and transplanted himself to Chicago where he ended up in a troubled marriage. That was all Willy recalled of his father's family tales. "Will it cheer up Benjy to read this?" he asked Elizabeth. No reaction. Willy believed that hopes for justice surface in every generation, as they did in his own. He stroked the cat's three shades of fur. "Easier to be a cat," he said aloud. "You have no idea of what goes on out there beyond that bird."

Soon enough, outside Benjy's unlocked door, Willy was shaking the clumps of snow off his boots, the copy book preserved dry in the inner pocket of his heavy pea coat. He'd called first and Benjy had said to come right over. He was finishing up some letters and they could go to the post office and then take a short chilly walk around town. It was no day for the woods.

"Warm, up first," he said now. "No, keep your boots on. We'll be going out shortly."

Through the living room window the sun was sparkling off the ocean and the air all around was bright with reflected whiteness. Benjy's apartment was always warm, partly because the couple below cranked their heat up and it rose through the uninsulated floors. Benjy had chosen to rent rather than own, more economical at his stage of life, and anyway there was plenty to leave

Becky's kids from Tom's estate. Unless, of course, he lived far into his nineties or needed super-expensive care. It wasn't something he could plan, but his old pal never even thought about such contingencies. He'd never planned for his future at all.

"I have something for you to read," Willy said stamping his rubberized boots and unbuttoning the pea coat he figured made him look more like a local.

Benjy took the frayed leather notebook, opened it and read the dedication aloud: "A present from his loving though absent father for Christmas A.D. 1859. With the request that each and every composition required of him by his teachers throughout the course of study be neatly transcribed into this book & be preserved thus as a faithful witness to himself and others."

"You love historical artifacts," Willy said. "That's my great-grandfather's book from before the Civil War. My great-great-grandfather wrote what you just read."

"You've had this in your keeping?"

"In my desk since Chicago. I never thought to show it to you, but I figured it might cheer you up. Keep it as long as you like. You'll find my family maybe wasn't always as nasty as they became later on."

Benjy was leafing through the pages. "Neat script he had. Sometimes these old diaries are indecipherable."

"It's not his diary. It's what he wrote for school. He orated some of them at what he calls the Athenian Society. He was a teenager in rural Ohio! Read the one about Indians."

Benjy nodded thoughtfully and said, "Thanks, I look forward to it. Hold on, let me get my parka. I want to catch the noon pickup at the post office."

They took their daily constitutional, or "unconstitutional," Willy quipped as a nudge toward political light-heartedness. And later they ordered hot chocolates and melted cheese-and-tuna sandwiches at the diner and brought them up to Benjy's toasty

194 | JONATHAN STRONG

living quarters where Willy asked about his travels with Tom, winters to some Caribbean island and summers flying out to Becky's with a stop in Indiana to see Tom's parents. Willy had never much left Chicago. He wasn't the vacationing type. The city provided all he needed back then.

After Willy had trudged off home to his cat, Benjy lay down on the window seat to read from the copy book. After the first pages about the hornet's nest and going fishing, written by a young teenager a hundred-and-sixty-odd years ago, he fell into a peaceful doze and, at some point, dreamed about himself and his sister paddling in the bright sunny cold water of the lake or maybe the ocean, but they weren't children. They were somewhere in their fifties, it seemed, and they had all their clothes on even though they were swimming. When they began to feel weighted down, soaked through, afraid of drowning, Benjy woke up and noticed Willy's great-grandfather's old book lying there on his chest. He opened it to a page with the title "Indians Wrongs" and read every word, stopping only to go grab his Latin dictionary to translate a phrase the boy must have learned in school. Coming to the end, he noticed the date: "Feb 8th 1861"—two months before the war against slavery began with the attack on Fort Sumter. But that date seemed to call up some historical significance of its own. Benjy went again to his bookshelves for the almanac. Sure enough, it was the day the first six southern states elected Jefferson Davis their seditious president. The schoolboy in Ohio hadn't yet heard the news. And Willy expected this to cheer me up! Benjy asked himself. An innocent kid's meditation on the course of human cruelty?

He lay his head back on the throw pillows that usually cradled him comfortably while he read or listened to music, safe in his aerie, as Becky called it. But now he was sunk again, and when he had just begun shutting out the recent images of those marauding fellow Americans, here they were again, centuries old and,

Benjy was convinced, for centuries still to come. As if to confirm his belief, he held the book up before his pillowed head and read the grim story one more time.

Indians Wrongs

Scarcely three & a half centuries have elapsed since these beautiful lands were inhabited by a race far different in every respect from those that now hold there ill gotten gains. It scarcely seems possible to one to reflect for a moment that so great changes could take place in so few short years. This vast expanse of wooded country has changed its form & flourishing cities & small villages are to be seen in the once wild wilderness. But whare are the many once flourishing tribes of Indians the lawful owners of these tracts of country. They are gone. "Gone is the mighty warrior & gone forever from oure elder states are the red men who like Saul & Jonathan were swifter than eagles & stronger than lions." Before America was peopled by the Europian nations, the Indian roamed through the valleys & over the hills lord of all he surveyed. We then saw them assembled together under the protection of a Chief or governor who led forth his people for the purpose of procuring the necessities of life, making war & soforth. Then Mr. President then were the happiest days the Indians ever saw & I fear the happiest he ever will see. Then it was that he had everything in common. No one claimed to be lord & ruled over the poorer class for they considered themselves to be equal breathren of whom there Chief was the common father. When they were sick they took care of them as if it wer for ther common interest & not as in our own country left to die of want & starvation because it was ther lot to dwell among the lowly. But to use the language of one of there own men "an evil day came upon us, your forfathers crossed the great waters & landed upon our shores." A sad day was that indeed to the poor Indian. At the time of the discovery of America those simple hearted inhabitants dwelling near the sea shore were struck with amazement when they saw the ships of Columbus approaching there shores they thought them to be birds to whome the hull answered for a body & the sails for wings. Would to God there conjectures had been true. Then we there unlawful successors would at the day of Judgment be free from the mountain like evils Which we as a nation have inflicted upon them. When God made man did he not impart into him that love of liberty which was to distinguish him from the mere brute. Why then do we have any reason to suppose that the Indian was destitute of this great love. But the contrary to this we know to be true & because he did not submit as if he wer bound in chains his character is drawn in as dark colors as all art could give. As the country increased in numbers the depredations of the whites upon the Indians raised to fury ther vengeance. As the country increased in numbers a counsel fire being called in which ther aged Chiefs would admonish there braves not to receave so great wrongs. Being thus encouraged they swore eternal hatred against there white entruders & seek an opportunity to wreck there just vengance & what Mr. President is the result. Fearful indeed. For many years the colonies have to struggle with ther determined foe. At last peace is proclaimed, but how long does it last, hardly until the distant war cry has seased, before it is broken by the whites. Agane the colonies are at war & agane peace is declared & so it continues for many years until the Indians might well have said "Timeo Americanos et dona ferentes." Finally the colonies so increased that they wanted more land. They did not go as far as a friend to the Indians & offer to buy there land. No, but how different they came and took forcible possession of it, slaying by hundreds all such as stood up in defense of there homes & there liberties. From that time the program of the American Aborigines to uter annihilation hass been steadaly but surely marked out. Untill the present day. "The winds of the Atlantic fan not a single region which they may call there own." But what have they done to merit such cruelties, nothing more thancivilized nations have done from the beginning of world & will continue to do until the end of time.

Feb 8th 1861

"There" for "their"—there, away, from what was theirs, thought Benjy. No, Willy, this doesn't cheer me up at all. You can't feel what I'm feeling now. You've always been the hopeful one. Yet I'm the one with the happier childhood! I'm glad if this makes you prouder of your family, even if it's back three generations. I don't even know who mine was three generations ago. Some of us came down from Canada, my dad used to say. The others? Up from the Lower Peninsula, moving the Indians on along the way, I bet.

Benjy didn't feel like thinking about it anymore, so he buried himself further into the throw pillows and tried to finish his nap.

March

Because it had sold for a low price, other buyers of Willy's small cottage would immediately have replaced the siding with bright cedar shakes and the asphalt roof with a dark red standing-seam metal one. Then they would have gutted the interior, wired and plumbed it anew, installed a more efficient heating system, rebuilt the stairs to the bed and bath tucked under the eaves (and perhaps added a dormer window), put in thermal panes and blond hardwood floors and a contemporary kitchen and modernized the bathroom—all this to use the place as a weekend getaway from their hectic city lives. But Willy left things exactly as he found them, not only because he lacked the funds but because he preferred the house the way it had been conceived over a hundred years ago. His neighbors' hopes for upscaling were soon deflated, but aside from occasional greetings on the street, Willy hadn't pursued connections with any of them. They were seldom at home, because either they worked long hours or had primary residences elsewhere.

The seaside town was fast losing its native character, filling up with ex-urbanites. At least, they contributed to the tax base. Somehow, Willy never thought of himself as belonging to that crowd. "Are we locals now?" he asked his cat over supper. But no Midwesterner could ever become a townie, no matter how downwardly mobile. After all his restless years in Chicago (restless in a good way, he reassured himself), Willy was finding himself quite devoted to his quieter routine. Fewer joys? It was a puzzling transformation. He didn't seem to need constant company or the bustle of the city streets or, strangest of all, the warm touch of yet another male body. Was it only his age or had the pandemic's enforced isolation hastened the change? Willy had cleverly told Benjy that he was experiencing Covid's Metamorphoses. It took a moment for the pun to register.

But one especially windy night, having watched his news ladies (still required to report the continuing subversions of democracy), Willy was delighted to see his favorite Nick once again maintaining the cleanshaven look. He had just swallowed the last of his vegetarian chili with fresh Italian bread and Greek salad from the pizza shop when there came a light knock at his door. He knew it wasn't Benjy, who of an evening would always call first. Then he heard the scratching of a dog paw. He cracked the door open and there stood Maxim in his "Science" mask with Brownie on a leash.

"Out for her evening pee," the younger man said, pulling off his leather gloves. "I saw your light. Could we come in briefly and get warm if I keep my mask on?"

Elizabeth had immediately skedaddled up the stairs to hunker under the bed. Because he, like Benjy, had received the second shot, Willy could safely say, "What a fun surprise, sure, come in. Just keep Brownie, I mean Catherine, on a leash is all." So in they came. "Will you have a hot tea? Kettle's on. It's definitely blustery out."

Maxim entered, holding the dog under tight control. She sat by his feet after he settled on the far cushion atop Elizabeth's afghan.

"Unmask for the tea," Willy said. "May I give her a biscotto?"

"Better not, but thanks. I hope we're not interrupting. It's that I was out and didn't feel like going home quite yet, but I was getting kind of numb and saw your light. Nothing like a lighted window on a dark windy night! No worries, my wife and I are being very safe."

"And an old man like me is pleased to have some company." Willy quickly wished he hadn't called himself an old man. That was Benjy's term, but his own subconscious mouth had apparently armed him with a layer of platonic insulation against any unwonted impulses that might arise.

Maxim was soon warming up his thick-fingered hands around the steamy mug Willy presented him with.

"Milk? Lemon? Honey?"

"Black's how I like it," said the lanky man, long legs spread out enclosing the dog, his familiar running shoes dripping from having splashed through puddles. That didn't much matter, but too bad Maxim was in a baggy pair of woolen slacks and not his trim jogging outfit. Wait till spring, Willy told himself—shorts weather! Maxim pulled his black knit cap off his pepper-and-salt curls and set it on the middle cushion beside his leather gloves. He seemed to have something on his mind.

"What's the news from your kids?" Willy asked to show he took an interest.

"The boy's in Manhattan working from his one-room apartment in Washington Heights, and the girl's in DC in a nice group house near Dupont, so you can imagine what she's gone through. She'd been interning for our congresswoman, I mean from our former district. She wasn't at the Capitol that day, but still, you know, a father worries."

"And your wife?" (The de rigueur question, Willy figured.)

"Lisa's good. We both work too much. It's why I have to get out into the fresh air and, wow, that wind tonight! Lisa's not as claustrophobic as I am."

Willy automatically supplied a mental image of skinny PBS-Lisa on the News Hour to stand in for Maxim's wife.

The husband on the couch with his large devotedly panting dog then asked, "Are you eligible yet for the vaccine or is it still limited to seventy-five plus?"

"That's me," Willy said. "At the clinic I was never before surrounded by so many oldsters, and I was one of them! Eighty-one if a day."

"No! I didn't take you for that."

Willy was on the lookout for any indication of flirtatiousness but decided the young man of forty-seven was merely being respectful, so he said, "I'm in pretty good shape for my age. Maybe it comes from not having to worry about a wife and kids, though I'm sure they provide their rewards."

"A bit of both, I guess," Maxim said into his hot mug.

"I do worry, however, about my friends," Willy went on, "and that can be stressful. At least, the cat's no trouble.'"

"Oh, did my Catherine scare her off?"

"She hid out upstairs at the first whiff of canine. She looks after herself. It's what I appreciate about Elizabeth. We've given our pets normal girls' names, haven't we!"

"I think of her as a girl," Maxim said. "That nut-job Sharon with her doggie nicknames—Brownie!"

"Or Pokey," Willy added, enjoying the private irony. He was absorbing the sight of those angular features, the scruffy stubble so unlike his two smooth-cheeked Nicks, and those stretched-out limbs with one loving hand stroking the dog's brown fur.

"It's taking some adjustment, you know, empty-nesting up here in our new house."

Here comes a revelation, Willy told himself. He gave his visitor a coaxing glance with an encouraging twist to his lips.

"My father, at my age," Maxim began but stopped himself.

"Your father?"

"Well, he left the family. I was about to go off to college."

"That must've been tough."

"He had a bit of a drinking problem." Maxim was avoiding Willy's eyes by staring into his dog's adoring ones.

"That must've been tough," Willy reiterated.

"At eighteen! Talk about adult child of an alcoholic! You know the syndrome. We just want safety, security, steadiness. I do my best to hold it all together."

"You grew up around Boston?" Willy said to keep him going.

"Well, New Hampshire. I went to college at Michigan to get away from home. Ann Arbor? But after grad school I came back and brought Lisa, who's from out there. She loves New England. I hope the kids come back to Boston, though they're away for jobs now."

"I get the feeling you're going through something," Willy said.

"Thanks," said Maxim. "I sometimes need to talk. I realize I'm horning in on your peaceful evening."

Willy ignored that and said, "It happens I have a friend living down by the beach in an apartment above the diner. He's from Michigan, too. He should meet your wife. I'm from Chicago myself, got here only a year and a half ago."

"Oh, wow," said Maxim pensively, as though he hadn't quite heard. "We haven't made any new friends here yet. Lisa could use someone to talk to besides me."

"And I've known Benjamin for years, since our younger days." Willy decided it was the moment to put in: "We had a brief affair fifty years ago, if you can imagine such a thing. His partner died awhile back. He retired up here, and later he found me this little cottage for my declining days—nearby old friends."

"You don't look like you're declining much," said Maxim, again the flatterer.

"By this point," Willy said, "life is largely maintenance."

"Mine too," said Maxim. "It's why I go running, keeping in shape."

"Looking trim," Willy said but stopped short of adding anything particular about the strapping body at the other end of the couch. He patted his own tender tummy in contrast, though it really wasn't at all out of proportion for his age.

"I don't mean to take up your time with my issues," Maxim said. "It's just the ups and downs of being married, I guess. Well, I should get this beast back to her poop corner. You know, that's the only spot she'll use."

"I remember."

"You're a good girl," he told the dog and set his mug on the end table.

"She's an excellent guest. Stop by anytime, Maxim—Maxim, right? And Catherine, not Brownie, forget the Brownie."

"Lisa will be wondering where we've gotten to. But thanks, William. I still can't bellieve you're eighty."

"Eighty-one."

"Wow." He stood up and tugged Catherine toward the door.

"Don't forget your cap and gloves," said Willy handing them over.

"Oh, stupid me. Thanks, well, we'll see you around? When

spring comes maybe we can meet outdoors with your friend from Michigan. Lisa always says gay men are better at staying friends. She says straight men are terrible at it once they're out of college."

"We do try," Willy responded with a chuckle. Mentally, he was nudging Maxim further off limits, but then you never knew about middle-aged married men with what they call their issues, he told himself.

Meanwhile, in his third-floor refuge, to the tumbling of waves whipped up by the northeast wind, Benjy was making his slow way through a massive biography of Lyndon Johnson, who he'd long ago come to consider the greatest—though tragic—president of his personal historical period. Now that he was into the next volume, he could call up his own memories of the events recorded and had begun to dread the coming volume in which Becky would lose her Dennis in Vietnam. Back then, Benjy had taken a two-month leave from the Northwestern library and settled in with his sister and her little kids in Ontonagon. He'd wanted to be an attentive brother and uncle and do all he could to supply some of the love they were suddenly missing. He knew his efforts had been forever imprinted on those three little ones. No wonder, now in their fifties, they wanted Zoom sessions, even if the boys left it to their wives to schedule them. His divorced niece Carol, after her son went off to be with his dad, had loved Benjy's chatty letters. He knew that all those bonds had never faded, and to his delight, they had been passed on (runaway nephew aside) to the youngest generation, though they only knew Great-Uncle Ben and Great-Uncle Tom from their summer visits once they'd moved to Boston. It all went back to their grandmother Becky and how tough she'd had it when Grandpa Dennis died.

Reading on that windy evening had taken him through time to his first Chicago years and meeting Willy and beginning, gingerly at first, to open up to his whole family, though his parents didn't quite catch on and Becky had, for some time, seen Willy as only the lively pal who was good for her bookish brother. But to go see Benjy on stage in that play was merely her excuse to take a bus all the way to Chicago and show how grateful she was for his months in Ontonagon the year before and to reassure him, in person, that she was coping okay now and the kids were doing fine and Mom and Dad were enjoying their snazzy new ranch house up in Houghton and being no less busy in their retirement. Benjy had loved showing Becky the lakeside campus and his funky Uptown neighborhood and taking her on the El into the Loop. She had never been in such a huge city, and for the first time since Dennis's death she managed to appear almost happy again. Becky always tried to put the hardest things in the gentlest light.

Benjy could still picture her round-cheeked face glowing from the second row of the half-filled theater, watching him pretend to be a bearded Russian named Semyon Nikodimovich, a silent guest in the birthday party scene. He thought wistfully of how in Chekhov's plays people are always in and out of each other's houses in the country, talking and eating and drinking tea from the samovar and complaining about their lives. Despite the occasional suicide, there was something cozy about it, especially looking back now during the pandemic when you can't visit anyone and everyone is behind a mask. He remembered the Wood Demon's crusade to preserve the Russian forest. If he had only known what the coming century would bring! Benjy thought of the pine woods in the UP of his childhood, still standing and properly managed, he hoped. Home! That was where Becky always knew she belonged. She couldn't leave the kids with Mom and Dad for more than that one short weekend. He picked up the hefty Johnson volume again.

And then the phone rang. It could only be Willy unless—for

a second, he feared something had happened to his sister. She'd looked weary the last time they Skyped. But of course, it was Willy in a particularly jovial mood. "How late is it?" Benjy asked, because reading all evening had made him lose track of time.

"Only nine o'clock. You're not in bed yet."

"Just reading."

"I was catching up on YouTube. Were you listening to your music?"

"Schumann before supper. I prefer hearing the waves crashing out there only while I read. It helps me concentrate."

"What book?"

"Still on LBJ."

"I don't know how you do it," Willy said. "Now, Benjy, old friend, do you happen to remember last fall when I got into a chat in the woods with a young jogger?"

"Was I there?"

"By young I mean in his forties."

"I don't think you told me."

"I must've. He's the one with the brown dog that gets walked by that gal Sharon."

"I remember those big dogs."

"Anyway, the point is, he showed up at my door this evening when I was finishing supper. He had Brownie, but her real name's Catherine, and he wondered if they could come in to warm up."

"You let them in?"

"He had his mask on. He sat at the far end of the couch. Besides, I've had the shots."

"What about your cat?"

"She snuck upstairs."

"I can't believe you, Willy. You let him in and you've only met him once?"

"Actually twice. He was running by the cottage awhile back and saw me out filling the bird feeder."

"I get a feeling you're up to something," said Benjy.

"I promise it's merely visual. He's married to a girl from Michigan. I told him about you."

"What about me?"

"That you're from Michigan. And that we'd had an affair fifty years ago."

"You are so crazy."

"I didn't want him to think I was just some old grandpa."

"I'm sure you flirted up a storm."

"You know what I've always said about middle-aged married men. A little mid-life crisis, got to get out of the house?"

"Give it up, Willy."

"An old man can dream."

"So now you're an old man, too."

"But not a depressed one," Willy said.

"Then go to sleep and dream of your dog man. I've just gotten to the second Stevenson campaign. Good-night, Willy."

April

They were walking in the woods of early spring when Willy announced, "Today is the Buddha's birthday."

"How would you even know?" asked Benjy, lagging ten yards behind.

"For a week I forgot to flip the calendar, and then there it was."

"But Buddhists didn't use our months."

"Neither did Jews, but we all mark when Jesus was born even if it's wrong."

"All I know," Benjy said loudly enough to reach Willy's far-ahead ears, "is my own birthday's in July when I'll be your age for six weeks."

"I will always be older than you," Willy said, "or dead," and he let out a hoot at the not-yet-budding treetops. "By the way, I finally got around to making an appointment with a lawyer. You've been pestering me ever since I moved out here. Not that I have much to leave, but the mortgage is almost paid and, since you'd never live there, you could sell it."

"You're leaving it to me?" Benjy hadn't ever imagined Willy dying before he did.

"I'll leave it to PBS if you prefer."

Benjy was puffing along trying to catch up. The path was scattered with stones and fallen brush and moldy mulching leaves.

But Willy was neither waiting for an answer nor for his friend to catch up. "I wonder if we'll run into Catherine and her dad," he said.

"Who's Catherine?"

"Brownie! I told you her real name's Catherine."

"You're not still on that, Willy! Wait up. Come on, I don't want to stumble. We should've remembered our trekking poles."

So Willy stood still and looked about for signs of spring poking through the underbrush, lady slippers and frogs croaking in the vernal ponds. So far it had been a silent and gray morning, but with the clouds blowing eastward, soft sunny rays had begun to fall through the barren branches and brush against his face. When old Pokey reached him, he said, "Turn around into the sun, pal. Warmth from ninety-three million miles away."

It felt good on their skin. They both stood awhile bathing in it until Benjy said, "You'd better think seriously about your wishes. Tom left me with plenty. I appreciate the thought, but I'm more likely to leave something to you than you to me."

"Not since I'm your executor," Willy said. "Conflict of interest. I've got your power of attorney."

"And your name prints out on my bank statements and they won't let me take it off, but I can still leave you anything I want."

"You leave it to those kids in Iowa and Wisconsin or wherever they are. It's what long-lost rich great uncles do."

"I'm not rich."

"Comfortably-off great uncles, then. Your live-in insurance man's whole thing was gambling on how long his clients would live."

"I've told you a thousand times, Tom was in home insurance not life."

"Still, it's all a gamble, and there he was teamed up with a con-firmed tightwad."

"It's my upbringing" Benjy said. "You were raised too soft in the suburbs. We couldn't be, Becky and I. It sticks, even if now I'm better off than you."

"Then Becky's the one I'll leave my cottage to. I always liked your little sister." And on they walked.

Later, tiring from the ups and downs of the twisty trails, with sunlight shifting back to front according to the turns, they heard the galumphing of paws speeding their way. Suddenly, there were those three labrador-like dogs with Sharon shouting from behind, "They're friendly! They're friendly!" As she drew closer, she called out, "Oh, it's the two guys!"

Catherine, in her role as Brownie, was sniffing Willy's pants legs as if her nose had recognized him.

"That's Brownie," Sharon called from behind her pulled-on mask.

"I know her, she knows me." Willy had pulled his on, too.

"And Blackie and Goldie, the three stooges." Next, slowly down the trail, came a young man in a grease-stained padded jacket and overalls clumping along in floppy black-leather boots. "Hey, Fitz, it's the two guys. I told you about them." Fitz raised a hand in greeting but said nothing. "I figured we'd run into them." Fitz nodded, his expression trapped behind his Boston Bruins mask.

Benjy had backed away from the dogs carousing underfoot. He was having difficulty getting the elastic loops over his ears.

"This here's William and that's Benjamin, did I get it right?" Sharon said. "And this is the famous Fitz, guys. I got him out of the yard for once. He needs exercise as much as the dogs."

Fitz was shaking his head and nodding and mostly looking away, though he stuck a smudgy hand up once more in greeting.

Sharon was rattling on: "They were wearing those gray cable-knit sweaters out on the rocks past the harbor, so I thought they were fishermen not professors, or whatever they were. Enjoying retirement, guys? I can't imagine what it'll be like when I get there. What'll I ever do with all that time?"

"I could use some" came out in Fitz's deep voice, muffled as it was, so Willy gave a cheery laugh to bring him into the imbalanced conversation. He supposed Fitz was used to Sharon's volubility and maybe even liked the way it kept him from having to say anything. But Benjy was sensing the young man's discomfort around two old gay men, assuming Sharon had clued him in.

"So Brownie's owner isn't out on his run today?" Willy asked.

"We don't say 'owner' anymore," Sharon put in. "We say her dad." All the dogs had charged off, chasing each other, dodging tree trunks, bounding into nests of dead leaves. "Between you and me," Sharon said, "I think he's going through some marital shit. I shouldn't speculate, but—"

Willy crinkled his brow in concern to get her to say more. Benjy was looking in the opposite direction from where Fitz's eyes were squinting after the dogs.

"Usually, it's him I see when I pick up Brownie," Sharon explained, "but today it was her, I mean the wife, and she said he was going into the office more now, all that way, because, and this is what she actually said, I quote, 'We're driving each other sorta crazy cooped up here.' She meant the damn Covid, but I could tell it was more than that. You think?"

Willy decided to steer clear of this, so he said, "I hope Brownie's all right."

"Listen, dogs pick up the family vibe. She's more nervouser than usual. Guess what though, she just did a big poop on our walk. First ever! I think it's nerves."

"Maybe she's more relaxed?" Willy suggested as if to sound hopeful for the marriage.

"It's that she's feeling safer with me! That's my interpretation. Fitz didn't realize what a big deal it was when she did that poop."

"Big deal? Dogs poop," Fitz said.

"Listen, I know dogs. Maybe I'm the stable influence in her life now. Maybe Max and Lisa—that's their names—they're fighting all the time. Dogs think it's their fault, like children of divorce. I know from experience. I don't mean my own, I mean you-know-who over there." She pointed at her distracted husband, if that's what he was. She'd never made it clear.

"You get to know lots of people through their dogs," Willy said.

"Most are neurotic worrywarts," said Sharon. "This pup's got one problem, that one's got another. It doesn't bother me. I get dogs and they get me. It's between me and them. Right, Fitz?"

He nodded, but Benjy could tell he was ready to move on. So were the three dogs, who had circled back and congregated around Willy's and Sharon's legs with Brownie once again pants-sniffing. Benjy hoped they'd avoid his.

"Fitz has to get back or we could hang out more. Blackie's due back at noon, then Goldie—all right, guys, here's your treats—but Brownie's mom has me keeping her till two so she can get some work done. I can't wait to tell her about that poop!"

"Come on, Share," Fitz said in his low voice. He was already heading down the path in the same direction Benjy and Willy had been going.

"See you guys around," Sharon called and, at her fast pace, was soon out of sight.

Removing his mask, Willy said, "It's too nice to go home yet. Let's find a sunny boulder to sit on. I feel spring's finally on the way."

"There's plenty of cold still to come," Benjy reminded him.

They soon spotted off the path a large granite erratic with a smooth flat top and took seats side by side and pocketed their masks.

"Let's not talk about inheritances," Willy said. "It's finally a warm day. Let's soak it in."

"You've been saying 'finally' a lot lately."

"Have I? I get stuck on certain words. Nick used to say 'and so on and so forth' and it drove me nuts. Or 'at any rate.' 'At any rate, let's go out for dinner and so on and so forth.'"

"And you say 'let's' a lot, too," said Benjy.

"But remember when we could go out to restaurants? In Chicago, I was out on the town three or four nights a week, or over to friends, or they came to me, or movies or theater. But theater got so commercial, slicker acting but it cost a lot and the new plays usually stank. And after Nick, I'd still go with other friends or whoever, but all that's over. You and Tom were such homebodies. I bet you miss your old Beacon Hill apartment."

"Sometimes, but I couldn't have stayed there. It got hard to be where we'd been together. I've told you that."

"And you're happy enough here," said hopeful Willy.

"By now it's familiar. Besides, we used to drive up for seafood and the beach, so it's not as if Tom had never been here. He even dreamed of us retiring to a town like this. I can't believe he was still working part-time. He was one of those sorts, even getting on toward eighty."

"Our generation doesn't like to retire," Willy said. "We tell ourselves we're still too young."

Benjy was propping himself up on his arms, palms on the cool stone, but Willy had hunched over, elbows on knees. Each man was lifting his face to the sun.

"Frogs?" Willy said.

"You hear them?"

"Maybe it's a bird. There!"

"I don't hear a thing."

"But isn't it great, Benjy, to walk up from town into all this wild nature? You can't do that in a city."

Benjy hummed a brief tune (Brahms?) then suddenly said, "What's all this really about, Willy?"

"All what?"

"What our lives have really been about."

"I'm expected to answer that?"

"But is there," Benjy began and hesitated, "I mean, I suppose you might ask is there a story to our lives?"

"I trust you're not going philosophical on me."

"Maybe not a story," Benjy said. "I don't mean there's some symbolic meaning but simply a question of what it all adds up to."

"You're thinking of that Rumanian queen's jigsaw puzzle you told me about?"

Benjy considered for a moment then said, "I don't necessarily mean a finished picture—well, that too, but more a series of events, a story, one thing leading to another that makes sense."

"One thing generally does lead to another," Willy said. "So what? We're still here. It's the Buddha's birthday. 'Just be,' as they say."

"I looked up life expectancies in my almanac," said Benjy. "We've already beat the odds for American men—seventy-six-point-two. Covid's probably brought that down. Japanese men make it to our age—eighty-point-nine."

"But they have to live in Japan!" said snide Willly.

Benjy didn't laugh. He was thinking something through.

Willy pointed out, "We're already well past the biblical allotment of three score and ten. The rest is gravy."

"But what I'm wondering," Benjy went on, "is what's the—I don't really mean the story, but what counts? All the small things as well as the big ones?" He lifted his palms from the rock and brought his hands to his lap, leaning forward to match his friend. "All I do is read books and listen to music and take walks and write letters and eat and nap and spend lots of time thinking."

"I never get bored," Willy said. "When I have nothing else to do, I talk to Elizabeth."

"Sometimes, I still talk to Tom in my head," Benjy admitted.

"That's fine as long he doesn't start talking back."

Benjy gave him a frown because, in fact, he did like to imagine Tom's voice saying the things he used to say. Benjy clearly wasn't in the mood for jokes. He didn't know why he'd fallen into this dreary state of mind. Maybe it hit after they'd been interrupted by Sharon and that Fitz of hers, and those dogs leaping about and all her babble and Willy getting the skinny on his jogging forty-something-year-old.

"I'm joshing you," Willy said. "Sorry. Myself, I talk to the news gals on TV."

"We've never talked about actual death, Willy," Benjy said as softly as he could and still be heard.

"What's to be said? We could live another decade, even two."

Then Benjy had to ask, "Is it only a matter of everything simply coming to a stop and we'll never know what comes after?"

"And that'll be a great relief," Willy said in all seriousness.

"Yes, but it's getting harder to contemplate, don't you think? It used to be only a concept. Ever since Tom died, each year, it's been more and more real. History stops for each of us. We won't see the seas rising or storms proliferating or the heat getting unbearable."

What else could Willy say?

"But remember what your great-grandfather wrote for school about how cruel we white people were to the Indians. I know you're proud of him for saying all that and thought it'd cheer me up, but it only made me despair of humanity."

"Funny how, for me," Willy said, "my great-grandfather is only his words in his copy book. Did he imagine there would be a me someday? By his standards, he'd be horrified to know how I've turned out. See, you don't want to know how history goes after you're dead. Anyway," he added to change the drift of the conversation, "I thought you'd be glad I'm finally getting around to seeing a lawyer."

"There's your word 'finally' again."

"Sorry, pal. Do you want to walk on?"

"But you always mix Tom up with the actuarial tables. He was in home insurance!"

"Sorry, Benjy. Come on, you'll feel better if we start walking. I'll pick us up vegetable fried rice with tofu for Buddha's birthday. We'll go eat in the park if the sun's still out." He arose creakily and held out a hand to detach his friend from the slab of granite.

Later, when it was still light after supper and Willy had headed home, Benjy went for a meditative stroll on the beach with the tide slowly slipping out. He was trying to remember something comforting he'd written into his notebook after Tom died, something about Socrates. He'd come across it in one of the old Modern Library editions with the bendable covers that Tom had inherited from his parents, academic folks so unlike Benjy's own. That set of small volumes, with gold lettering on dark green spines, had been lined up on the mantel on Beacon Hill. In the empty lonely rooms, in his stunned and aimless meanderings, lost without his mate, sad listless Benjy had flipped randomly through those century-old books hoping to land upon some words of solace. He saw a pencil mark in a margin and a light scribble in what must've been Tom's father's handwriting that read: "death of Socrates." On the beach now, Benjy couldn't quite recall what he'd copied down, so he turned toward the stone steps to the street and saw Milly and Jack coming down.

"Isn't it wonderful, still light at this hour," Milly said.

"We got our first vaxes," said Jack, "but we still wear our masks, and I see you do, too. Good, we've all got to stay careful no matter what the Republicans say."

"I've had my second," Benjy said.

"But we can still be carriers," said Jack.

"Is this ever going to end?" Milly lamented.

"At least, there's serious smart normal people in charge again," said her husband.

Benjy waited at the bottom of the steps to let them pass, then with "Enjoy your sunset walk" he made his steady way up to his door, shook and dusted off his shoes on the mat, and went in to find what he'd preserved in his notebook back in 2016. There it was, quoted from a novel—if that's what it was—by Gabriele D'Annunzio, who presumed to represent the thoughts of Socrates on his death bed. Benjy, as a reader of history, knew how that proto-fascist, with his own band of Black Shirts, had taken the city of Fiume from the Austrians and ruled it as a dictator after World War One. Why do I always dwell on the awful stuff? Benjy asked himself. He had a tendency to let miseries creep in with no Tom there to snap him out of it. Unfortunately, Willy usually produced the opposite effect.

He found the right page and read what he'd copied down: "He felt that perhaps after all, there was nothing beyond, that his finished existence was enough unto itself, that prolongation in the eternal might be nothing but an appearance—like the halo of a star—produced by the extraordinary splendor of his humanity."

It seemed so long ago that those words had given him comfort. They didn't quite do so now. A halo of a star, yes, that was Tom, but that was all he was now, and his human splendor belonged to Benjy alone and would soon be gone forever. Tears were coming to his eyes, but when he had at last stopped crying, he felt somewhat better.

May

They hadn't left town in months, but it was full spring now, and Willy kept suggesting they rent a car to take a drive into the country, if only to see a different world. Despite politics and the pandemic and their hesitation and fears, they could set out on the road under their own power again. Neither needed a car to do the local shopping, and their doctors and dentists were in walking distance. If they needed a hospital, it was a short trip on the regional bus service, and there were ambulances if it ever came to that. Benjy's landlords at the diner took care of his garbage and recycling, and Willy toted what little accumulated (he composted and avoided plastic) in two canvas satchels the half-mile to the transfer station.

Benjy had resisted the road trip idea to the point that Willy was threatening to rent a car on his own because he was going a bit nuts. There weren't enough trails in the woods or back streets in town to explore anymore. It was all too familiar, which is what Benjy liked about it. But now an opportunity had come up: Benjy received an email from a former colleague of Tom's who had retired to an old farmhouse over the New Hampshire line. Isaac and his partner Jim were the other male couple at the company, a decade younger and much grander in style, but they were pleasant enough and once in a while it was fun being treated to an elegant dinner party with stimulating conversation among well-heeled middle-aged guests of various sexual orientations. Tom, who made as much if not more money than Isaac, had been brought up in dowdier academia and preferred a modest home life, but he rose to the occasion and made sure Benjy felt included.

But when Tom's old friends (Benjy's, too, he had to admit) invited him to come picnic outdoors at their "farm," it offered a chance to get Willy out of town. He called and got Jim on the phone. Because Tom and Isaac worked together (Isaac was in life insurance), Jim and Benjy were often relegated to spousal conversation. Benjy didn't mind Jim, a graphic designer of some description, and was always mildly amused by his name-dropping and brand-awareness.

"It's Ben. I got Isaac's email. Good of you two to think of me. I'm fully vaccinated now, and—"

"So are we! Isaac's doc got us in early. Had to use up some unclaimed doses. People are so irresponsible."

"I wonder though if I could bring a friend."

"Oh my god, you're seeing someone? There's hope for us all!"

"No, but he's an old friend from Chicago who moved out here. Well, we did once have a brief relationship, but that was fifty years ago."

"Flames can be rekindled," said Jim with a lilt in his voice.

"Not this one, I'm afraid, but you'll like Will. He's a retired newspaperman," Benjy added because Jim always needed to know what people did.

"For sure, bring him. Remember when you and Tom came to inspect after we bought this place? Just for weekends then. Now we're year-rounders, but we have a condo in Cambridge, not to become total hicks."

It was all arranged, and Willy was delighted. Meeting new people, especially gay ones, had been missing from his life. He couldn't subsist on the rare Maxim sighting. So now a week later, in a rented Kia Soul they were following Isaac's overly-detailed emailed directions on a sunny warm dry spring day. "What could be better!" singsonged Willy behind the wheel as evidence of human habitation dwindled and the road narrowed. One final turn and they sighted the promised bright yellow mailbox and pulled up to a long red-clapboarded and black-dormered old colonial house with a one-story kitchen wing leading to an open woodshed and then a blond-shingled barn, as yet unweathered. A coral-colored Crosstrek, adorned with Biden stickers, shone from its wide doorway.

Willy parked on the crunchy gravel, and out through the woodshed came two tall men, Jim now bearded and Isaac noticeably older than when Benjy saw him at Tom's memorial.

"It's been way too long," he shouted. "Ben, you haven't changed, man! Welcome, I'm Isaac and you're Will?"

"I'm Will," said Willy.

"And here's my mountain man Jim. Like his new look, Ben? No need for masks outside now that we're all safe."

"This is the first we've been out of town," Benjy said.

"First time seeing anyone else's mouth," said Willy.

"Things are getting better at last," Isaac said. "So come around to the deck. We're all set up back there. We've cleared the view now so you can see the mountain."

There was plenty to catch up on, as Isaac put it, but without Tom connecting them, Benjy felt strangely independent of those two blue-jeaned, flannel-shirted men settling down in the other pair of Adirondack chairs. Willy, however, was doing his fair share of the talking, starved as he was for fresh interlocutors. Their hosts were drawing him out equally eagerly. Isaac and Jim, maybe from their years in business, knew how to please new acquaintances. Tom had that skill, too. Benjy was always amazed at his genuine ease in social situations even though what he loved best was being home, just the two of them, where he could slow down and read and listen and be together. Benjy had provided a refuge, and Tom kept Benjy from retreating as he was always in danger of doing.

After admiring the sight of the purplish rocky heights of Monadnock rising beyond the gap in the pine and maple forest, the four had dived into the lunch (delicious, as Benjy had predicted it would be) elaborately set out on colorful plates and bowls in the sun on the low table between them. Willy kept spooning up dollops of garlicky hummus and spreading it on Jim's home-baked bread, and he sampled all the cheeses from a local dairy and scooped handfuls of almonds and speared with a toothpick the florets of cauliflower and spicy braised brussels sprouts. Benjy, meanwhile, tackled the rolled-up prosciutto with cream cheese and capers and the many other savory items.

"We hope you don't mind finger food," Isaac said. "It's simpler al fresco." And later, "More vino? You're doing the Pinot, Benjy?"

"I'm good," Benjy said because neither he nor Willy was much of a wine drinker. Tom himself usually had a German beer after dinner to mellow out, but beer made Benjy feel bloated, so he declined that, too.

They got talking about their travels, how great it used to be to hop on a plane in January and go somewhere warm or in August somewhere cool. "Didn't you and Tom always fly to some volcanic Caribbean island?" Isaac asked.

"A dead volcano," Benjy assured him. It was a resort of open-air cabins on the mountainside, very downscale and restful. The Dutch couple that ran it expected their return each year. They had sent Benjy a thoughtful note after Tom died. Of course, he had never been back.

"And you'd also visit your sister in the summer, right, and

Tom went to see his aging folks in Indiana. We've never been to the Midwest," Isaac added.

"I never much left Chicago," said Willy. "I relished my sweaty summers by the lake. I even appreciated the cold winter winds and snow."

"You're a heartier soul than I, man," said Isaac.

Then Jim explained how they liked to explore different destinations, the Azores or Northumberland, and in winter they'd head way south to Montevideo or Cape Town and once even New Zealand where it was high summer. "Don't make us sound so fabulous, Jim," Isaac put in. "It really isn't that expensive if you travel simply. But when," he groaned, throwing up his hands, "will we ever get to travel again!"

There was one touchy moment, after they'd polished off as much of the "finger food" as they could, when Isaac, who was suddenly determined to talk politics, said how gratified he was to watch good old Joe Biden in the Oval Office with that bust of Bobby Kennedy behind him, and Willy blurted out, "That carpetbagger, that clerk to Roy Cohn! I worked hard for Eugene McCarthy. Our theater did some major fundraisers."

Tactful Isaac, after a sharp glance from Jim, said, "We all had our causes in those days. But you have to admit Bobby came a long way."

Willy shrugged his shoulders, smiled, and the tension deflated.

"I was only eighteen when he was shot," Isaac said. "King, too. Jim here was, what, twelve?"

"I was twenty-eight," Willy said. "That whole year left one hell of a mark on me. It was the year we only did Brecht."

"You worked in theater out there?" Jim asked to be clear it wasn't Broadway.

"On the side. I wouldn't say worked because it was too damn much fun. Wasn't it, Ben?"

"Was that how you met?" Jim wanted to know. "I love first-meeting stories."

"Well," Willy began, as if deciding how much to tell, "this young Ben here, a year younger than me as you can plainly see—well, he was shelving books at the university library. That was in seventy, the year after we did Brecht's Chicago plays." He stressed the *Chicago* and went on: "*Saint Joan of the Stockyards*, *Happy End* with all those great songs, 'Surabaya Johnny,' I loved Lotte Lenya records—and then that surreal homoerotic play *In the Thicket of Cities*. We couldn't get the rights to *In the Jungle of Cities*, so we had a grad student do our translation and he preferred *thicket*. It's *Dickicht* in German, after all. That was our agitprop year."

Benjy could tell that even one glass of Pinot Grigio had loosened Willy's tongue. He worried his old pal was showing off to a detrimental effect, but Isaac was taking an interest and maybe the wine was helping. "You know a lot, man," he told Willy.

"But how did you two meet!" said mildly irritated Jim.

"Okay, so young Ben, the skinny shy librarian, helped me locate some plays for our next season."

"Will was sort of the stage manager after his day's work on the paper," Benjy explained.

"Because we were a co-op and barely scraped by," said Willy. "And there wasn't much money in a leftist underground weekly either." Benjy could tell he was enjoying making a distinction between their hosts' style of living and his own. "And our artistic director—you have to understand, I'm an entirely inartistic character myself—he figured we'd get more critical notices in the big papers if we gave local premieres of obscure plays by classic playwrights. We didn't always fill the seats, but it was a noble effort. Ibsen's *Love's Comedy* was a crowd pleaser, but Chekhov's *Wood Demon* not so much. I did manage to entice my reluctant friend Ben here on stage as a silent guest in a party scene. Those Chekhov plays are nothing but people in the country sitting around, as we're doing now, talking and squabbling over moral principles, the way I spouted off about old Bobby—"

Everyone gave a chuckle, and without masks it was possible to read the degrees of each other's smile. Benjy admired Willy's ability to retrieve good feeling after having committed a social faux pas. But he really should cut it short, now.

"And so you two were involved at that point?" Jim prodded.

"Would we have called it 'involved'?" Willy asked.

"I certainly was involved," Benjy replied, which elicited another set of chuckles.

"But to my discredit," Willy went on, "I eventually took up with someone else the way we horny boys did in those days. Still, we had a fun year, didn't we, Ben? I can't believe I got you pretending to be some old Russian in front of a maybe-not-quite-sold-out house."

"I preferred it backstage," Benjy said.

"Double entendre?" said Jim.

Willy didn't pick up on that. He was going on: "And Ben's little sister came down all the way from the shores of Lake Superior to witness his acting debut, didn't she?"

"She did."

"She'd recently lost her husband in Vietnam," Willy said, suddenly somber. Benjy feared the conversation might turn awkward again, but it didn't because Willy went on to the Shaw play and the bare-chested Hindu god with the bronzed torso, which intrigued Jim, but luckily Isaac, having drained his second glass of wine, stood to clear off. "Just sit, we got this," he said, passing the empty dishes and silverware and delicate goblets through the kitchen door to Jim, who'd popped inside. "And then we can take a post-prandial stroll around the property."

Which they did. Somewhere in the woods, on a path strewn

with pine needles, the delicately balanced political situation arose again after something Willy said about forests and climate change, and Isaac said he hoped the progressives wouldn't fuck up Biden's efforts to bring the country together, and now it was Benjy who gave a warning glance to Willy and made a zip-up-the-lip gesture behind Isaac's back. Jim had been leaping along well ahead.

When they returned to the house, Isaac asked if they'd feel safe coming in for a tour. "We're all pretty much immune, we're a bubble and you're a bubble—whoever thought we'd be talking about bubbles!"

"I'd love to see it again," said Benjy. "When Tom and I were last here, you'd only had the place a few months."

"I miss Tom," said Isaac. "Sorry, Will, but I'm glad you didn't stay 'involved' with this dear man here because then we wouldn't have had Ben and Tom in our lives. At the office, Tom was like my big gay brother. So come on inside. We've done a lot with the place."

It was the same sort of overly detailed account as Isaac's map directions. Benjy supposed that such attention to minutiae was what made Isaac a successful life insurance man. Tom, though not as obsessive, also took a carefully methodical approach to everything, which was reassuring for Benjy. Upstairs and down, even out to the woodshed and the recently re-shingled barn, Isaac gave all the credit to Jim's excellent design sense. Then, when they had regrouped on the deck and Jim brought out coffee "for the road" and his own crunchy lemon squares, the conversation turned again to the past.

"What happened to break you two up?" Jim asked Willy. "If you don't mind my wanting the other end of the story."

"Oh, after fifty years, who even remembers!"

"I bet you remember," Jim said to Benjy.

"Jim's shameless, isn't he?" said Isaac.

"Will was making it with the actor and his magnificent torso?" Jim guessed.

"And I was in the wings working the angel's pulley for the Judgment Day scene," Benjy said with a wry smile to seem a good sport about it.

Willy was clearly enjoying himself. He hadn't been the center of attention like this in well over a year. It was more delightful than spinning fantasies about Maxim because these events had actually happened. Don was real and not at all as vapid as the character he portrayed—well, Willy told himself, maybe a bit vapid, but what a body! This was the sort of fun stupid talk that Benjy never indulged in, and it was harmless, so why not!

The coffee had energized them all, and soon stories were flowing freely with Benjy and Isaac playing the raised-eyebrow sidekicks while Jim kept egging Willy on. After swapping stories of the early seventies (from Willy) and the mid-eighties (from Jim), the talk turned to the current young folks' locked-down year: All they were unable to do, how everything they saw and said and felt was largely virtual. "It's going to be a big adjustment," Isaac said, "to be together physically again. They'll be way out of practice. Hard for all of us, too, I imagine."

"But we know who we are now," said Willy, "and they don't yet. They've lost a full year of finding out. I sure didn't know who I was way back when."

The sun was now down to the treetops, and it was getting time to head home. There was much talk of "doing this again" and of their hosts making the drive to the seaside, not to lose touch—and fond words about missing Tom and of their pleasure in meeting Will and, even if they weren't "involved" again, Isaac was glad there was someone nearby to keep an eye on old Ben.

"At our age, that's enough," said Willy, thinking of Elizabeth on her afghan and his news gals and TV-Nick along with the

YouTubers he reserved for late in the evening—and of Maxim in shorts with his brown dog running in the woods on a summer day still to come.

"I like your car, Will," said Jim as they came around front. "It's so cute and boxy."

Benjy took it as faint praise. "It's a rental," he said. "Neither of us needs a car."

"But how do you get into the city, man?" Isaac wondered.

"There's the commuter train, but we don't take it. We may be vaccinated, but still—"

"Ben makes us stay careful," said Willy. And when they were at last on the road, he asked, "Did I talk too much?"

"They enjoyed you."

"Poor things, they didn't get to Tahiti this winter. Sob! But was I being too obnoxious?"

"Let's say they were good about not taking offense."

"I kept waiting for Isaac to start putting down the Green New Deal. I'd have slung it right back in his self-satisfied face."

"You were having a blast, Willy."

"Getting out and doing something different! Look at this beautiful day we've still got—windows down, breezes blowing. Did you and Tom see a lot of them?"

"Not so much. They had a big house over in Watertown."

"Tom must've made as much as that Isaac."

"Tom wasn't a spender."

"I never had the choice," Willy said. "No, but I had a good time today. And thanks for paying for the Kia. Thanks for dragging me along."

"I couldn't have stood it alone," Benjy said. "I'd have been remembering being there with Tom."

"But they mustn't come visit us! Your apartment's a third-floor walk-up and I live in a shabby little shack."

"They won't come. They were only being polite, Willy. I'll send a thank-you note and leave it vague. Don't worry."

"And we didn't even think to bring flowers, Benjy! We're simply not proper guests, man."

June

They were sitting, unmasked, leaning against the seawall, their pale bony feet digging into the sand. No dogs were allowed on the beach after Memorial Day, so there was no danger of Sharon and either her small trio or her large one showing up, or of Fitz, who was in his busiest season putting boats back in the water. There were a few dozen other beachgoers, some masked, some not, in a diverse array of summer dress: a number of bare but unremarkable male chests, lots of chubby ladies in one-pieces, a few lithe teenage girls in bikinis, and many screeching children.

Benjy and Willy were in their close-knit pod, or bubble as Isaac put it (he and Jim had recently sent a postcard from Yellowstone), but Milly and Jack had extended their own pod to include Benjy and Willy. Their balcony over the beach, a feature Benjy's apartment lacked, was too chilly after the sun went behind the building, so a few nights ago they had served the older men supper indoors, all vegetarian, having considerately asked about dietary restrictions. Benjy wondered why, before Covid, he had never gotten to know his downstairs neighbors because they had proved quite congenial and not the sorts to become intrusive. Willy had also established one particularly private pod with Maxim (sometimes with Catherine, sometimes not), but he was growing tired of hearing about his marriage issues. Even the sight of those supple thighs wasn't quite the compensation he'd imagined it would be.

But that afternoon it was just them, two old geezers, as Willy liked to say, with their slightly numb blue-veined feet burrowing into the cool sand and their craggy blotchy countenances (well-smeared with protective lotion) pitched toward the sun for the restorative baking effect. They knew better than to court such lethal rays, but who could resist the first true beach days when the ocean was as yet too frigid to swim in but the air was so crystalline you felt virtuous soaking it in?

"This morning I was reading up on the Four Temperaments," Benjy announced. "Renaissance medicine had a philosophical dimension. The imbalance of your bodily fluids may seem an absurd idea now, but in a metaphorical sense they were onto something."

"I'm totally ignorant of what you're talking about," Willy confessed.

"Well, you can picture it as a graph with two axes, positive–negative and active–passive. Didn't I ever tell you about when I went to consult a college counselor about homosexuality and he asked if I was active or passive and I had no idea what he meant. Anyway, this isn't about that. On the graph I'd place you in the positive–active quadrant. They'd have said you were sanguine with a preponderance of red blood."

"I should hope so," said Willy.

"Whereas I'm in the negative–passive quadrant, too much black bile."

"What the hell is that?"

"Actually, there's no such thing, but they called it being melancholic. Regular bile would make you choleric, negative-active, which means angry but energetically so."

"Like my two damn brothers."

"And my sister's more positive–passive, which they called phlegmatic, low spirited but benign, plodding along without complaints, always agreeable in a passive sort of way."

"You spend too much time thinking, Benjy. You should get out more."

"We're out right now." He stretched his arms wide as if presenting the scene to his crabby companion, who was crushing up the paper cups and sandwich boxes from their take-out lunch and stuffing them in the paper sack. The tide was low, and a few little kids were wading in and screaming then running back up the sand to their moms.

"It's going to be hell this summer with all the tourists coming back," Willy said. "We'll have to retreat to the woods."

"I forgot to tell you, Willy, with Becky flying out for my birthday, my niece Carol wants to come along to look after her mother and make sure she doesn't get lost changing planes in Detroit or making it to the train up here."

"I've never met Carol," said Willy. "That'll be fun. She's the divorced one?"

"She's a lot like her mom, but funnier. They can share my bed, and I can sleep on the window seat. But anyway, I know I think too much, but what I was pondering all morning was a puzzling question: why do I, who have plenty of money and a loving family back home and had a long happy life with Tom, why am I the melancholy one while you, who have only enough to squeak by and no family looking out for you and you've always been pretty much all on your own, why are you the sanguine one?"

"I had a delightful string of boyfriends," Willy gave for an answer.

"But if you and Nick, let's say, had stuck it out, even if you kept having fun times on the side, you'd feel more secure, wouldn't you? I know I'm being more me than you."

Willy had lowered his sun-bathed face to look straight out to sea. He pointed and said, "It's all that water out there. Doesn't it get to you, seeing it coming in and going out, over and over? It's what the lake used to do for me, all that water sparkling in the sun or growling in a storm or flat and silent under a full moon. I couldn't have been an inland person. I need that emptiness with no people on it other than the occasional boat passing by."

"What does that have to do with not having a steady boyfriend?"

"Enough of this, Benjy. You also grew up by a lake. You're not an inland person either. We just turned out differently."

"Maybe I'm not an inland person," Benjy said. "but sometimes, when the huge waves are pounding on the shore, I'm a little terrified. It's why I have my bedroom on the street side. It's not so bad when I'm reading, but not for listening to music. The headphones almost drown it out, but I can still hear the waves pounding out the wrong measures."

"Being up a few blocks I can't hear it, and I don't get as much of the wind off the water."

"I knew when I saw that dumpy little cottage in the hollow of the hillside that you belonged there."

"I still can't believe I made the move," Willy said. "A leap of faith, I guess."

Benjy pondered awhile. A pair of teenagers, girl and boy, was slumping past, ignoring each other as if they'd been having a fight. They were overdressed for the beach in sweatpants and long-sleeved T-shirts.

"And you?" Willy nudged him. "Why did you move up to the ocean?"

"After Tom died, maybe it seemed like a substitute for his living presence. On Beacon Hill, I was feeling sealed up once he wasn't there."

"I admit I can't know what it's like to lose someone the way you did, even if I did lose my whole dumb family once, but that was a happy thing."

"Maybe a relief, Willy, but not happy."

"Happy enough," Willy said, "but without them hanging

over me I soon became the totally sanguine fellow you know and love."

"And I was melancholy from the start," said Benjy. "It almost makes me believe in the Four Temperaments."

"No," Willy said, "you're just more attentive to the woes of the world instead of plunging ahead like me. I suspect we're the only people on this beach talking such analytical bullshit while everyone else is prancing about in the sun."

"It comes with age," Benjy said. "But I've always been the pensive sort. Becky will tell you when she gets here."

"And I've always been restless. Let's go get ice cream. It's time for dessert."

They picked up their shoes and the paper sack of the remains of lunch from the Beachfront where the same teenage girl—or was she the same?—had reappeared with the good weather. Willy dumped the garbage in the barrel at the top of the steps complaining how tricky it had become, standing themselves up from the sand, and they went and sat on an ocean-view bench to brush the grains from their soles and between their toes before putting on socks and Willy his topsiders, Benjy his loafers. Then they strolled into town, masked once again because there were plenty of passersby and it was still considered the civic thing to do.

The familiar-looking teenage girl greeted them at the ice cream window. She already knew that Willy would have Coffee Heath with hot fudge in a dish and Benjy would have a baby sugar cone of chocolate-vanilla twist, baby being what in his youth would have been a large.

"How did you know?" he asked the girl.

"Last fall you were regulars. Masks help me remember, your plain gray ones."

"Gray's our color," Willy said.

She gave them the 2021 discount card after punching it twice. "One free when you get to ten."

They went to sit at the wharf on a granite block near the rack of colorful rental kayaks with only a series of contented mmm's and ah's as they licked and spooned. When they had wiped their lips clean, they saw coming down the wharf the short figures of Milly and Jack who weren't yet sure who they'd spotted, but soon she gave a wave and Jack shouted, "Afternoon!" They took the perpendicularly-placed other block. "We're your pod," Milly said, "so we're removing our disguises. Hers read "BLM" in white on black and his bore the Celtics logo. "What have you been up to?" Jack asked.

Willy said, "I was planning on doing some yard work, not that I have much of a yard, but that damn knot-weed from next door is invading, and ivy is creeping up to my kitchen window. Also, I plan to put on a fresh coat of blue paint over the flaking gray shingles."

"Don't get up on a ladder, Will," Milly said.

"I wouldn't at your age," said Jack.

"Speaking of shingles, we've had our shingles shot now, as well," Milly said.

"Willy hasn't yet," Benjy said.

"But I can at least paint the first floor," Willy put in, "and I've got a young fellow who's volunteered to climb up and get the peak."

"Young in his forties," said Benjy.

"We're glad to have no maintenance worries, right, Ben?" said Milly.

"That's why I rent," he said. "In Boston, it was the condo association that had to come to a consensus. It drove us crazy."

"After all our years in Arlington," Jake said, "with too much grass to mow and too many leaves to rake and snow to shovel, we swore never again. Our son's in a high-rise because he grew up hating to mow and shovel and rake. The younger generation's big on low maintenance."

"They don't yet realize that at our age most of life is maintenance," said Willy.

"Not much for that cozy little house of yours, though," Jack said. "But trim those bushes in front before they get leggy."

"It's a charming place," said his wife.

"I'm all about charm, aren't I, Ben?"

"It gets him away with a lot," said Benjy.

Milly was swinging her short legs against the block of granite, her sunny smile shining forth. "Isn't it a comfort to have an old friend who's known you forever, Will?"

"I'd say he knows too much."

"How was the ice cream?" Jack asked.

"Too expensive but worth it," said Willy. "Tourist prices!"

The four of them chatted on about out-of-towners till Benjy mentioned the initials on the mask dangling under Milly's chin. "Isn't it surprising," he said, "walking around this nearly totally white-people town and seeing all the Black Lives Matter signs and those colorful ones about science and gender and welcoming immigrants—you know the ones. I wonder what Black tourists, and there have been some, make of those signs."

"They're put up by the Unitarians," Jack said, "and probably some Congregationalists. Maybe even the Catholic priest's pushing them. I doubt it's the Chamber of Commerce, but you never know. I'd imagine tourists of color will feel safer, won't they?"

"But you don't necessarily feel safer when you're a rarity any more than if you're taken for an entering wedge," Benjy said.

"He always sees the downside," Willy explained.

"But true, there's more racism in rural areas," Milly pointed out. "In any case, I'm all for those signs. The America I love is showing up again. My parents, you know, left the Soviet Union when I was only two."

"You were actually born in Russia?" Benjy had had no idea.

"Can't you tell? Milly's short for Ludmilla. I'm sure you know Glinka's overture to Russlan and Ludmilla. I hear your classical music sometimes in the stairwell."

"I'm sorry, I try mostly to listen on earphones."

"Oh no, I love it. Of course, my husband's an old uncultured Bostonian still trying to lose his accent. You can catch him on words like 'sports' or 'warm' or 'weird.'"

They went on with their family histories. It turned out Milly and Jack also had one daughter. Willy contributed his suburban upbringing of no interest even to himself. Then, Benjy told of his sister and niece coming out from Michigan for his birthday next month.

"Seventy-five, seventy-six?" Milly wanted to know.

"Eighty-one!"

"No, you can't be."

"I'm eighty-one already," said Willy, "eighty-two after Labor Day."

"You're both such admirable specimens," said Jack.

"Will they be staying with you? Because," Milly proposed, "we go off to Vermont in July and you could put them up in Number Two. They could sit out on our balcony and have the guest room twin beds. They would air out the place. We hate leaving it shut up all month, and our daughter has no use for it, she's such a city girl."

The offer was enthusiastically accepted. Benjy wouldn't have to go sleep on the window seat with the waves counting off the hours.

Jack and Milly decided to go and get some ice cream for themselves, and Willy and Benjy went the other direction, threading through the weekend crowd that was spilling into town where the shops had at last opened again and the restaurants were serving on improvised sidewalk patios with reduced capacity indoors for the fully vaccinated. Benjy ducked in alongside the diner and back to his entryway, and Willy tramped on up the slope to his cottage under the hill, where he found Maxim (and Catherine) sitting on his stoop.

"I was about to give up," said the dropper-in.

"I was getting ice cream. What a day, isn't it, Catherine!" Willy patted her brown furry head and stroked under her somewhat slobbery chin.

"Lisa and I are so much freer now. It's been two weeks after our second shots. Even the kids have gotten their firsts. They can come visit next month. So what about that paint job?"

Willy promised he'd be getting around to it but Maxim really didn't have to—he surely had plenty else to do—but no, said the younger man, it was the least he could contribute after dumping all his problems and receiving such great counseling. So Willy invited him and the dog in for iced tea from the tall pitcher in the fridge. Elizabeth made herself scarce up the stairs but snuck a peek or two from under the bed. Maxim was in rather clingy running shorts and sockless tennis shoes, and that was enough to focus Willy's interest. He also did take some pride in passing on his store of wisdom to the rising generation.

Benjy had closed his unlocked door and felt a sudden rush of fatigue. He had intended to get back to reading the heavy tome he'd borrowed from the town library called *The Modern Construction of Myth*. Fascinating as it was, once he'd lain down on the window seat and dived into the small typeface for a few pages, he felt the book, of its own accord, descending to his chest and his enervated hands folding together across it and his eyelids drooping to a close. The distant lapping of waves and the fading squeals and shouts from the beach down there sent him off into an immediate deep slumber.

An hour later he awoke from his nap, half of him still in a vivid dream. He'd been out in a dark forest and come upon what was more like a river than the trickling brooks he and Willy had to hop across on their springtime walks. Sharon was standing on the near bank with a dog that looked like Brownie (or was it all three dogs?) and she was tossing sticks into the river for them to plunge in after, and over on the other bank he thought he saw Tom in the dim sunlight filtering through the canopy of leaves but didn't quite dare check, and when he couldn't help but turn to see for sure, it wasn't Tom at all but that silent Fitz who waved a hand, not in greeting but in farewell.

Benjy woke up, the picture still in his mind's eye. He asked himself, perhaps out loud, "What will I ever do without Tom?" before he was fully aware of where he was.

July

Willy was sitting beside Benjy's niece Carol on the second-floor balcony, late enough on a hot day for the shade to have encroached even down to their toes. They were giving Benjamin and Rebecca (wry-humored Carol's names for them) a chance to have the undisturbed brother-sister talk they obviously needed. So the other two were now having a private chat of their own.

"My dad named me for Carol Burnett, if you can figure that. He apparently used to crack up over her show. Thinking about it probably kept him happy in Vietnam. And I've ended up looking like her."

"I don't see a resemblance," Willy said. His baggy swimming

236 | JONATHAN STRONG

trunks and sagging T-shirt were slowly drying out, and the effect of that loins-chilling dip in the sea had completely worn off.

"I have her chin," said Carol, "and I can do her drooping-one-eyelid thing, see?"

"So you can."

"I never knew my dad. I was only three."

She was tall like her uncle Ben, raw-boned she'd say, gawky and hearty in a North Woodsy way. Willy knew that the death of her father and the departure of her son Bob to go live with her ex-husband out west must lie behind her self-deprecatory sense of humor.

"I keep trying to get Mom to give up her crappy house in that development and come up to Houghton with me. I've got my grandparents' place, and if she moved in, it will have housed four generations if you count little Bob's first dozen. My brothers think of it as the family homestead. It's where we have holidays. Their kids have sweet memories when they were tiny of visiting the great-grandparents. Oh, they all took pity on me after the big Bob took off, so I got the house. With that loser out of my life, I figured I'd have better opportunities in Houghton than Ontonagon. But puberty hit and little Bob got to throwing his selfish fits and had to storm off after his dad. I'd be surprised if they weren't in some militia out in Washington State. East of the mountains, that's rebel country. Well, the UP isn't much better, but we have our summer crowd to keep us half decent."

"You're not in contact at all?"

"Nary a peep. I truly screwed up as a mom. I had to do it all, and who appreciates that in a woman? I should've been a cut-up like Carol Burnett, but I had to be the disciplinarian. That kid was a handful—like father, like son. And now I've got to keep old Rebecca under surveillance. But she won't move. She needs her distant view of the lake, and I'm in the middle of a town. She's getting to be a chore."

"She seems great to me."

"Because she's here with Benjamin. They go way back. He's part my dead grandpa to her and part dead Dennis, part even of her sons, my big and little brothers, and she loves Benjamin as if he's all of them wrapped up together."

"How are your brothers, Carol? Do you get to see them?"

"They'll be up next month when it gets too sticky down in the farmlands, and they do come home for Christmas, at least one of them does because they have to alternate with their wives' families. Dennis Junior's the one in Madison, and Wayne's in Iowa City. How did stupid me ever get brothers working at universities? I only made it through one year at Northern Mich."

"You had a lot to cope with, Carol."

"That came later. But what did I know? I married right out of high school. Rebecca was ripshit."

"You've held it together pretty well."

"I still like my work and my gal pals at the office, and I've got the house spruced up. Denny and Wayne don't begrudge me for it. They like me keeping the home fires burning."

"But you do worry about your mom."

"See, she hopelessly wishes Uncle Ben will come live with her so she can look after him."

"And he can look after her."

"Maybe, not that she'll admit it. I don't know what she'd do if anything happened to him. I mean if he died before she did."

"Your uncle has been worrying about death a lot lately. He's perfectly healthy for his age, but he thinks too much. He may be the slowpoke on our walks, but I'm the creakier one. Ben's one of those steady types that don't much change. He's got the soul of a philosopher, always studying. He keeps writing down quotations for me. It's the archivist in him. Lately, it's been death, bits of wisdom about its meaning or lack thereof. He's putting the pieces of his life together."

"Because there's no Tom anymore," said Carol with a sigh.

For a couple of minutes they sat quietly contemplating the smooth line of the horizon fifteen miles off shore.

Carol was wrapped in a bright yellow terrycloth bathrobe that must have been Milly's because it was short on her. "He's got it good out here," she finally said. "I don't ever see him leaving. Mom knows that. She worries about him way too much. She's super grateful you moved near him, though. She always talks about you as his best old friend from his early Chicago days before he met Tom. She didn't know about his orientation yet. Is that what we call it now? But she met you at the play he was in, and she appreciated how you got him out of the library to have a little fun for once. If you don't mind my asking, didn't you two have a thing back then?"

"Now it can be revealed," Willy said, a tinge of red blushing up his neck to his jowls. "But it was short and sweet. I don't think Becky even knows."

"I figured. And then Tom came along."

"A much better match," said Willy without accounting for much. "I was a kind of transition, for him at least. My life was nothing but transitions back then."

"So why did you move out here after all these years?"

Willy was finding it strangely comforting to be asked such questions. Carol was the right person, not as close as Becky and of a generation more used to confidences, so he said, "One day he wrote me about the old fisherman's cottage for sale. I was turning eighty. Chicago was too much for me. It's not like we hadn't remained friends over the years. I'd go for suppers when he and Tom lived in Lincoln Park or we'd take a picnic to the lake. They were a solid anchor in my footloose life. Unlike you, I didn't have much of a family. The theater wasn't solvent enough to keep on after another year, so I threw in with the newspaper, full-time. Fifty years later, though, I still miss doing plays. Behind the scenes, I mean."

"I'd have figured you for a real actor," Carol said.

"Oh no, underneath I'm shy as hell."

"I wonder what they're talking about upstairs right now."

"Have we given them enough time?" Carol asked. "It's almost supper hour. After the big birthday bash I'm all cooked out."

"You're off the hook. Uncle Ben's taking us to that high-end place with the patio by the harbor."

"I won't say no," said Carol, "but I could always warm up the leftovers." Willy shook his head. "Then, I'd better go shower and get rid of this salty feeling. I'm a fresh-water person. The ocean makes me sleepy."

Willy stayed on the balcony, enjoying the view of sea and sky from this new angle. But he soon began filling his head with images of Maxim on the ladder with the can of sky-blue paint and splotches on his arms and chest, bare because it had been hot that day, and though he was no bronzed Don, he had an appealing build for a man in his forties, chest hairs graying but youthfully trim at the waist, and those ratty sneakers and flimsy running shorts left the rest to an old goat's memories of livelier days.

Up in Number Three, at either end of the padded seat below the picture window, sat Benjy and Becky, bolstered by throw pillows, her bare feet tucked under and his stretched out almost touching her bent knees. Now and again, she'd give his toes a tickle. They had been talking about everything. Or that was what it felt like. They had gone over in full detail the lives of junior Dennis's family in Wisconsin and Wayne's over in Iowa, updates on all the offspring, especially the engineering girl who had so appreciated her great uncle's letters. "It's how much you mean to all those kids," Becky had said. "You may not realize it, because they're not good at reciprocating in kind, but you're a guardian spirit to them almost as if you're not made of flesh and blood. You could say they take you for granted, but it's bigger than that. It's a touch of something they can't know about yet. Listen to me, talking like an English teacher!"

Benjy had told his sister how much he missed the kinds of talks they used to have in high school, senior and sophomore, shy and studious and unpopular and hardly noticed by the cool crowd. Now they were going on to talk about her own Dennis and his Tom. She did not resent Benjy's long coupledom because, she said, loss is loss whenever it occurs and she had her children and Mother and Dad right there, whereas he had found himself suddenly alone in a distant city with no one who knew him from his youth. That led them to talking about Willy.

"Whatever happened to his theater career?" Becky wanted to know.

"Career's hardly the word. You saw the peak of it. They spent too much money on the next show, flying an angel in from above and constructing a Hindu temple. The affair I wrote you about didn't last much longer, either. We were and still are such different sorts."

"So were you and Tom."

"But we had the right balance."

"So did Dennis and I when we had the babies, one, two, three. Wayne never even saw his father, and Denny barely remembers him. Carol says she has a feeling about his being there but can't put it in words." She gave Benjy's left foot a prolonged squeeze.

After their swim, they had dressed for the heat, Becky in a flowery bright muu-muu that concealed her pinkish plumpness and Benjy in a pair of light linen pants and a striped short-sleeved jersey such as he'd worn every summer of their teen years. Becky's fluffy hair tinted golden and Benjy's gray, relatively ample for a man just turned eighty-one—both shone in the light reflected off the still sunny sea, which was all they could observe beyond the glass without leaning close to spy down on the beach and the late-afternoon bathers.

"You and Tom, Dennis and I," Becky began, "we were two fine pairs, like Mother and Dad, and my boys have been lucky, but it's Carol I worry over. She can't turn to either big or little Bob for any consolation. She keeps putting herself down, being the comic, I know, and she's coping, and her office-mates make a big difference—she does have a jolly social life, but there are too many single or divorced or widowed middle-aged women up in Houghton. She wants me to move in with her so she can take care of me. Frankly, it's she who needs the company." Becky pointed out the window. "See, we both have places near water. I wish it could be the same place, Ben, but I understand why you need to stay here. It's as if you're still with Tom." She looked carefully over at her brother, right into his eyes. "Isn't it, Ben?"

"I feel suspended here, in between. It's the music he and I heard together that's still in my ears, the books we read aloud, the meals we ate, the bed we slept in. I suppose it's my private myth. I've been reading a scholarly book about how the modern world had to invent the concept of 'mythology' for what the ancient Greeks took as truths, as a deeper sense of reality. Lots of their stories are about death, aren't they? Orpheus trying to bring back Eurydice or those nymphs Apollo turned into a laurel tree or pan pipes or the Great Bear in the night sky. I once copied out from one of Tom's books something the dying Socrates was supposed to have said." He stretched his feet out to tickle Becky's pudgy hip with his toes like a bothersomely affectionate older brother.

"What about Socrates?"

"Oh, it had to do with what's left of us when we're gone and that it's only an appearance, like the halo around a star, if I remember it right. I wrote it down in my notebook."

"That's how you see Tom? Maybe it's how I still see Dennis."

"But Dennis died so young and in a terrible war, and Tom luckily died with morphine keeping him comfortable and me at his side holding his hand even if he couldn't speak or even be sure it was me. I'm sorry, Becky, for having witnessed a better ending."

"Death is still death, Ben, and we'll never see them again."

"But all your years alone, and I've only had five—"

"Years are only years. It's not a matter of how many."

"But it is."

"No, I sometimes think they might as well be one same day, one same year. Not that time doesn't pass, but that one moment never moves. Past, future, it's all one thing. I've come to think so anyway."

"How have you done it, Becky?"

"There's always been something accepting about me. Don't ask me why. I find myself just going along."

"While I'm, well, the word I've been using lately is melancholy by nature. Wasn't I always like that back home?"

"I'd have called you pensive, in your head a lot. I could almost see your thoughts rumbling around inside. Maybe it had to do with your feeling you were inclined to love the wrong people, you know, the way things were in those days."

"Who knows how it starts," Benjy said. "Don't worry about me, though. You've got Carol to worry about."

"And she worries about me. But I'm not moving to Houghton!" Becky announced with cheerful decisiveness.

"And I'm staying right here," said Benjy. "But I'll visit, I promise."

"I'm just glad Willy's up the street. He's my spy. And I suspect he's even gladder to have you here."

"Speaking of Willy, what are he and your daughter up to downstairs? I don't want her doing any more cooking. I'm taking you all out for a big dinner by the harbor."

When they had joined the other two, Benjy said he hoped

they hadn't been bored. "Bored!" exclaimed Willy. "We've been having what an old Jamaican boyfriend of mine used to call a heavy-heavy. The things I've learned about you two!"

"I trust," said Carol, "that Rebecca and Benjamin have done enough sibling bonding that we can talk about more happy things like the pandemic and racism and the economy."

"Very droll, Carol," said her mother.

On the way to the restaurant, where Benjy had thought to reserve a table at the water's edge, they were walking two abreast down the busy sidewalk, politely masked despite the prevalence of visible mouths and noses on other pedestrians, when they nearly bumped into Willy's jogger, unmasked, and what could only be his wife Lisa, who looked nothing like PBS-Lisa. She was rather chubby and had a bright self-assured smile.

"So you're the mystery gal from Michigan!" Willy said. "And here are my Michigan friends. You remember hearing about my old pal Ben, Maxim? His sister Becky and niece Carol are visiting from the Upper Peninsula."

"I'm from Petoskey!" Lisa nearly shrieked.

"Top of the Mitten," Benjy explained to Willy.

They all stepped off the sidewalk to get out of the way. From behind their masks, they exchanged stories of home and hit on remarkable coincidences. As a kid, Lisa had spent family vacations at a resort on Trout Lake and splashed in Tahquamenon Falls, and she and Maxim, in college, had gone climbing and camping in the Porcupine Mountains. They'd all even patronized the same Dairy Queen in Marquette. "I transferred from there to Lansing," Benjy offered. "And we two met in Ann Arbor," said Lisa. "I only made it through one semester in Marquette," Carol threw in, "and then I went and married the wrong man."

Benjy was worried they'd be late for their reservation. It took a series of well-wishes and good-byes and hopes of meeting again: "How long are you here for?" "Only the rest of the week." But

Willy helped move them along, Willy who had at last seen the woman about whom he knew too much, and yet there she was, and the two of them were trying to work it out. Love's comedy, he thought. "But where's Catherine?" he asked over his shoulder as they went their separate ways.

"It's too hot for her," Maxim yelled back. "She prefers staying home in the air-conditioning."

Willy was pleased to note a few remaining smudges of sky-blue paint on the splendidly tight T-shirt the young man had nonchalantly peeled off halfway through the job when he got to the sunny side of the house. For once it was Willy who had to speed up to join Benjy along the sidewalk, crowded with out-of-towners.

August

They were in the deep shade of the woods. They made a point of walking some distance every day, however hot it was, but July had ended so rainy and cool and depressing, and now the continuing Republican obstructionism wasn't helping Willy's mood. The climate in DC had even broken through Benjy's defensive armor, and he was paying attention once again.

Ahead lay a fork in the trail, blue markers to the left, yellow to the right, so Willy waited for Benjy to catch up on his poles. When they could stand side by side and consider which path to take, to his old friend's surprise, Willy said, "I want my ashes scattered in these woods."

Benjy took a step back to take in Willy as a whole. "It's come to feel like home to you then? Where you belong?"

"It's where I'm ending up. It's as good a place as any I'm likely to find, far from the evil ways of the world."

Benjy felt some satisfaction at having brought him here. "And as for me," he said, "I'd like my ashes tossed into the ocean. It's where Tom's are, except for the half that went to Indiana with his sisters."

"I didn't know," Willy said. "How did you manage it?"

"It wasn't me alone. One of his colleagues had a sailboat. We went out of Nahant and up the coast. Not that I felt it helped, but the insurance company wanted to do something for me. It's what they came up with. I appreciated it."

"I'll be gone first," said Willy, "so I won't be able to do it for you."

"You won't be gone first. I will."

"Neither of us has a thing to say about it, Benjy. So let's just follow the blue markers to the swampy place and look for pitcher plants."

They encountered no one on the trail, no Maxim, no dogs. It was a particularly silent summer morning. Down the slopes, deeper in the trees, there wasn't even a hint of distant traffic or any birdsong.

"Hold up, Willy!" Benjy had to shout when he lost sight of him around a bend.

"I may not be as speedy these days," said the pathfinder, "but I don't like to dawdle. My feet get itchy."

When they had stepped onto the rotted-out narrow boardwalk that the scout troop had constructed through the low wetlands, Willy went hunting for his favorite plant. He was like a city boy just discovering the wonders of nature. When he spotted one in reach, he didn't touch it but squatted to inspect it up close and see if it still held any water after all that July rain.

"Don't tip over, old man," Benjy warned. Hands on knees, Willy creaked his way up with Benjy standing close to steady him if necessary.

It was a long, slow trudge up and over the hills on their way back. They made it to the final crest with its view over the roof-tops of town to the ocean's horizon that somehow appeared to rise higher than the land. Of course, given the earth's curve, it was in truth incrementally lower. Fifteen or so miles hardly accounts for the planet's roundness.

"You have to stop forgetting your trekking poles," Benjy said. "They really do help. Want to use mine for the downhill?"

"I like swinging my hands free."

"And then you slip and fall on some sharp stones and I have to run for rescue."

"Run?"

"Or walk very fast."

"You could fall as easily as I could," Willy said.

"That's why I remember my poles."

Squabbling, they descended the paved road into town and, at the crossroad, turned toward Willy's freshly-blue cottage so they could collapse with glasses of lemonade and whatever else could be rustled up.

Willy had taken Jack's advice and clipped back the privet out front and weeded the grass between the bricks of the path to the door. Elizabeth sat eyeing their approach through the window screen, and when they stepped inside, she hopped off the back of the couch and strutted directly into the kitchen, meowing and whipping her tail.

"Yes, lady, sorry I'm late. You'll get your liver and egg."

Benjy sat, tuckered out, on what had become his end of the couch, knowing he would be of no help in the kitchen. Willy quickly assembled meals for both his cat and the old codgers, as he now called the two of them: rye crackers spread with goat cheese, applesauce from tangy Bancrofts, one ripe Bosc pear each, and a sort of organic cookie plus some raisins and nuts. It wasn't Benjy's idea of lunch, but the lemonade made it go down easily. It was good to be sitting, even if Elizabeth, after gobbling her food, had come to stare at him and eventually insisted on crawling onto his lap.

"Cats aren't like dogs," Willy said. "Dogs know instinctively who loves them and are all over you. Cats can tell who isn't especially fond of them, and that's who they go for."

"I'm getting used to it," Benjy claimed. He noticed on the side table that Willy hadn't yet re-shelved his great-grandfather Albert's high school copy book that he'd returned weeks ago. It was peeking out from under a sloppy stack of magazines. Benjy had read the whole thing as a document of history—tales of hunting squirrels and shooting ducks and rowing on a river, but of more interest was the long report of Albert at seventeen standing guard over a boat full of southern prisoners of war heading down the Mississippi to Vicksburg for an exchange with wounded Union troops, all Americans but sworn enemies. It had affirmed Benjy's hopelessness for the future. No one ever learns anything. Greed and self-aggrandizement rule the day. All the science in the world can't put us on a better track because no one really wants it to. It's only getting worse now with this Delta variant and those damn Know-Nothings refusing masks and vaccinations. We're doing it to ourselves again, as we always have.

If he said any of this out loud, Willy would jump in with predictable sanguinity, praising Biden and Harris and Secretary Pete and the whole crew, though even Willy was finding it harder to keep the faith and mostly kept his spirits up for Benjy's sake. How lucky that Tom had died believing Clinton would be the next president. What Benjy said now was: "Your great-grandfather's book here reminds me how recent our own history is. When Becky visited, we got talking about our grandparents, and then about our parents and us and her kids and her kids' kids, and I realized how that's five generations right there! You take my grand niece, the engineer: so for her, my own father is her great-grandfather. She's in the same relation to him as you are to the boy who wrote those papers for school before the Civil War. And young people now see World War Two when we were born as ancient history. Even Vietnam! Do they have any idea how quickly it all goes?"

"They don't," Willy said, "and neither did we at their age. It's better that way."

"But no one learns anything!" Benjy moaned, and then: "Could you coax this cat off my lap, please? She's digging her claws into my pants."

"Here, pussycat, cookie?"

Elizabeth yawned and then slowly made her way onto the arm of the couch toward the dangling crumbly treat.

"Is that good for her?"

"No, but there's something to be said for her quality of life."

"There is indeed."

"We've had it, haven't we, Ben?" He only called him Ben when he was getting serious. "We're so unbelievable lucky. Compared to most of the world, we've landed on our feet. Doesn't that fill you with some joy?"

"Or some sadness for other people."

"Ah, so you're an armchair Marxist like me."

"At heart, I guess," Benjy said, "but Marx was hopeful for the future and thought we could improve everyone's life."

"And so do I," said Willy and added, "Emphasis on the could."

Benjy gave him a closed-mouth frown and a sharp shake of the head.

"Now let's not give in to the urge for naps yet," Willy said with sudden vigor. "Let's saunter out to the rocks above the harbor, and we can stop for ice cream on the way back. We should make the most of this day."

After he had piled their few dishes in the sink, they set out, careful of the door because the one anxiety Willy was unashamed of was that Elizabeth might somehow slip out into the wider world, a place she knew only through windows. She could disappear for good, perhaps flattened by a car or eaten by a coyote in the woods. Willy worried about his cat's life more than his own.

The rocky headland was catching a strong breeze from the northeast. They hadn't felt it in town but decided to brave it anyway because it was warm enough and bracing. At last, they took their seats, side by side, on Ruth Brown's memorial bench.

"I feel protected sitting here," Willy said, "as if I, too, will live a hundred years."

"You're being superstitious," Benjy quibbled.

"What about you, wanting your ashes mingled in the vast ocean because that's where you think Tom is?"

"It was a sentimental gesture that his work friends suggested."

"Bullshit," said Willy, "it meant something to you."

"I can be sentimental," Benjy admitted. "It doesn't mean I believe in magic, but it's what I do get from certain pieces of music, a comforting feeling of sadness and happiness both together. I was listening to Schubert's B-flat sonata last night. The first movement especially does it to me. Surely you miss people, Willy. A person doesn't have to die to be missed. What really happened between you and Nick? You must think about him. I only met him that once when Tom had a conference back in Chicago and we went out with you two for lunch. I'd hoped you'd settled down at last."

"We won't go into all that on this beautiful day in this bright fresh air," Willy declared.

A sharp gust caused him to grab the brim of his cap, the green one Becky had brought him from the Porkies, oddly with a black bear on it, not a porcupine. She had given Benjy one, too, but he seldom wore it because he didn't want them to walk through town looking like a pair of weird old twins.

"Enjoy it now because we may soon have to go back everywhere to masks," Benjy said loudly into the wind. His cap-free grayish-whitish hair was flapping and flopping about. He had more of it than Willy did.

"Hey, you guys!" came from behind them as the gust died down. Three little pups suddenly began scampering in between their legs. The yippy one was bouncing up to Willy's knees. The stinky one had evidently been rolling in something foul. "Down, boys!" squawked Sharon as soon as she reached the bench. "Hey, sorry about that. Pokey, get out from under there. They're such a handful, worse than the larges. I don't know what's best, off leash or on. On, they get tangled, but off, they have no manners at all. I bring them out here for exercise because it's another month before we're allowed on the beach again. Watch it! Get away from the edge, you stupid little shits." They scampered back, and Sharon took a stand in front of the bench, bare-legged and bare-headed in a red corduroy sort of jumpsuit with suspenders. They'd finally seen her wide chattering toothy mouth, but at a respectful distance. "Isn't it too windy out here for you guys?"

"We're hardened to it," Willy said. "But where are the big dogs? Don't you ever mix your threesomes?"

"Are you kidding? You establish a pack where they know each other. Otherwise, they'd be hashing it out every time from the get-go. It's not size, it's attitude. Yippy would boss poor old Brownie around, and the other larges would be all over Stinky because of how he smells."

"They're all boys?"

"Yeah, but fixed, thank you, Jesus!"

Benjy couldn't find an opening in the conversation. What could he engage in about dogs?

"Is Brownie still going home to poop?" Willy asked.

"Afraid so. Remember when I thought we had a breakthrough? But her dad and mom are doing better. He's working from home again. Covid has sure stressed some people out. Hey, they're saying it's cranking up again. I thought we'd all be back to normal and my business would really take off. I mean, when they have to do a full eight hours away from home, plus commute, that middle-of-the-day bathroom break, they can't leave that to chance. Unless they have a fenced yard, but then you run into the barking issue. The point is, I'm what should be designated an essential worker. At least, we don't have to be masked on the street yet. Some shops are requiring it again, though, but I'm vaxed as I'm sure you guys are, and here we all are, out in the real world again."

"And glad to have survived," said Willy.

"Unless," Sharon said with a toss of her blondish locks, "maybe those killer variants do their thing. I'm sure glad I don't live down south in Florida or somewhere." She began corralling her charges and got all twisted trying to leash them. Finally, aiming them toward town, she was off with her usual, "See you guys around," adding, "It always makes me happy seeing you guys. Out here's where we first met. Wasn't that like about this time last year? Can you believe all that's happened since?" Her voice was fading out, but they could still hear her say, "You guys always seem the same, though. Stop tangling the leashes, you little bastards!" Those were the last words they caught.

"She didn't mention Fitz," Benjy said. "I trust they're both doing okay."

"You're invested in Fitz and Sharon now?"

Benjy shrugged, but he knew he did want people to stay together. He'd had that upsetting dream awhile back where an apparition of what he'd thought might be Tom turned into Fitz who seemed to be waving good-bye.

"Sentimental Benjamin," said Willy.

"Sentimental's good, as long as you don't take it for more than it is."

"Maybe it's your interest in history, my friend, that makes you turn to the past."

"I'm a librarian by nature. An archivist," Benjy conceded.

"And I stumbled on you shelving books in the stacks. I was searching for some forgotten plays. Roger—you remember Roger, our director—he thought it was his mission to keep the old stuff alive, but even in those days audiences were already turning off the classics. By now, only Shakespeare draws a crowd. Good old Roger kept trying anyway. He was gay, of course, not that anything ever really happened between us, but—our final season, the Balzac play about the criminal underworld of Paris with a sinister homo subtext, that's what did us in."

"Willy, Willy, and you think I live in the past."

There was a colorful catamaran passing below into the harbor, partiers aboard, young and sun-bronzed and beer cans in hand, all a bit sozzled at that early hour.

Willy said, "Past, future, who even knows, but your question's still bugging me: whether I've been useful, I mean in the Marxian sense."

That set Benjy to mulling over how orderly his daily routines were, how every other day was shampoo and shave (because his beard, unlike Tom's, grew slowly), and in between came bubble bath days, and Sundays he doled out his pills for the week and every morning he let the bed air out before making it after breakfast, and the list kept going, so he had to say, "What was that, Willy?"

"I was asking if we've been useful. If one hasn't been useful, one simply disappears."

"We all disappear either way," Benjy said looking out and down the cliff side at the waves churning against the rocks, thinking only for a moment that Tom was also down there. "You're talking about death, aren't you, Willy?"

"But who disappears from memory and who lasts at least a little while?"

"A melancholy question coming from you."

"Characters in plays!" Willy exclaimed. "All my years on the paper were nothing compared to moonlighting at the theater—because characters in plays aren't gone or, anyway, don't have to be. They disappear when the curtain comes down, but there they are again the next night when it goes up. At the end of the run, they may seem to be gone forever, but if the play gets a revival, with different actors of course, the characters themselves will appear again in human flesh. I'd like to think of myself, Benjy, as a character in a play."

"Let's leave it at that then, Willy, if it's a comforting thought."

JONATHAN STRONG is the author of seventeen previous novels, short or long, so these *Endpapers* constitute numbers eighteen and nineteen. Born in 1944 near the Illinois shore of Lake Michigan, he lives now with his spouse Scott Elledge in Massachusetts by the Atlantic, and they retreat to a Vermont log cabin for the warmer months; all three home turfs provide settings for this book.

Strong retired in 2019 after fifty years teaching fiction-writing, mostly at Tufts but also at UMass Boston, Harvard, Wellesley, and the Bread Loaf Master's program. Along with Grid Books, his work has been published by Quale, Pressed Wafer, Zoland, Ballantine, and Atlantic-Little, Brown.